AS EASY
AS MURDER

Quintin Jardine

AS EASY
AS MURDER

headline

First published in 2012 by
HEADLINE PUBLISHING GROUP

2

Cataloguing in Publication Data is available from the British Library

978 0 7553 4027 9 (Hardback)
978 0 7553 4028 6 (Trade paperback)

Typeset in Electra by Avon DataSet Ltd, Bidford-on-Avon, Warwickshire

Printed and bound by CPI Group (UK) Ltd, Croydon, CR0 4YY

Headline's policy is to use papers that are natural, renewable and
recyclable products and made from wood grown in sustainable forests.
The logging and manufacturing processes are expected to conform
to the environmental regulations of the country of origin.

HEADLINE PUBLISHING GROUP
An Hachette UK Company
338 Euston Road
London NW1 3BH

www.headline.co.uk
www.hachette.co.uk

This is for the lovely Frida Teixidor Hoverstad,
and her lovely daughter.

One

She's a truly sad person, she who can harden her heart against the joyous sound of children at play!

... but sometimes the incessant squeal of a swarm of the little buggers would grate on the nerves of the Blessed Virgin herself. Was there never a time, maybe from the years 3, to 6 or 7AD, when she didn't turn on Him and yell, 'For Christ's sake, Jesus! Would you allow me five minutes of peace and quiet? Is that too much to ask?'

In Plaça Major, the centrepiece of the village of St Martí d'Empuriès, the enchanted Catalan village that I, Primavera Blackstone, Phillips as was, and my son Tom, have called our home for the last five years or so, the fourth Arrels del Vi . . . the proper name of the annual wine fair . . . was in the fullest swing. Since it moved a couple of those years ago from its original, smaller site, it's become a magnet for family groups. Now Mum and Dad can bring the nippers along while they wander among the stalls and sample the best that Emporda can offer, knowing that they have room to play in front of the church, and my house, which is bang next door.

Until that evening I hadn't really appreciated the fecundity of the current generation of young adult Catalans. The place was swarming with under-fives, all too young to have any sort of meaningful volume control, and the din was huge. Not only that; a quick bump count among the women in the crowd was enough to tell me that the breeding programme was still in place.

At any other time, I'd have been amused, probably even charmed, but that was not the best day of my life. I'd arrived home with Tom from a clothes-shopping trip to Girona . . . for him, he's ten and seemed to have been taking a growth hormone (now there's an ironic analogy) behind my back; I'm not short, yet he's up to my shoulder already, and solidly built with it . . . to find that when we'd been out the post person had called, on her wee yellow scooter. I knew this because Ben Simmers, who created and runs the fair, had spotted a letter sticking out of the top of my mail box, and had rescued it, and three others, before anyone else could. Two of those others were bills. The third was a letter acknowledging my resignation from a part-time job I'd held for a couple of years. I'd been a sort of . . . how best to describe myself? . . . honorary consul, with a remit to promote Scottish interests and business on behalf of the Edinburgh government.

The role had involved lots of travel around Catalunya and beyond, throughout the rest of Spain. I'd enjoyed it for a while, but it had only been possible because I'd been able to employ a young woman called Catriona O'Riordan to look after the house, Tom, and Charlie, our amiable idiot Labrador retriever, during my weekly absences. When I was there she took it upon herself to run all three of us, and I was fine with that. Catriona was great;

irreplaceable, as it turned out. When family circumstances forced her to go back to Britain, I'd looked apathetically for a successor, but none of the CVs that I was sent appealed to me, and so I decided, after not too much internal debate, that since being a full-time mum is what I'm best at, that's what I should go back to doing.

The job had been useful at the beginning, though. Not because we needed the money . . . we don't, and we never will . . . but because it took me out of myself, and out of St Martí at a time when, without it, I'd probably have spent too much of my time sitting around brooding.

About what? Not what, whom: a man, of course, the only one who's ever come close to making me go all domestic, other than Tom's dad . . . although here I need to volunteer that my brief attempt at a conventional lifestyle with Oz Blackstone ended in disaster so acrimonious that our son was three and a half years old before his father even knew of his existence.

God, I can't even tell this tale without getting myself sidetracked, all screwed up with angst and regret over my years with that guy. When they were over, irrevocably, as death tends to be, and I was able to consider them, and him, from a distance, I did some internet research that led me to a pretty unshakeable conclusion. When I looked at fifteen behavioural traits indicative of anti-social personality disorder, I found that my former husband ticked fourteen of those boxes. The experts say that particular condition is something you're born with, but none of them ever knew my ex. The Oz Blackstone that I met was lovely, open, honest and brave, just as his son is growing up to be.

But things happened, and they transformed him.

I had a rival for his affections. She won out for a while, but then she was killed, murdered, and that, I am certain, triggered a change in him, and turned him into what he became, a classic sociopath.

And yet, I loved that Oz too. Having admitted that, I made myself go deeper and looked at myself in the same context, to be faced with another truth. There was a period in my life when, in my relationship with him if nowhere else, I was pretty similar myself.

But it's over, Primavera, it's over, he's dead. Forget the bad that he was, and concentrate on the good that he's left behind him in our son.

Fine, with an effort of will, I do that and I come to the man who's come closest to filling what others . . . but not I, never I . . . see as a gap in my life. There was a time two years ago, a brief moment when I thought that all things might have been possible. If Gerard Hernanz had asked me to, I might even have left St Martí for him. It would have been difficult for me to walk away from paradise, but I believe I'd have given it a try. So would Tom, I'm sure, because he liked the man too. He didn't worship him in the way that he keeps his father's memory alive in his heart, but if I'd put it to him he'd have followed my lead with only a little regret.

However, it didn't come to that. Once again, unforeseeable events got in the way. Gerard lost someone very close to him, and he felt that he needed to go away to consider his future at length, to discover whether he was able to turn his back completely on a previous relationship, one that had been his career also: his priesthood within the Roman Catholic Church.

The fourth item in my Saturday post was his decision. I won't burden you with the text of his letter . . . I couldn't anyway, even if I had a mind to, for it went through the shredder that same evening . . . but what he told me was that while he wasn't returning to his ministry, he wasn't returning to me either. He'd spent two years teaching in a monastic school in Ireland. There, he said, he'd found the sort of peace that had eluded him all of his life. He had thought about coming back to St Martí, to build a life with Tom and me, but he had realised that it would involve challenges that might be beyond him and he was concerned about the damage that failure would do to all of us, and most of all to Tom, whose interests he placed above our own. And so, with the blessing of his abbot, he had decided to commit his life to his cloistered pupils.

It was after my second reading of his epistle that the noise below my balcony began to grate on me. I could do nothing about it, so I took the letter off to my bedroom, which has a secluded terrace overlooking the sea, and went through it another couple of times, looking for any sign that he might really be expecting me to respond, to fight my corner against the bloody Benedictines, to write back to him protesting, 'Bollocks to that, get yourself back here.'

But there was none, I concluded. What he was telling me was unequivocal, with no sign at all of an uncertain man waiting to be persuaded. The more I studied what he was saying, the more my respect for him wore away. The way that I saw it, he was using my ten-year-old son as cover for the blatant lack of guts he was displaying, either in not taking a chance on life, or in not telling me he didn't really fancy me. He'd come to know Tom well, and he must have appreciated that the real boy was a lot tougher than the one he was describing. Tom seemed to have dealt with his father's early death and built on his spirit; in truth there had been moments when his strength had reinvigorated me. If we'd tried, and it didn't work out between Gerard and me, the same thing would happen, I was sure. He'd give me a hug and we'd move on.

But what about me? What did I really want? Two years before, Gerard had asked me to give him space, and I'd done that. Eh? Pardon? Me? I frowned at the page, and asked myself a straight question, for the first time. Wouldn't the real Primavera, if she'd wanted him badly enough, have gone to Ireland a long time before and laid it on the line for him? 'Dinner's in the oven, sunshine. Get your ass back home!'

Of course she would. So why hadn't she? For make no mistake, that woman still exists.

I didn't have to dig far for the answer to that. The bald truth was that even if Gerard Hernanz had never gone, if instead he'd stayed put in St Martí two years before, and I'd taken him into my home and into my bed, he'd always have been second best.

Inside, the real Primavera would still have dreamed that the dead might arise and walk once more, as she'd done herself in a manner of speaking, after a spell of hiding in mistaken fear.

Inside, she still does.

'Are you all right, Mum?'

I turned in my basket chair. Tom was standing in the open doorway; still only a boy, a child, but with a look of adult concern in his eyes as he gazed down on me. 'Of course,' I replied lightly. 'Why shouldn't I be?'

'Because you promised you'd come out to the wine fair with me, remember. I sniff, you taste, that was the deal. You never forget a promise, so something must have upset you.'

He's not a boy you can fob off. 'I've had a letter,' I told him. 'From Ireland. From Gerard.'

'And he's not coming back.' There was no question mark left hanging in the air.

'No, he's not. I'm sorry, Tom.'

He shrugged his shoulders, in a Scottish way rather than his usual Catalan. (Linguistic shrugging is complex; it has to be seen to be understood.) 'I'm not,' he declared, firmly; then he paused. 'Well, I'm sorry for you, Mum, if that's what you wanted. But not for myself. I don't need . . .'

His years and his vocabulary weren't yet at the point where he was able to articulate the concept that while he might have liked Gerard as a man, he had no room for him in his life as an added authority figure, but that's what he meant.

The letter hadn't brought the merest hint of mistiness to my eyes, but that did. Before he saw it and misunderstood, I jumped to my feet, beaming. 'And neither do I,' I declared. I slung an arm round his shoulders, something that I'm able to do these days without bending at all. 'Come on, kid. Time for you to do some serious sniffing.'

We strolled out into the square, leaving Charlie on guard duty in the garden, and joined the crowds. The kids were making more din than ever, but I didn't mind any more. In any event their parents, after a few tastings, were beginning to drown them out. I bought a ticket, exchanged a tear-off for a tapas from La Terrassa d'Empúries, our newest restaurant, and began to explore the exhibitors' tables. Unlike too many other fairs of its type, only the best is on offer at Arrels del Vi. It's become a showcase for the growers of the Emporda comerc, and they're keen to show the world how good they are.

Miles, my brother-in-law, dabbles in the wine business, like many rich Aussies. Some time before he'd acquired a winery, a bodega, near Cadaques, and he'd been nagging me for a while to become involved as a director, since he lives in California and can't be hands-on himself. With the government job off my hands, I had told him that I'd do it, so my tour around the stalls wasn't entirely for fun. I knew many of the wines that were on offer so I concentrated on those I didn't, looking to compare them with our range and to see where it might be deficient.

I'd just taken a sip of a very nice white, one hundred per cent garnaxa grape, and let Tom have a noseful, when a hand fell on my shoulder.

'I knew I'd find you here, gal.'

'Hello, Shirley,' said Tom, before I'd had a chance to turn around, but I'd known who it was anyway. Very few people are allowed such familiarity.

'And hello to you, young man. God, but you're growing fast. I'll bet you're pissed off with people telling you that.'

He was, but he was too polite to agree with her, plus, he liked her. Shirley Gash, my best lady pal in L'Escala, the town of which St Martí d'Empuriès is a slightly detached suburb, is one of the most likeable people I know. She's had tragedy in her life, more than I've had, the sort that would have destroyed a lesser woman, but she's overcome it, as far as the world can see. She's tall, blonde, buxom but elegant with it, and she looks after herself so carefully that people who meet her for the first time don't have a clue about her age. I'm privy to the secret, and that's what it shall remain.

'Hey,' I greeted her. 'Where have you been and what the hell have you been up to?' She'd been away from her big house on the far side of L'Escala for a few weeks. Her departure had coincided with one of my away trips, and I'd known nothing about it till she was gone.

Before she could tell me, my gaze fell on a man, standing slightly behind her, but not so far that he was in the Duke of Edinburgh position. One look, and I didn't need an answer any more. I knew the 'what', if not the 'where'. He was at the upper end of middle-aged, as dark as Shirley is fair, solidly built but not gone to fat, dressed, immaculately, in slacks, white shirt and gold-buttoned blazer, looking as if he'd just stepped off a very large yacht. All it would have taken was an apricot scarf, and Carly Simon might have been singing about him.

Or might it have been someone else's song? Not 'You're So Vain?', rather 'Just a Gigolo'? I fixed on my smile but focused a little harder: no, I reckoned I was being suspicious without a reason. His eyes were soft, warm, and there was a degree of uncertainty in them. I've seen quite a few professional Romeos in my time, and in each of them there was the look of the shark.

'This is Patterson,' Shirley announced. 'Patterson, with two "t"s and never Pat, Cowling. We've been on a getting acquainted trip, now he's come to stay for a while, and maybe even for longer than that.'

I extended a hand. 'I'm pleased to meet you, Patterson.' He shook it as gently as if I'd been the Queen of Spain. His fingers were thick, like sausages, but soft, like those of a lawyer or a banker. If he had come off a yacht, he'd been on the bridge, captain rather than crew.

'Likewise,' he replied. 'I've been waiting for this meeting for a while now. You're Shirley's number one topic of conversation. It's easy to see why.'

Brownie points, Patterson, I thought. That could have made him sound like a smoothie too, but it didn't, just a friendly, open guy. I frowned at my pal. 'Oh yeah? And what's she been saying about me?'

'That you're the best friend she has. That you're the unofficial mayor of this place. That you're a sort of roving ambassador for HMG. She's told me everything about you and yet nothing, nothing about what you were or what you did before you came here.' He paused, and grinned at Tom, who looked back at him, deadpan, as if he was still weighing him up, which he was. 'Oh yes, she says your son's a bit of a character as well.'

'I'll take all those, save the roving ambassador part; I've chucked that. And yes, he is; the loveliest boy in the world, until someone upsets his mum.' I turned back to Shirley. 'Are you just here to show Patterson off, or have you come for the fair as well?'

She waved their tickets at me. 'What do you think?'

They joined us on a leisurely tour. We didn't visit every producer . . . there was no need, since the event was only in its first day and the weekend weather was set fair . . . but I made sure that we stopped at Miles's bodega's table. The representative there knew who I was, but I didn't let Shirley in on the connection until she'd tasted, and pronounced the red that she tried, 'excellent'.

'This is the one?' she exclaimed, when I'd told her. 'The place your famous brother-in-law bought a couple of years ago? I'd forgotten about that until now.' She peered at the bottle. 'You wouldn't know from the label.'

'Miles doesn't take a high profile in any of his sideline businesses,' I explained. 'They have to succeed through the quality of the product, not because of his name.'

'What is his name?' Patterson asked. 'His other one, that is.'

'Grayson.'

His thick eyebrows rose. 'Miles Grayson? That Miles Grayson? The movie director?'

'That's him. He's married to my kid sister.'

'Jesus Christ!' He paused, making a mental connection. 'And your second name's Blackstone. Does that mean that Oz Blackstone, the actor, was —'

I cut him off. 'Yes. I was married to him for a while. He was Tom's dad.' Indeed he hadn't been kidding when he'd said that Shirley had told him nothing about my past. I felt my son stand just a little taller beside me, and sensed the squaring of his shoulders. We don't discuss his father very often, and his name means nothing to his school and village contemporaries, but he is intensely proud of him. The only Oz that he ever knew was loving, generous and caring, and it's my firm intention that he will never hear of the other one.

Patterson had the good sense to realise that I was going to say no more about the subject, and the good taste not to follow it up. I headed him off anyway, by spotting an empty table outside Esculapi, and securing it with a wave to Salvador, the front of house man. (There's no point being the unofficial mayor of anywhere unless you make it work for you from time to time.)

There was a football match on telly that night, so I let Tom order a takeaway; I could see the house from the table, so I had no worries about letting him go home on his own. To be honest, I was quite pleased; it gave me more freedom to interrogate Mr Patterson Cowling, and for that matter Mrs Shirley Gash.

I started on her as soon as the wine arrived. 'So, woman, explain yourself,' I challenged.

'How did this new liaison come about?'

'It was Tom's doing,' she replied.

'Tom!' I repeated. 'You turn up with a new bloke and you're blaming my ten year old?'

'Ten going on eighteen, Primavera.'

'Maybe so, but still . . . More,' I told her. 'I need more.'

'Well, one day last autumn, when the two of you came up to the house and you were in the pool . . .' She broke off. 'She likes my pool, Patterson. Puts it to good use every chance she gets.' I'm too brown to go pink or I might have; we both knew what she meant, and with whom I'd gone swimming. *A warning shot across my bows*, I wondered, *lest I spill too many beans?* ' . . . I got him to show me how to use Google. You know I'm crap on the internet. I got him to search for dating sites.'

I'm rarely surprised by anything these days, but I gasped. 'You what . . .'

'Single people sites, mature singles, you know,' she continued, nowhere even close to being abashed. 'We found one that I thought looked respectable and he showed me how to find the form. He didn't fill it in for me, Primavera, honest: I did that myself.'

'Bloody hell! Why didn't you just ask him to get you a plastic chair and a parasol and pick you out a nice spot at the roadside with the other working girls?'

She beamed. 'Because I wanted quality, not quantity. I sent it off, then I forgot all about it, for a couple of months, until I had a reply from this one here. Not directly, through the agency; they sent me his entry and a message form if I wanted to get in touch with him. I decided that I did, and he replied, and I replied to him and then we exchanged email addresses. Oh, and photos: I had to ask Tom how to work my scanner. I hadn't a clue about that either. After a while we spoke on the phone . . . it was all very gradual, you understand. About three months ago we decided to meet. I flew over to London and we had dinner. A month after that Patterson flew to Barcelona and we did it again . . . just dinner, mind,' she added quickly. 'Finally we decided to go on holiday together.'

I looked her in the eye. 'Separate rooms?'

'Not by that stage. Come on, love,' she chuckled. 'At my age? How much quality shaggin' time have I got left? But we split the bill,' she added, 'fifty-fifty.'

'I did offer to pick up the whole tab,' Patterson volunteered, quietly.

She nodded. 'True, but if I'd let him do that,' she explained, 'I might have wound up feeling like one of those roadside girls.'

'To some people that might be not a lot different from putting your name on a website.'

'Sure,' she snorted, 'to the same people who read the small ads for hookers and their services in the Barcelona papers.'

'Hey, I'm not judging you,' I insisted. 'Obviously it's worked out for you both. It strikes me as just a bit risky, though.'

'True,' Patterson conceded: then he smiled, 'but I've survived.'

'So far,' Shirley laughed.

I studied them. They seemed truly relaxed in each other's company, no question of that, and I still hadn't detected the faintest whiff of bullshit from him, not that he'd had much to say up to then. I waited until our meals had been served before I switched my interrogation to him.

'So, Mr Cowling,' I began, 'what's your tale?'

The smile left his face. 'Widowed, like Shirley,' he replied. 'I suppose that makes three of us.'

'No,' I corrected him, 'I'm not the official widow. She lives in Monaco with their two kids. I'm the divorcee, the second Mrs Blackstone.'

'The second?'

'Yes, but that's a long story. Summarised, he dumped me to marry number one, she died young, and I picked up the pieces for a while.'

'Then why do I get the impression that you feel like a widow?'

He was a sharp one, was Patterson. He'd hit on something that I'd never really articulated for myself, and he was right. Oz and I might have been divorced, but we were never really apart. I suppose we were a little like Jack Nicholson and Kathleen Turner in that movie where they played a married couple, both hit people, each with a contract on the other. Mutually self-destructive, but never out of love.

I felt my throat constrict, and took an easy escape route. 'Perhaps it's because I still see him across the breakfast table every morning,' I told him, 'when I look at our son.'

I was forced to admire the way that he had turned my attempted interrogation back on myself, but he wasn't going to get away with it. 'How many Mrs Cowlings have there been?' I continued.

'Just the one. Jennifer. She died seventeen years ago; brain tumour, very sad. She was only thirty-seven.'

'I'm sorry. Do you have any kids?'

'Two daughters, both flown the coop; I have two grandchildren now.'

'You'll fit into L'Escala very well in that case. The place is overflowing with Brit grandparents.' I glanced towards the church where the unofficial crèche was still as lively as before. 'And Catalans, for that matter,' I added. 'Was there much of an age difference between you?'

The grin returned. 'I'm going to take that as a compliment. The very fact that you're asking means you imagine I could still be in my fifties. Jen was eleven years younger than me. I've just turned sixty-five.'

'And retired?'

'Yup. That was one of the reasons for my foray into the partnership site. I've always been pretty busy since . . . since it happened, initially as a working single parent, more recently as, just a worker, I suppose. I had no time for a personal life and no inclination to pursue one, to be honest.'

'What shook you loose?'

'My younger daughter, Ivy. She's quite a lot like you, frank and forthright. She sat me down about a year ago and told me that with two kids to raise, her life plan did not include time as a carer for her father in his dotage, so I should get out and find myself some appropriate companionship. Then she showed me how to do it, pretty much like young Tom did for Shirley.'

'And your older daughter? What did she think?'

'Fleur has always delegated paternal management, as she puts it, to Ivy. The fact is, she doesn't have much choice. She's in the army. Major Cowling, in fact.'

I sensed, or perhaps I only imagined, a sudden tension in him. 'Active?' I inquired.

He winced 'Very. She's a surgeon, in the field. Bloody awful job. I told her not to join, but she was adamant. I don't know how she does it. I don't know how any of them do it, her people or the boys they patch up.'

'As far as I'm concerned, she's a heroine.' Then I tried to put myself in his shoes. 'That said, if Tom ever announces that he wants to join the armed forces, here or in Britain, I'll . . .'

'What?' he asked. 'What will you do?'

'Lock him in his room, possibly. But more likely I'll go all weepy Mum and beg him not to risk breaking my heart.'

'Is it likely that he will?'

Good question; I had to take a few moments to consider it. 'At this moment, I'd say no,' I decided, aloud. 'He goes to martial arts classes, but as a discipline, not to encourage aggression, or even to work it off. His teacher's very strong on pacifism and he's being brought up by me to believe in the sanctity of life. Somehow I don't see him with an assault rifle in his hand, or launching a missile.'

'There's always bomb disposal,' Shirley chipped in.

'Fuck!' I barked at her. 'Don't even think that. I've seen *The Hurt Locker,* thank you very much. I take it you weren't in the army, Patterson.'

He laughed. 'Me? No, boring old civil servant, me. I spent most of my career in a suit in Whitehall.'

'Mmm. A mandarin, no less. I've met a couple of them.'

'Nothing so exotic.'

'Senior, though.'

'Eventually.'

'Were you one of those who earn more than the Prime Minister?' All of a sudden he seemed a little fidgety. 'You were,' I exclaimed, 'weren't you?'

'Well, yes,' he admitted. 'But most of us would argue that the Prime Minister isn't paid nearly enough. It's reasonable to suggest that the people who run the country are worth more than footballers . . .'

'Or silly birds with artificially big tits who're famous for being famous,' Shirley added. 'Every time I log on to AOL and see the shit on the "Welcome" page, it makes me want to throw my computer out the bloody window, and my breakfast after it.' She paused. 'You're right, love,' she added. 'MPs shouldn't have to fiddle their expenses.'

'My dear,' he said, quietly. 'As long as there are expenses, people will always fiddle them . . . apart from civil servants, of course.'

'What was your department, Patterson?' I asked.

'I moved around. But I spent most of my career in the Foreign Office. It was balls-aching boring stuff, most of it. You'll appreciate that, given the job you've been doing.'

I shook my head. 'Actually I enjoyed mine, while it lasted. The expenses were crap, though,' I added.

'So why give up?'

I leaned back in my chair and took a long, leisurely look around the square, with its cafe restaurants, full of happy people, then sideways towards the crowds under the tents of Arrels Del Vi, and finally at the ancient church, and at our house.

'I understand,' he murmured.

'It's very quiet in the winter, mind,' I pointed out. 'But Miles's wine business should keep me occupied. That and writing.'

Shirley stared at me. 'Writing?' she repeated. 'When did you become a writer?'

'As soon as I handed in my resignation from my job,' I told her. 'That's one of the things I plan to do.'

'What the f . . . are you going to write about?' Then her mouth fell open. 'Here, you're not going to do a biography of Oz, are you?'

I whistled. 'No danger. And I will block anyone who tries. No, I'll possibly write about . . . about this place, and about the things that have happened since we settled here. Dunno yet. I've still got to work it all out in my head.'

'How about children's books, with Tom the boy detective?' Patterson suggested.

'Mmm. His grandmother did that; she was quite successful too. But that might give him too high a profile, and I don't think I want to draw attention to him. Maybe I'll write a cookbook instead. Anybody with a shilling for the gas meter seems to be doing one of those these days.'

Actually, although a village portrait was on my agenda, I knew very well what I was going to write about. I was planning to undertake a biography of my father, one of life's great eccentrics, a quiet, creative Scotsman who's managed to keep much of the twentieth century at bay, and all of the twenty-first. I even had a title: *The Man Who Makes Monsters*. (He creates wonderful, hand-carved, chess sets, populated by creatures weirder than any you'll see in a video game.)

We moved past the cross-examination stage, and on to general chat, although I was left with the nagging feeling that I was losing my touch, and that Patterson had got more out of me than I had from him. However I was impressed that he hadn't asked me anything about Miles and Dawn, even after he'd learned of the relationship, and very little about Oz. I have an automatic antipathy to people who meet me and quiz me about them, but he didn't fall into that trap. Okay, they were famous, but he seemed to be interested in me for what I was, not for my link to them.

One thing I did learn was that he had revived Shirley's interest in golf. He asked me for a rundown on the courses in the region and I was able to help him. Tom and I are members at Platja de Pals, the oldest course on the Costa Brava. He's been hitting balls since he was five; he shows promise, not only in my eyes but in those of his Grandpa Mac, who's no slouch himself. The game's big in the Blackstone family, as it happens. Oz was a low handicapper, and of course there's … but I'll get to him, in due course.

'I'll take you both along next week,' I offered. 'We can't start too early, because I've got to get Tom off to school, but it isn't desperately hot during the day just now.'

'Sounds good,' said Patterson, 'but I've got plans for next week. There's a European Tour event, the Catalan Masters, at the PGA course at Girona, wherever that is, and Shirley and I are planning to go along. The pros will be practising from Monday, I'm assuming. We were going to take a look at them before it gets too busy. Fancy joining us?'

I doubted if it would ever get too busy, since golf is still very much a minority sport in Spain, but it sounded like a nice day out. 'Okay,' I agreed. 'Who knows, I might pick up some tips.'

'Or even a nice young golfer,' Shirley suggested, with that gleam in her eye.

'At my age, love,' I pointed out, 'if I was on the prowl for talent, I'd be eyeing up the senior tour. I'll be older than most of next week's field.'

'Nobody's going to believe that without seeing the date on your passport.' Shirley is damn good for a girl's morale; it's one of the things I've always liked about her.

Once we had finished eating, I left them to carry on exploring the fair and went back home, to rejoin my son. The game was approaching a climax, but he seemed to have only one eye on it. I took a couple of Fanta drinks from the fridge, handed one to him and sprawled on the sofa. He jumped up from his usual place on the floor beside Charlie, and came to join me, pressing against me, his head on my shoulder.

'Are you all right, Mum?' he asked.

'Sure. Why shouldn't I be?'

'I thought you might have been sad about Gerard.'

I ruffled his hair. 'I stopped being sad about Gerard a long time ago; that's if I ever was. If he'd wanted to be with us as part of our family, he wouldn't have taken two years to consider it. He could have stayed but he didn't.'

'So we forget him?'

'No, let's not do that,' I decreed, firmly. 'It was nice to have known him for a while. You'll find that, love. People come into your life, and then they go out again.'

'Like Dad?'

'Not in that way. I didn't mean by dying. Nobody stays in one place for ever; our circumstances change, and we move on, from place to place.'

He frowned. On screen someone scored, but he barely seemed to notice. 'I don't ever want to leave St Martí,' he murmured.

'You say that now, but you will. One day you'll go to university. Even if it's no further away than Girona, it'll take you out of here and into a bigger circle. One day you'll have a career.'

'Maybe I'll start a restaurant here, like Cisco.'

'I don't think Cisco and the rest would be very pleased to have you as competition. And anyway, I don't see an opening in St Martí, ever. No spare premises.'

He considered that for a while. 'Then maybe I'll make wine; I could go and work for Uncle Miles. That's not very far away; I could work there and live here.'

'And put someone else out of a job? It's not a very big bodega, Tom, and most of the people there will still be around when you're old enough to be starting a career. Anyway, the last I heard you wanted to be a cop, like Alex Guinart.'

'Yes,' he conceded, tentatively.

'Then you could wind up anywhere in Catalunya, somewhere you couldn't commute from.'

He frowned up at me. 'You're not going to move on yourself, Mum, are you?'

He touched my heart yet again. 'No, my darling,' I promised him. 'I have done plenty of that in my life, but finally I've arrived where I want to be.'

'You lived here before, didn't you? With Dad?'

That wasn't something we'd ever discussed. I'd told him, years before, when I'd brought him to live in St Martí, but he hadn't pressed me about it; until now.

'Yes,' I replied, then waited for the follow-up that I knew would come.

'And yet you moved away then,' he pointed out, a little anxiously.

'I was younger then, and sillier. I wasn't ready to settle here, and neither was your dad. There were things he had to get out of his system.'

'Did he?'

'Honestly? I don't think he ever did.'

'Sometimes I wonder, Mum,' he murmured, pensively. 'If he hadn't died, would he still be in Monaco with Susie Mum and Janet and wee Jonathan, or would he be here with us?'

I ponder the same question myself, often, for all that I try to avoid it. I'm no nearer knowing the answer, and I wasn't going there with Tom, so I settled for a vague, general bullshit response. 'I'm sure he'd have found time for everybody, love.' *Heaven knows,* I thought, *he shared himself around when he was alive.* I've often wondered what happened between him and that girl from Singapore, the one who showed up just in time to stop him getting on board the plane on which I came so close to meeting my Maker.

He sighed. 'It's not fair, Mum,' he said, with a hard edge to his voice that startled me. I'd never heard it before. 'Why did he have to go and die?'

'He didn't plan it, Tom. Don't blame him.'

'I'm not blaming him,' he snapped, pulling himself upright on the sofa. 'I asked Gerard once, if God's so good, why did he let it happen? He said that God operates on a different level, and that as people, we have to take the rough with the smooth.'

'What did you say to that?' I asked, knowing that he couldn't have been any more than eight when the conversation took place.

'I told him that if God was only a sort of Presidente del Gobierno in the sky, then he wasn't much good to ordinary people.'

Gerard had told me once that Tom didn't believe in the Man Upstairs. If he'd been encouraged to see Him as a celestial prime minister, it was pretty clear why. Nobody believes in those people.

'Well,' I said, 'leaving God out of the discussion and going back to your dad, the truth is that none of us knows what each day will bring. Some things we can change, if we want to. Others, we can't. If we're bitter about them, the more we will hurt. And when I see you in pain . . . I feel it too.'

'I'm sorry, Mum,' he exclaimed.

'No, no. Don't be. We all go through these things in life. I still miss your grandma, and I always will. It's a part of being, and I suppose when you're very young, it's not something that's easy to understand. You've reached the age when you do. Now you have to learn to accept it. You have to learn . . .'

He glanced at me. '. . . that shit happens?'

My mouth fell open. I snapped it shut. 'Where did you learn that expression?'

'Grandpa Blackstone.'

'That figures!' I snorted. 'When?'

'I asked him the same thing, why Dad had to die. That was all he said.'

And that was pure Mac Blackstone, I had to concede. Oz's father is not a man to tiptoe around his feelings. 'Succinct, but spot on, kid. Life is about accepting that, and putting it in perspective. You know what the word "grief" means in English?' Tom's multilingual, naturally, given his Scottish parentage, and the fact that he's spent most of his life in Monaco and Spain. He has a lot of words inside his head, but I don't assume that at his age he understands all of them.

'I think so. It's what you feel when you're very sad, isn't it?'

'That's right. Well, there's a saying: "Grief is the price we pay for love". I find it beautiful. I hope you will too, and that you'll try very hard to accept it, and to believe that it's a price worth paying. If you do, then however sad you are when someone dies, it will never overcome you, because you will appreciate what you've had from that person and know that nothing can take those good memories away.'

He was gazing at me. 'D'you understand?' I asked him.

He nodded. 'It's much the same as "shit happens", only not so rude.'

Two

Deep discussion over, Tom went to bed with *The Fellowship of the Ring* . . . he's taking a break from Harry Potter. I read Gerard's letter one more time, ran it through the shredder, wrote him off as a memory, and saw off the rest of Saturday with a coffee on our first-floor terrace, overlooking the square. The day died slowly; there were quite a few stragglers from Arrels del Vi, and the restaurants were busy until almost midnight. But eventually, the village turned in and so did I.

Tom and I spent the first part of Sunday with Charlie on the only beach in our area that allows dogs in the summer months. It allows nudists too, although going naked is not obligatory. (No, I don't! When I feel like getting all my kit off, I do it in the privacy of my terrace.) We had a late lunch at Vaive, our favourite xiringuita (that's beach bar to you), then wandered back home, so that we could be showered and reasonably dressed in time for the last session of the fair.

Business around the stalls was even more brisk than it had been the day before, and there were even more pre-schools playing in front of the church. But I was in a sunnier mood so that was fine.

The salesman from Miles's winery tried to quiz me about the owner's view of his performance, but I gave him no more than an encouraging smile. I wanted to speak to my brother-in-law, to make things as official as they were going to be before I started to act on his behalf.

Tom and I knew most of the people there so we spent a happy couple of hours schmoozing the crowd, me sipping, him sniffing. Shirley and her new beau were in evidence again, getting full value for their tickets.

Before we'd left for the beach I'd done one thing. My time in the ambassadorial thing had given me a few contacts in the Foreign Office. I called the best of them, a man named John Dale, on his mobile, and ran the name Patterson Cowling past him. His response had been immediate. 'Never heard of him. One of ours, you say?'

'I don't, he does. He told me he spent most of his career in your set-up. Fairly senior at the end, but I couldn't wheedle any more out of him.'

'Is he giving you cause for concern?'

'No, but if my eventful life has taught me anything it's never to take anyone at face value. My friend's involved with him, so if there's anything she should know . . .'

'I'll check, soon as I can, and get back to you.'

Fortunately I was some distance away from the man under discussion when the opening bars of 'Born to Run' sounded in my pocket. I took out my mobile, apologised to Alex Guinart and his wife, to whom I'd been chatting, and took a few steps away from the throng.

'Primavera?'

'Of course, John.' I was surprised. Although I knew him well enough to have called him on a Sunday, I hadn't expected a result for a couple of days, at best.

'Can't be too careful. Are you alone? There's a lot of background noise.'

'I can't be overheard and anyway, most of the people making it don't speak English.'

'That's good, because this conversation will never have happened.'

My eyebrows rose, my forehead ridged. 'Oh yes?'

'Definitely. I asked a couple of quick questions about your new friend. Wow! I'm not so high up the ladder that I can't still get my arse kicked, and it didn't take long for it to happen. I've been instructed to tell you to stop asking questions about Mr Cowling, and to take him at face value, as a retired civil servant.'

I reached a very quick conclusion. 'Oh hell,' I moaned, 'you're not saying he's a fucking spook, are you? I don't like those people.' That was very true; about three years before I'd had real trouble with an MI5 woman, in something that a renegade cousin of mine dragged me into. I'd sorted it out, and her, but I hadn't forgotten her. If she had anything to do with Mr C . . .

'Primavera,' John cut in, 'I'm not saying anything, and neither are you. Understood? If this man gets the faintest notion that you know about his background, there could be hell to pay, for me, personally.'

'But he seems like such a nice guy.' *Yes,* I thought, as the banality escaped, *and Eva Braun loved Hitler.*

'I'm sure he is. They're not all licensed to kill, you know; most of them are linguists, or IT experts, or graduates who had no clear career plan when they left university.'

'Fine, but what about Patterson?'

'I don't know about him!' He was beginning to sound exasperated. 'The person who gave me my orders isn't one to be cross-examined.'

'Okay,' I said, to mollify him. 'Thanks for that. Who were we talking about again? I've forgotten his name already.'

'Good. And not a hint to him, remember.'

'Promise.'

'You'll be held to it, be sure.' He paused. 'Hey, about your resignation: are you firm on that? The people in the Barcelona consulate are going to miss you.'

'I'll miss them too, but not enough to change my mind. Nothing's going to do that; my boy needs me more than my country.'

'I can understand that. Be happy, and keep in touch.'

I pocketed my mobile and turned back to face the throng. Alex and Gloria had moved along, with Marte, my god-daughter, tagging along in Tom's care. She's getting disturbingly close to school age, another constant reminder of the passing years. I was about to rejoin them, when Shirley's bellow stopped me short. 'Hoi, Primavera, you haven't forgotten tomorrow, have you?'

I stared as she and Patterson approached, focusing on her alone and trying not to look at him at all, in case something in my expression betrayed me. Spooks must be experts at reading people, I reasoned wildly. 'What about tomorrow?' I asked, puzzled.

'Golf,' she exclaimed. 'Girona. Christ, you have too.'

She was right. I had; stuff had intervened.

'Leave the girl alone, Shirley,' Patterson laughed. 'Not every-one's as keen as you to watch guys whacking balls around a field.'

'It's the guys we're going to watch,' she retorted. 'Isn't that right, girl?'

'If you say so.'

'I do. What time are you picking us up?'

'Eh?' was all I could gasp.

'Come on, you don't want Patterson to have to drive, do you? Not on his first trip here. Let him see the countryside.'

'I'm all for that,' I replied, 'but can't he see the sights with you behind the wheel?'

'Sure, but who's going to point them out? Besides, I'm a terrible driver.'

The only thing that makes Shirley's driving terrible is her insistence on approaching Formula One speeds on public high-ways, but that was reason enough for me to agree. I had spent a few journeys in her passenger seat with my eyes shut tight. 'Okay,' I conceded. 'Nine o'clock, your place. But we'll have coffee and croissants before we set off.'

'Done deal.' She frowned briefly. 'Oh, by the way, Ben was looking for you earlier.'

'Did he say why? Does he have a problem?'

'Maybe he wants you to look after the baby.'

Benedict Simmers, our village wine merchant, had settled down; he had fallen in love with a beautiful girl from Barcelona called Tunè, and in June of the previous year they had produced a small angel, name of Lily. She had pushed all my 'broody' buttons, and I'd become a regular volunteer babysitter. I looked around trying to spot him among the crowd, and eventually I did, paused in mid-bustle, talking to his mother and sister. He saw me at the same time, and waved me across. 'No problem,' I told him, as he approached. 'Do you want to leave her with us, or have us come to you?'

His eyes said 'puzzled' until he worked it out. 'Oh no, no,' he said, hurriedly. 'It's not about that. Someone's been looking for you, that's all. He phoned my shop asking for your phone number. Jordi's in there just now, looking after things, and naturally he wouldn't give it, not just like that, to a stranger. So he told the guy to leave his number and you'd call him back, if you felt so inclined, that is.'

He fished in his pocket, produced a scrap of paper, and handed it over. It took me a few seconds to decipher Jordi's scrawl, but eventually I made out the name 'Wigwe', and a phone number that could have been an American mobile, to judge by the format.

'Wigwe?' I muttered, wracking my brains. 'I don't know anyone called Wigwe. I'm absolutely certain of that. Never have done.'

Ben grinned. 'Remember it was Jordi who took the message. The name's as likely to be Smith or Jones.'

True, but I focused on Wigwe in the meantime. Forename or surname? Whichever, where the hell could a handle like that have originated? It couldn't be an intermediary from Gerard, could it, I wondered as I scratched around for a clue? From the postmark, his letter had taken ten days to reach me. Could he have been hoping that I wouldn't accept it, that I'd want him enough to fight for him? If so, he'd bet on the wrong horse. But still . . .

'Only one way to find out,' I declared, digging out my phone once more, and walking away to give myself some more clear space. As I did I saw Tom looking at me; I waved to him and smiled, to let him know that everything was all right.

I keyed in the numbers that Jordi had written down and pressed 'call'. It took a few seconds to make the connection, but when the ringing tone began it came in single pulses, a clue that the owner was in Spain, or some other part of Europe. It sounded six times, and then it switched to voicemail.

'Hello,' a deep, confident, cultured baritone greeted me. 'This is Uche.' *What the hell happened to Mr Wigwe?* I wondered. 'I'm afraid that I can't take your call just now, but if you tell me what's on your mind, then I promise I'll do something about it.'

What was on my mind was 'Who the fuck are you?' but I decided not to share that with him. Instead, I killed the call. He wasn't linked to my former job, that was for sure, and I didn't take him for a friend of a friend. If a chum of mine had known anyone with a name like that, more than likely I'd have heard about him and it would have stuck.

That left only one other likely explanation: journalist. It doesn't happen very often but it has done. On two or three occasions I've had approaches from hacks digging into Oz's life and death. In every case I've refused to speak to them: more, I've left them in no doubt that if they bothered me further, I had friends in the police force and elsewhere who would bother them.

'I think I'll just sweep you under the rug, mate,' I whispered to myself.

'Sorted?' Ben asked as I moved back towards the shade of the entrance tent.

I shook my head. 'A mystery,' I replied, 'and that's how it will remain. If he calls again, you've never heard of me.'

I went back to Tom and to my happy day.

When the next one dawned, there were clouds in the sky. That suited my son, because he had school, and I didn't mind either. In my experience golf courses are best avoided, either as player or spectator, when the temperature heads towards the nineties as it can here when you least expect it. Tom took his bike to school, with a packed lunch in his haversack. The former was normal, since it was no more than a ten-minute cycle; the latter he likes to do more often than not.

I'd never been to the PGA Catalunya course, but I had a feeling that it would be even more upmarket than the Emporda norm, which can be fairly posh, so I chose a designer outfit that I'd bought in Barcelona, sticking a lightweight rainproof jacket in my shoulder bag as a precaution, just in case those clouds were water-bearing.

I arrived at Shirley's a couple of minutes ahead of schedule. The bitch in me hoped that I might catch them on the hop, or even on the job, but they were ready and waiting. Shirl had coffee on the hob and fresh croissants warming in the oven. I was determined not to let Patterson have a whiff of my precautionary interest in him, but I couldn't stop myself from sneaking the occasional glance at him, trying to catch him off guard, to see if anything showed in his eyes other than the bonhomie so evident at our first meeting.

There was nothing; if anything he was even more laid-back. Those laugh-lined eyes of his were positively twinkling. So, indeed were Shirley's. I reckoned that they must be getting very well acquainted. Looking at the pair of them made me wonder about myself. They were twenty years older than me and obviously at it like rabbits. So what had I become? Wasn't I a woman any longer? I hadn't fancied anyone since Gerard left, not for a second.

It passed quickly, though, as I told myself why that was. In the couple of days that had gone by since Gerard's letter, I'd come to think of him as a lucky escape. I'd found him attractive, sure, but . . . a lapsed priest, for Christ's sake!

The fact is, my sexual career hasn't been very exciting or very extensive. I won't list all my partners: suffice it to say that I'm well short of double figures. And here's the truth, boys. Of that number, only Oz really knew what he was doing down there, or to put it another way, cared about what he was doing for me. The others ate, shot and left, more or less. A wise and cynical lady, whose name I've forgotten, once said that the two saddest times in a woman's life are, one, when her partner can't find her clitoris, and two, when he finds it. I've had enough sadness in my life, and I'm not about to go looking for more.

Our leisurely breakfast behind us, we hit the road. I didn't take the scenic route. Patterson had to make do with the scenery from the autopista. It took little more than three-quarters of an hour to find the championship venue. The newish PGA course is set between two trunk roads, just south of Girona Airport, but not so close to the flight path for it to be a major nuisance. It's tree-lined, with undulating fairways (for non-golfers, those are the close-mown bits where the ball's supposed to land) that look odd, given that they're still surrounded by forest, the rest of which was cleared so they could be made. It's a lovely course, though, and on that day had been beautifully presented for play.

Patterson was surprised to find that the visitors' car park was far from full. In fact, the place looked deserted. In the distance I could see vans standing beside a giant marquee; it was the exhibitors' tent, I supposed, but they all seemed to be dropping off stock, so I realised that it wouldn't be open for business for a few hours, and probably not that day.

'Where do they sell tickets?' Patterson asked.

'What makes you think they will?' I countered. 'They might charge a few euro admission during the tournament itself, but not on the practice days.'

'If this was Wentworth,' he began, 'even on a Monday . . .'

'But it isn't Wentworth,' I pointed out. 'It's Spain, and in this country, golf is still very much a posh people's sport. Sure, there are plenty of courses around but they're mostly used by Brits, Germans and Swedes. You can walk up and play on them, but they're not cheap. As for tournaments like this . . . when this starts properly, you'll find that most of the spectator announcements will be in English.'

As I spoke I wondered whether I should have talked them into waiting until Wednesday or Thursday; but what the hell, I'd shown them the way. If they wanted to come back when the action started, they could. In the meantime, we were there, and there was nothing to do but go in search of whatever there was to be seen.

As we left the car park we saw that there was more bustle about the place than we had realised. Plastic seats were being fitted on the spectator grandstands, a television camera was being winched up on to a stand and a giant leader-board was under construction, beside what I guessed had to be the eighteenth green. The tented village was being set up just behind a big modern clubhouse, around which, happily, there seemed to be plenty happening. There were tables out front under a sun awning; all of them were occupied, exclusively by men, some in blazers like Patterson's (I had begun to think of it as his uniform), others in what seemed, from a distance, to be designer golf gear. None of it, I reckoned, had been picked up for a couple of euro at the Palafrugell street market.

'What do we do?' Shirley asked.

'Find the practice ground?' I suggested.

'How?'

I looked around for any sort of public information, but saw none, not even a layout of the course. Then I glanced back towards the clubhouse and saw three men appear. One, in a T-shirt and shorts, was carrying an enormous golf bag covered in logos, the second, who wore slacks and jacket, had a phone pressed to his ear and was in mid-conversation, and the third, in golf gear and with two-tone footwear that looked hand-crafted, had ginger hair tied back in a ponytail. I recognised him from telly as a pro.

'Let's follow them,' I proposed.

We did, at a discreet distance. The path they took led past a bronze statue of a man straddling an enormous golf club . . . five or six iron, I guessed . . . and past a hotel complex on our right, before opening out into a wide field, at one end of which around a dozen golfers stood in a long rank, some with caddies, others with coaches as well, each with a bucket of balls at his feet, each engaged in whacking them into the distance.

'This is more like it,' Patterson beamed. 'Practice range.'

Maybe so, but I felt instantly self-conscious. Although there was a small tiered grandstand behind the players, with half a dozen rows of seats, they were empty, and there was nobody else around who looked even remotely like a spectator, or who didn't know what they were doing there. Someone else thought so too. A tall white-haired man with tanned, leathery skin came walking towards us. Fortunately he was smiling.

'Morning,' he began, in a refreshingly Scottish accent. 'Can I help you? I'm Clive Tate, the practice ground manager. Are you looking for anyone in particular? If you're media, your tent isn't open yet, but I saw the Tour press officer on the clubhouse terrace with some of the early arrivals.'

'No, no,' I told him, hurriedly. 'We're not journos, God forbid.'

The smile became a chuckle. 'I didn't really think so; I know all the regulars. But occasionally we have people turn up at these Spanish events saying they work for ex-pat newspapers; websites too, these days.'

'That's not us, I promise. We're punters, simple as that.'

'In that case you'll have the stand to yourself.' He reached behind his back and pulled a rolled-up magazine from a trouser pocket. 'Here,' he said as he handed it to me, 'on the house for a fellow Jock. It's the programme for the week, with all the players listed. You won't be able to buy one of these until Wednesday. That's how early you three are. Still, if you stick around for a few hours, you should see quite a few of the top guys. This event has a high-quality entry field.'

He left us to it and headed back towards the Portakabin that seemed to be his office. We chose seats in the top row of the not-very-grandstand. One or two of the players glanced in our direction, but most of them stayed completely focused on what they were doing.

Shirley and I sat on either side of Patterson, who seemed to know his stuff as he played 'spot the golfer'. He named quite a few stars even I'd never heard of, proving himself right when in doubt with a quick check of the programme. I concentrated on the ponytailed chap we'd followed. He was one of the oldest on the range, built like a man who'd enjoyed a few good breakfasts in his time, and with a distinctive practice routine which I guessed that he had been following on other ranges for at least a quarter of a century, and probably more. He loosened up before every shot with a huge, furious swing of the club, but when he put a ball at his feet, he struck it with a slow, controlled rhythm, sending it off into the distance with a perfect left to right fade.

I watched him for a while as he worked his way through all the clubs in his bag, then switched to another player that I recognised, a former US Open champion no less. Patterson remarked that his very presence was a sign that the Catalan Masters event was being taken seriously, and that the prize fund was attractive. I studied his form for a while. At one point he turned to speak to his coach, and noticed us in the stand. He smiled, and I heard him say, 'Hey, we've got a gallery already.' He waved in our direction. I formed the conceited impression that it was meant specifically for me, and found myself smiling back.

'He's a new one on me,' Patterson murmured, drawing my attention back to him. 'I wonder who he is.'

I followed his gaze and saw a well-muscled young man of medium height with braided hair, and skin like shiny ebony, carrying a huge golf bag along the back of the range until he found a space between two players. 'Yes indeed,' I whispered, as he swung the clubs from his shoulders and planted it firmly on the ground.

'No,' said Patterson, 'not him; he's a caddie. I mean his boss.' He pointed to a guy who was following him, a few paces behind. He was quite a bit taller than the other, and his tanned face was set in serious concentration.

If we hadn't been sitting I'd have fallen over. I felt my heart hammer as it jumped from the normal sixty-something beats per minute to rather more than twice that. My head swam, and for a split second I didn't know who or where I was. Bizarrely, I wondered if I was dead, like those cops in purgatory in that TV series, for it was as if I was looking at someone I knew better than any man in the world, only it couldn't be him, for he really was dead, and anyway this version was only half the age he'd have attained if he hadn't been. My right hand was at my mouth. I bit my fingers, hard, to restore a semblance of reality.

Shirley had been looking at me. 'Primavera,' I heard her call out, 'are you all right?'

I gulped and nodded, but I was speechless.

Patterson had been oblivious to my near faint. He'd been too busy leafing through the programme. 'Got him,' he exclaimed. 'It's that new lad, the kid from the last Walker Cup team. He's just turned pro and this is his first event.' He thrust a page in front of me. 'There he is. Sinclair, his name is: Jonathan Sinclair.'

I had worked it out for myself by that time. I'd placed him, even though I hadn't seen him since he was a precocious, pre-pubescent youth, not since the days when I'd been married to his uncle, his Uncle Oz. I knew how his life had developed, though; his Grandpa Blackstone was vastly proud of him, and had kept me in occasional touch with his progress as a golfer. I knew that he'd gone to university in America, on a sports scholarship, and that he'd made a name for himself on the amateur circuit. But I hadn't seen Mac for a while, and so, while I'd been aware that turning pro had been on the cards, I'd no way of knowing that it had happened.

'Jonny.' I only whispered the name, but Shirley heard me nonetheless.

'Who?' she asked, loud enough to make the former US Open champion's caddie throw a frown in her direction.

'Jonny,' I repeated. 'I'd forgotten what his dad's surname was. He's Oz's sister's older boy.'

She stared at me, then at him, then back at me. 'Oz's nephew? The kid who was here when you and he were married? He's turned into that?' She looked at him again, a little more closely. 'Now you tell me, yes, he does look like him. Not as much as Tom does, of course, but still . . .'

Of course. It came back to me; Shirley had met him, when

Grandpa Mac, Ellie and her boys had come for Christmas to the house in L'Escala that Oz and I had bought not long after we were married. For several reasons, that place, that whole time, had been a disaster for us. The only positive had been Tom's conception, just as his parents were falling apart as a couple. Things had been pretty bad also for Shirley then. But she hadn't reacted by taking flight, she'd done so by correcting a mistake, and buying back the house she'd sold believing wrongly that she'd be happy some- where else. Still, tough and all as she was, my instant concern was that being hauled back to those days wouldn't be good for her.

I should have known better. 'Wow,' she whistled. 'What a honey. What age will he be now?'

'Hmmph,' I snorted. 'Trust you, Mrs Gash. Young enough to be your grandson.' I did a quick sum. Jonny would have been . . . what? . . . eleven back then, so . . . 'He'll be twenty-two, I reckon.'

'Well, if I can't have him, what about his caddie? He'd look great in my garden.'

'Hands off!' I warned. 'I saw him first.'

'Actually,' Patterson pointed out, affably, 'I did.'

Shirley looked at him and raised an eyebrow.

He laughed. 'Don't worry. There's nothing I haven't told you.' He turned to me. 'What are you going to do, Primavera?'

I leaned closer to him, as if I was trying to make myself as inconspicuous as possible, which, in all probability, I was. 'I don't know,' I murmured. 'I don't want to interrupt his practice, that's for sure. God, I may be the last person in the world he'd want to see. There was a lot of shit happened between his uncle and me.

His mother probably hates me, so he'll have had his card well marked about me.'

'If he has,' he said quietly, 'there was an up-to-date picture on it. He's staring at you.'

'You're kidding.'

'I wouldn't, in these circumstances. No joke.'

I forced myself to look back towards the practice range. He was right; Jonny was gazing up towards the spectator stand, and there was nobody else he could have been looking at. He was frowning. Most of me wanted to be out of there. I thought about jumping off the back of the structure and legging it, but my dignity wouldn't let me take that way out. So I let my eyes meet his.

And when I did, he smiled. 'Auntie Primavera,' he said. I could hear the laughter in his voice, and see my past in his wide, friendly smile. He started to move in our direction. I knew that if I stayed where I was he'd climb up to us. I didn't want to involve Shirley and her man in such an unexpected reunion, so I rose and headed towards him, stepping over the empty seats in front and jumping down on to the ground.

'Auntie Primavera,' he repeated, as I stood in front of him, then he swept me up and off my feet, into unexpectedly strong arms and hugged me tight. And I hugged him back. I was feeling lots of things, but none of them was very clear to me at that point. I didn't know whether I was happy or sad, whether I was really hugging him or whether he was a surrogate for the dead. I kissed his neck, the nearest part available, then whispered 'Lovely to see you, Jonny. Now put me down. At least three Major champions are staring at us.'

I was overstating it; there were only two. Back on my feet, I took my first close-up look at Jonathan Sinclair as an adult. He was slightly taller than his uncle had been, and maybe not as naturally heavily built, but he had the sort of gym muscles that you find on young pro golfers these days, since power became all-important to many of their coaches. There was a slight facial resemblance to his father, a first-generation computer nerd who'd been more interested in his job than his family, until finally Ellie Blackstone had binned him, but mostly he took after his mother. Other than temperamentally, it seemed; my former sister-in-law is most kindly described as formidable, a woman given to making her point.

'So Uche's message did get to you,' said Johnny. 'The sod never told me you'd called him back.'

'I didn't,' I replied. 'Well, I did, but I decided not to leave a message, since I'd no idea who he was. Who the hell is he, anyway?'

'He's my caddie.'

'You've got a caddie?' I gasped, inanely, as if it was natural in my world for a pro golfer to carry his own clubs.

'Of course I have, Auntie,' he chuckled. He nodded, over his shoulder, towards the black guy, who had closed in on us. 'This is Uche,' he continued. 'Uche Wigwe. He's my mate really; we were at Arizona State together. He hopes to join the tour as well, but he's caddying for me until we can both go to qualifying school.'

'That's if we both have to, ma'am,' Uche intervened. 'If Jonny makes enough money through sponsors' invitations, he'll earn a playing card automatically.'

He was beautifully spoken, much better than Jonny, much better than me for that matter. 'Your accent,' I began.

'African,' he explained. 'Nigerian, to be precise. My father is what the British media delight in calling a "princeling", the implication being that our nobility isn't nearly as grand or important as yours. It's a slur that doesn't trouble us, however, for aside from his old tribal title, he's filthy rich.'

'Uche was at Winchester School before Arizona State,' Jonny added. 'No scholarships, by the way. In theory we have the same manager, but it's harder to get sponsors' invites for him.'

'Why?' I asked, naively.

'Why do you think? I played on the Walker Cup team; he didn't.'

'Jonny.' The posh bag-carrier nudged him, gently.

'I know,' he said. 'Auntie, I have to hit some balls. Stay and watch and we'll talk when I've done. Can we have lunch afterwards?'

'On one condition,' I told him. 'Stop calling me "Auntie", will you?'

I climbed back up to my perch, and Jonny went to work. From that moment I wasn't looking at anyone else, not at any of the champions on parade, only my nephew . . . technically he hadn't been since Oz and I divorced, but I was claiming him anyway. I know a little about golf, from the telly and from playing myself. It didn't take me long to work out that the swing I was watching wasn't the one he had learned from his grandfather and his uncle, classic Scottish amateurs both, conditioned to hit the ball low, and under the wind. His flight was high, and long. At first I thought that his natural shot was a fade, until he started to hit it the other way, drawing from right to left.

I heard Patterson murmur beside me. 'See how straight his back is?' he whispered. That hadn't escaped my notice; everything about him seemed perfectly balanced. 'He hits it like a dream,' he added. 'I wonder what his short game's like?'

'If he's anything like his Grandpa Blackstone, it'll be deadly. Mac's a bandit around the greens.'

'You sound as if you're still in touch with him.'

'Why shouldn't I be? He's my son's grandfather too. Mac's a regular visitor.'

'Why isn't he here for Jonathan's debut?' he wondered aloud.

'I can tell you that,' I said. 'He and Mary are on a long cruise, out in the Far East. He may not even know about it.' *But if he had, would he even have told me?* I wondered. A loose, unofficial pact had grown up between Mac and me. While he had given me occasional reports of Jonny's golfing progress, we never talked about events past, and rarely about people from it. Tom was our shared future and we concentrated on him.

The thought was still in my head when I noticed that Jonny and Uche seemed to have been joined by someone else . . . at least I assumed they had, for she, the only woman on the range, was standing beside the caddie, talking to him, but watching Jonny, while filming him with a handheld camera. He stopped, to change clubs and to take on some water, and I managed a look at her in profile. She was well over thirty, maybe even my age. Her hair was blonde, without being lustrous, and her skin was brown, but weather-beaten rather than tanned. She was dressed in pale green trousers, golf shoes and a polo shirt. Although I couldn't see the front, it looked a match for the Ashworth that the guys were wearing, and it had the same car manufacturer logo that was on their sleeves. I'd noticed her earlier, near the clubhouse, talking to a large blond guy and two kids. One of the team, I guessed, but who was she?

Once again, Patterson came up with the goods. 'That's impressive too,' he remarked. 'That must be Lena Mankell. She's Swedish, a swing coach . . . the only woman doing that job on the men's tour, so it's got to be her . . . and she's reckoned to be one of the two or three best around. If she's working with Jonny, and it looks as if she is, that's a statement in itself.'

From then on, I watched her as well. Two or three times she stopped Jonny to play him back the video she had shot, and once adjusting the position of his hands at the top of the backswing, but otherwise she seemed happy with what she was seeing.

They worked on; that upright swing never seemed to vary, but gradually I could spot the slight differences in the set-up that triggered the differences in ball flight. When the session ended, and Uche put Jonny's driver back in his bag, I checked my watch and found that they had been at it for well over two hours. By that time I was on my own, Shirley having pleaded a combination of sore bum and hunger before dragging Patterson off to find refreshment in the clubhouse.

As his caddie shouldered the enormous bag and headed for the locker room, Jonny was left in conversation with the big blond guy, who had joined him just before his practice broke up; it didn't stop him waving me down to join them. 'This is Lars,' he said, 'Lars Martinsson; he's married to my coach, and he's a pro as well.'

'By the skin of my teeth,' his companion added, in comfortable, if accented, English. 'I don't play so much these days. Lena's work takes her to the big events, mostly. I don't get to play in them very often, but I don't like to be away from her and the kids, so I don't spend too much time on the minor circuit. The one time I did win, seven years ago in Malmo, she wasn't there to see it.'

Nice, I thought, *a golfer who follows his wife, rather than the other way around.*

'Come on, Auntie,' Jonny interrupted. 'Let's go to the players' catering. I need to take on some carbs for this afternoon's session.'

That sounded like a good idea, so I bade farewell to Lars, and fell into step alongside him. 'You're not finished?' I said.

He shook his head. 'I have to take advantage of today. It's going to be really busy here tomorrow, so I want to get out on the course while I can. I'm due on the tee at two fifteen in a four-ball with . . .' He rattled off three names; one of them was the former US Open champion, another had been captain of the previous year's Ryder Cup team, and the third was likely to be his successor. 'They're curious,' he explained. 'They want to see how I shape up. Plus they're all good guys, to be sharing practice time with a newcomer like me. But this is a generous sport, Auntie Primavera.'

I smiled. 'Hey, I told you not to call me that.'

'I like calling you Auntie. You're the only one I've got.'

'Not so,' I pointed out. 'There's your Auntie Susie, in Monaco.'

He stopped smiling. 'She doesn't count. I don't like her. Now that Uncle Oz is dead she's off the list.'

'That's a bit harsh, Jonny.'

'No it isn't. Mum can't stand her either, and Grandpa and Mary only tolerate her because of the two grandkids, Janet and my namesake. They've never forgiven her for the way she came between you and Uncle Oz. I was too young to know what was happening at the time, but now I do, and I feel the same as them.'

I was still pondering this as we walked into the catering tent, the only part of the tournament's canvas village that appeared to be working. I chose a salad from the buffet table, but Jonny helped himself to an enormous plate of rigatoni, with a rich meatball sauce.

'You know,' I told him, 'your grandpa's never said a word against Susie to me.'

'He wouldn't, for Tom's sake, but that's how he feels, trust me. Mum and him always liked you, Auntie P. Mum says that Susie's man, the one she was engaged to before, was hardly in the ground before she set her cap at Uncle Oz.' He grinned, and I could see the kid that still lived within him. 'She doesn't actually say "Set her cap", but you know what I mean.'

'I know,' I admitted, 'but I put that behind me a long time ago. It's history. Yes, Susie might have thrown herself at Oz, but he didn't have to catch her, especially not since we were technically on honeymoon at the time. But the truth is I wasn't perfect either. Your uncle managed to get the both of us pregnant at the same time, but I was so mad with him that I kept my condition to myself . . . for four years, as it turned out. It wasn't really Susie he left me for, you see, it was her baby. If I'd told him about mine . . . about ours . . .'

'That's what Mum says too. She says your problem then was being too nice about it.'

I chuckled. 'That's not something I've ever been accused of before. So anyway, how is your mother? I haven't seen her for years, since the last time I saw you in fact.'

'She's still the same; fearsome as ever. She hasn't changed a bit.' He paused. 'Well, she has in one respect. She's Lady January, now that my stepfather's a Court of Session judge, and a lord. She and Harvey live mostly in Edinburgh now, since my brother left to go to university.'

'And how's he? How's Colin? He was a wild little bugger, as I remember.'

'He's tamed. He learned to wipe his nose when he was about fourteen and got all serious with it. He's doing a maths degree at Oxford; I hardly ever see him.'

I thought of the Sinclair boys when first I'd met them, in the French village where their father had parked them and Ellie while he worked all the hours God sent. Urchins, both of them. What fifteen years could do. 'Will that be two graduates in the family?' I asked. 'What do you golf students come out with? I don't know.'

He smiled. 'I've got a Bachelor's degree in agribusiness; majoring in golf course management. If I don't make it on tour I can fall back on that; maybe I'll do an MBA, and go to work for Brush, or somebody like him.'

'No worries there, son. You'll make it all right. With a swing like that, how can you not?'

'We've all got swings like that, Auntie. That's why we use people like Lena Mankell. You saw her, did you?' I nodded. 'This is the first pro event I've ever played, and Brush has got me invitations to six more here in Europe, that's as many as you can have, and another five in the States.'

'Who's this Brush you keep mentioning?' I asked.

'He's my manager.'

'Our Jonny; with a manager.' I shook my head and smiled. 'You do realise you're making me feel ancient?'

'Not you,' he said, gallantly, and quickly enough for it to sound sincere. 'We all have, even as amateurs, some of us. His real name's James Donnelly, but everybody calls him "Brush", because he sweeps everything up.'

'Sounds handy. So how does the invitation thing work? Who invites you?'

'The event sponsors; it gets you past pre-qualifying. Like I said, I can have up to seven this year, but if I manage to finish in the top ten in a tournament, I get automatic entry to the one the next week, and I don't have to use up an invitation, if I have one. In theory, I could be playing full time for the rest of this season, and make enough money to get my playing card for next year. But on the other hand I could use up all my invites, miss every halfway cut, and not make a cent, then go to tour qualifying school and get cut again halfway through. If that happens, the sponsors that Brush has got for me will disappear,' he snapped his fingers, 'just like that.'

'Do you believe,' I asked, 'that is what's going to happen?'

'No.' His answer was instantaneous, and firm. 'I believe I'm going to win this week and never look back. I really mean that. I did sports psychology in my degree; if you can't manage your head, you'll never manage your game.'

'Is your mum coming to see you?'

He frowned. 'She can't. She had a hysterectomy a couple of weeks ago, and she's not cleared to travel yet.' He saw my expression. 'Don't worry, it's nothing life-threatening. It was serious, though. She developed a condition called endometriosis, a couple of years back. It really floored her. They tried all sorts of treatments, lasers and things, but nothing did much good, and finally, surgery was recommended as the only way. She'll be fine now, they say.'

I'd heard of that complaint, and thanked my lucky stars it hadn't come my way. Anything that could floor Ellie Blackstone January was not to be messed with.

'I'm glad to hear it's sorted,' I told him, and I was, very glad. I'd assumed that Ellie had set her face against me forever, and was hugely pleased to learn that she hadn't. 'So, since she's not here, can I come and watch you?'

'I hope you will. That's one reason why I asked Uche to try to get in touch with you. I'm sorry if he confused you, by the way. Grandpa's out of touch, so I couldn't get your number from him. All Uche did was look up the local Yellow Pages and call the first number he found with an address in St Martí.'

That filled in all the blanks. 'No worries. It's a date, then. I'll bring Tom at the weekend too.'

'Good. I'm looking forward to meeting him. What's he like?'

My son had met his Aunt Ellie on a few occasions, at first with Oz, and since then once or twice when we'd been visiting my dad in Auchterarder, and Grandpa Mac had picked him up and taken him to Fife for the day. He knew his cousin Colin as well, and Harvey, his newish uncle, but Jonny had been away on each visit, so their paths had never crossed.

I took a photograph, the one that goes with me everywhere, from my bag; Tom and Charlie, taken a few months before, on the beach in winter. 'He's the one without the tail,' I said. My nephew's eyes misted for a second or two as he looked at it. 'Yes,' I murmured. 'He is like his father, isn't he?'

Then I had another thought, a very big thought. 'Where do you live, Jonny?' I asked.

'This week? Brush has rented a house for Uche and me, plus Lena and her crew. It's not far from here, in a place called Caldes de something or other. We're all staying there.'

'No, not just this week; I meant permanently.'

He shrugged his shoulders and gave me that awkward Blackstone grin. 'I don't know,' he confessed. 'I've just left college, so I don't have a place yet, other than Mum's house.'

'But you'll need one, won't you, for the weeks you're not involved in a tournament?'

'I suppose, yeah.'

'Somewhere with decent weather and near good practice facilities? Somewhere central to the European events you're playing?'

'Yeah, but to be honest I haven't thought much about it, not yet. I've been too full of this week.'

I took the plunge. 'Then come and live with us; make our

place your European base. It ticks all those boxes, the weather's a hell of a lot better than St Andrews, plus it's forty minutes from an airport. We've got room, Tom and me.' Then a question that I'd overlooked popped into my head. 'Or do you have other involvements? Do you have a girlfriend?'

He shook his head. 'I'm between, you might say.'

'Then what's to stop you coming to stay with your old . . . scratch that, middle-aged auntie?'

He blinked. 'Nothing, I suppose. But things tend to get busy around me; the phone's going all the time. Uche would need to be close by as well. My caddie goes where I go, during the day at any rate.'

'We can find him somewhere . . . when I think about it, I could squeeze him in as well.'

'No thanks, I wouldn't want him that close.' He grinned. 'Neither would you, for that matter. Uche's a night owl; he's a playboy. Lovely guy, but he needs to get his mind more focused if he wants to make it as a golfer.'

'There are places available around St Martí that would give him his freedom, don't you worry.' I smiled at him, feeling a warmth akin to the way that Tom makes me glow. 'Are you up for it?' I asked again.

'Well,' he said slowly, 'if you're sure.'

Strangely, I hadn't been surer of anything for quite some time. 'Entirely. I'll tell you what. Why don't you come home with me tonight, and see how it feels?'

'All right,' he agreed. 'But what about Tom? It'll be a big change for him. Doesn't he have a vote?'

'Yes, but I know how he'll cast it. You'll be a hero to him; think of the bragging rights he'll have at school.'

He grinned. 'The dog in the photo? Is he yours?'

'Yes, but don't worry about Charlie; he does not have a vote.'

'I'll pay my way, mind,' he warned.

I looked him in the eye. 'And do you with your mother? The truth now; I'll ask Mac if I have to.'

He shook his head.

'Right you are, then. Jonny, we're family. If you like, you can take us for a meal whenever you make a big enough cheque; that'll be an added incentive for you. Every time you're over a twelve-footer on the last green that's worth a few grand, you can think of me done up to the nines in the best restaurant in L'Escala.'

Three

That's how I came to be a den mother. That's what Ellie christened me when, to my surprise, she called me that evening. Jonny hadn't even arrived in St Martí when she phoned. He was still in mid-round with the superstars when I had to leave the course with Shirley and Patterson, to be back in time for Tom coming home, but he had his own wheels, supplied by his German car sponsor as part of his deal, and equipped, naturally, with a navigation system.

I'd given him my home and mobile numbers. When the phone rang I imagined it might be him, having second thoughts, or having been leaned on by the mysterious Brush . . . whom I still hadn't met . . . to stay within camp, so when I heard his mother's voice instead it set me back on my heels.

'It's a funny old world, Primavera, isn't it?' she began; no preamble.

'You can say that again,' I sighed, recovering. 'Jonny tells me you haven't been too well. How are you feeling now?'

'Champing at the bit; that's a good sign, I reckon. I'll make it to his next event; I've told my surgeon as much.' She paused.

'This is very good of you, you know, taking my boy in like this. I've been worried sick about how he was going to look after himself, being dragged around Europe by that manager of his.'

'The sweeper-up?'

'Hah!' Her laugh was brief, cut off short; my nursing background told me that it had tugged at her stitches. 'Jonny thinks that's how he got his nickname, but there's another reason, a bit more obvious. They called him Brush when he was playing because he was as daft as one, they reckon. That was what Harvey was told, at any rate. He did some checking up on him when Jonny was choosing a management company. There were a few after him, you know,' she added, with evident pride, 'including the two biggest players of all, but Jonny did his own research and decided to go with Donnelly, because he liked the frankness of his approach, plus he liked him personally. On top of that he only takes twenty per cent, where some others can take up to fifty, when a lad's starting out. I have to say that he's done well by him so far. I didn't expect him to be in any tournaments at all this summer, but Brush has filled up his dance card. The event down your way was the icing on the cake; he got in there at the last minute. There's a huge prize fund, he says. Mind you, he has to make the cut on Friday to collect any of it.'

'He will,' I assured her, 'don't you worry.'

'You're confident.'

'I've just watched him practice, and I spent some time with him on the course. There's an air about him, a certainty, and it's very impressive.'

'Were you going to say that it reminds you of somebody?' she asked, quietly.

'Hell, no!' I retorted. 'When we were together Oz flew entirely by the seat of his pants. He never planned a bloody thing; everything had an uncertain outcome. Jonny seems to have his whole career mapped out.'

'Both of those are true, I suppose,' Ellie conceded. 'But you have to admit that when my brother did set his sights on something, nothing stopped him. It was when he got hitched to that wee Glaswegian bitch that everything started to change.'

'No,' I countered. 'It was when Jan died, surely.'

'No, love.' The term of endearment took me aback, but pleased me. 'You kept him on the rails after that. I've never said this to anyone before, but the fact is I never liked him and Jan together. I don't know why; I just didn't. Mind you I never liked her mother either, from when she taught me at primary school. To this day, I'm only civil to Mary because it would hurt my dad if I was otherwise.'

I was astonished, not only by her intuition . . . I knew, because he told me, a lot more about Jan's relationship with, and to, Oz than she or her father did, and the background to her instincts . . . but also because I'd known Ellie for all those years, yet she'd never been so frank. 'I'm standing here gobsmacked,' I told her. 'Is there any woman who's come into contact with your family that you do like?'

'Yes, you silly cow! You! Why do you think I'm so chuffed that you're taking my boy in hand? I'm laughing at the very thought . . . or I would be if my wound would let me. Imagine, you, the wild

Primavera, mothering Tom, Jonny and that simpleton dog that my dad likes so much. It'll be like the fucking *Jungle Book* in your house.'

I heard the gate bell ring, and Tom yell, 'I'll get it.'

'I'd better go,' I told her. 'I think that could be Baloo the Bear arriving, and I haven't told Mowgli about him.'

My son beat me to the door, comfortably, although he'd been beaten himself by Charlie, who'd stopped barking as soon as it was opened, confining himself to his usual jumping up and down in the presence of a stranger.

'You'll be Tom, then,' Jonny was saying, just as I arrived.

'That's right,' I told him, unnecessarily. 'Tom, this is Jonathan Sinclair, the cousin you've never met. He's coming to stay with us for a while.'

'Jonny,' Tom exclaimed. 'The golfer? Grandpa's told me a lot about you.'

Our new boy grinned. 'He's told me a fair bit about you too, chum.' He held out his hand and they shook. I knew there and then that they'd be blood brothers; Jonny had treated him like an equal and that's all my lad ever requires of any adult.

I showed him to what was to be his base, above the living room, with a view over the square and a bathroom that he'd share with Tom. The case he'd brought with him was vast; I took that as a sign that it was more than a trial visit. He noticed me looking at it as he dumped it beside the bed. 'That's only half of it,' he told me. 'My clothing company sponsor bombards me with stuff. Give me your size, and Tom's, and I'll get you some. Golf shoes too; and trainers.' He smiled and I felt that shiver again, the one that had sent me spinning earlier, the first time I saw him.

It must have showed on my face. 'Auntie P, is this going to be difficult for you?' he asked. 'I mean . . . Hell, I don't know how to say it. If I'm a reminder of . . . anybody: I'd understand if you changed your mind about this.'

'Jonny, suppose you were, you wouldn't be nearly as big a reminder as the guy who opened the door for you. And why should I be bothered? Don't you like to be reminded of your uncle? I know that you and he were very close.'

'There isn't a day goes by when I don't think about him. I carry his picture in my bag for luck; he's done pretty well for me so far. He's always looked out for me, and he's still doing it, in my head at least.'

I smiled at him. 'Just don't let him read your putts,' I said. 'That was always the weakest part of his game. Come on; I'll show you the rest of the house, and the pool.'

'You've got a pool?'

'Yes, it's out the back. It's big; stretches all the way to Italy and beyond.'

His eyes shone when he saw the Mediterranean from my terrace. 'Windsurfers!' he exclaimed. 'That's my other sport. If I buy a board can you store it for me?'

'Sure, right beside Tom's, in the garage. It's vast; there's room for your car too.' I raised an eyebrow. 'I didn't think there'd be much opportunity for windsurfing in Arizona. I lived in Las Vegas for a while and there wasn't a hell of a lot there.'

'There is in Fife. I have a feeling it'll be a lot warmer here, though.'

'You can use mine for now, if you want,' Tom volunteered, from his bedroom doorway. 'It's big enough for you.' I'd taken some persuasion to allow him to graduate to a larger board, but Ben Simmers, his unofficial coach, had assured me that he was good enough and strong enough to handle it. In fact, his real passion, and Ben reckoned his real talent, was free surfing, but the big waves in the Bay of Roses come too infrequently for him to concentrate on that alone.

'Maybe tomorrow,' I said, 'if Jonny has time. Tonight we have a date, all of us. Patterson and Shirley . . .' I told my nephew who they were, reminding him that he'd met Shirl when he was a kid, '. . . have invited us to supper in La Terrassa d'Empúries. It's their thank you to me for driving them down today, plus Patterson's a golfer and he's dead keen to meet you, Jonny . . . if that's okay with you.'

He nodded. 'Sure, that's very kind of them. Do you know the place?' he asked, not quite casually enough.

'We live right on top of it. Why? Don't tell me you're a fussy eater?'

He shook his head. 'Not me. I'm a Fifer, remember. But,' he added, 'I'm also a professional sportsman, and these days even golfers have drug testing.'

'Is it so strict that you're worried about going to a local pizza place?'

'No, I don't suppose it is. We're given a list of banned substances, but you hear these horror stories about athletes being banned for buying a brand of cough mixture where the formula's different in different countries, so . . .'

60

'. . . you can't be too careful,' Tom concluded.

'Exactly, cuz. The testing's supposed to be random, but I'm the new boy this week, so I'm more than half expecting to be asked to pee in a bottle at some point.'

'That's bloody ludicrous,' I protested. 'This is golf we're talking about, for Christ's sake.'

'Quite a few players agree with you, but everyone has to accept that it's part of the age we live in. We play every week around the world for millions of dollars, euro or whatever, and most of that money comes from or is underwritten by sponsors. We have to show them that we have nothing to hide.'

'Is garlic banned?' I asked him.

He stared at me. 'Garlic? No, of course not.'

'Then you're fine here,' I promised him, checking my watch. 'Come on; they're probably waiting for us.'

They were. Two tables had been drawn together to accommodate the five of us. Charlie wasn't eating, but there was a bowl of water on the ground, ready for him. There was also a bottle of cava in an ice bucket. Shirley and Patterson hadn't been closer to Jonny than the viewing stand, so I did the honours, and we took our seats. Patterson arranged things so that my nephew and my son were on either side of him, with Shirl and me left to our own conversation and devices, but since neither of us had brought any . . . we exchanged a glance that said, 'Ah, what the hell, he's paying,' and let him get away with it.

While our host began a gentle interrogation, with Tom listening in, we took the 'little woman' route, and talked between ourselves.

'Seems like a nice lad, your Jonny,' Shirley declared. 'He scrubs up well, too.' She had a point. He had arrived on my doorstep freshly shaved and immaculately dressed, but not with the air of someone out to make an impression, rather that of one who knows no other way. 'What age did you say he was?'

'Twenty-two.'

'Going on thirty-three, I'd say.'

'I agree; how things have changed. When I met him he was seven, going on six. Yes, a very presentable young man.'

A gleam of pure wickedness shone in my friend's eyes. 'Primavera,' she whispered, 'you're not thinking about . . .'

I shot her flight of fancy down, well before it reached cruising height. 'Absolutely not,' I told her. 'I'm in loco parentis here. If I was in any doubt of that, I had a call from his mum to remind me.'

'In that case, you might think about putting an ad in the British Society magazine making it clear, 'cos, my dear, there will be those that says otherwise.'

'Just like they said about me and Gerard,' I reminded her. 'But as before, none of them will have the stones to say it to my face.'

'If they say it to mine, I'll put them right.' I knew that was a promise, and also, that our chattering class, i.e. most of the ex-pat population, would make their way to Shirley's door sooner or later. My reputation, and as a mother I did care about it, was in safe hands.

'What about that Swedish coach of his?' she continued. 'Do you think she's the mother type too?'

As she finished, I saw Jonny throw the merest glance in her direction, and a smile flicker at the corner of his mouth. 'Come on,' I called out. 'What does that grin mean, other than that you've got hearing like a . . .'

'Yes, Lena is the mother type,' he laughed, as Patterson and Tom stared at me. 'She and her husband have two kids, ages two and four. Lars won the Scandinavian championship in his playing days; he's a great big bloke who's about as given to smiling as she is, that being not a lot.'

Unkind, I thought. *He'd been friendly enough with me, in our brief conversation.*

'He never let her coach him,' Jonny continued. 'He says she's too scary on the practice ground. Pity, he might have done better on tour if she had.'

'Where did you find her?' Patterson asked him, just as the waitress arrived to take our meal orders.

'I didn't,' he replied, once she had headed for the kitchen. 'She found me. People like her are always on the lookout for young golfers to add to their stable. She took a look at my game, and liked what she saw. She told him she was sure I could make it as a pro, and Brush made the arrangements between us. That was the moment when I truly made the mental commitment to going on tour.'

Something about the chronology of that struck me as odd. 'So that means that Brush was your manager even before you decided you were going to be a pro?'

'Yes, but that's not unusual. As I said, quite a lot of promising amateurs have people looking out for them.'

'Your mum told me that quite a few people wanted to manage you, including the top agencies.'

He nodded. 'True, but they only approached me this year, after I made the Walker Cup. Mum insisted on Harvey taking a look at them all, and I let him.' He turned to Tom. 'You will find out, mate, that as far as mums are concerned you will always be fifteen to them.'

'Hey,' I protested, 'don't say that. He thinks he's fifteen already.'

'Then don't hold him back, Auntie P,' he laughed. 'No, the fact is that I'd made up my mind to go with Brush long before that.'

'Why?'

'Because it felt right; that's all I can say.'

'How did you find him?'

'I didn't. He found me, like Lena did. He approached me last summer, when I was on vacation, working as a bag monkey . . . they paid us peanuts, hence the name . . . at a private club in East Lothian and practising there in my time off as an added perk.'

'He found you?' Patterson repeated. 'How? Did he approach your parents? Or did the college put him in touch with you? Data protection laws in the US are patchy at best, but I'd have thought that a university would have to respect its students' privacy.'

'Mine did,' my nephew agreed. 'I have no idea how Brush found me, but I know it wouldn't have been through Arizona State. It's a very protective place. As for Mum and Harvey, no, he didn't contact them at all. But why should he? For all I indulge them, I'm over twenty-one, Mr Cowling. I'm my own man.'

'Sure, sure. Forget it,' Patterson said. 'I'm making too much out of it. Trust me, I know how easy it is to find people.' He paused, then added, 'Unless they don't want to be found, in which case it can become very difficult. Even then nothing's foolproof. I know of someone who thought he was completely anonymous, only to discover . . .' He stopped, smiling, his eyes suddenly a little distant. He didn't throw the faintest glance in my direction, but he didn't have to; message transmitted, message received. 'Still,' he continued, abruptly, 'for this man to walk up to you at a fairly obscure golf club, one among hundreds that must employ young people like you in the summer . . .'

'No,' said Jonny, firmly, 'that's not how it happened. He contacted me by email.' He saw my eyebrows rise, and nodded. 'That's how he did it, Auntie P. I checked my box one day and found a message from "brush119@aol.com". It said that he'd been following my college golf and that he'd be interested in knowing my future plans. I wrote back and told him that I didn't have any, none that were firm at any rate, but like most young amateurs at competitive level I was interested in finding out exactly how good I was. He replied and said that he was an ex-pro who'd never really made it on any tour but who did know the business, and who was putting together a stable of young players, "out of the clutches of the global golfer production lines". That's how Brush describes the big agencies. I asked him what made him a better bet than them, given that their record of success hasn't been too shabby over the last half a century. He said "I care"; simple as that. He also attached two draft management contracts. One was the standard deal offered to new pros by the GRA, the biggest company in the world, and the other was his. He guaranteed me a level of financial support through sponsorship as soon as I joined the professional tour, and he guaranteed that all my affairs would be handled by him, rather than by some salaried employee with a couple of dozen people like me, maybe more, in his group, every one of them expendable. I asked him for a list of his clients. He said he didn't have any, that he was just starting out, but that his promise to me was that he would never have any more than six. I reminded him at that point that I didn't even know for sure whether I would turn pro, and if I did, whether I could cut it on tour. His reply was that he wasn't making his approach without having seen me play, and having faith in me, and that part of his job would be to help me make that first decision. Finally he proposed that we work together on a gentlemen's agreement, not just until I turned pro, but until I made my first cut in a tour event. Lena's fee, Uche's wages; Brush has covered those, for now at any rate. Almost all of the sponsor money we've had so far is still in the bank . . . not that there's all that much, just initial retainers. Only my travel and living expenses since I left college a couple of weeks ago have come out of that; Brush hasn't even taken his commission. As of now, there is no contract; but I have one with me, and if I'm still in the tournament after Friday, I will sign it.'

Patterson peered at him. 'So it's all on a handshake . . . but he still has your money.'

'The money's in a bank account in my name; I have to authorise every transfer.'

'Bloody hell, Jonny,' I laughed. 'You must have a hell of a powerful handshake. What does this guy look like? How bright is his halo?'

66

He smiled once more, but a little awkwardly. 'Well,' he said, 'that's the thing. And this is what you probably will find weird. I've never actually met him, not face to face. Everything's been done by email or by phone.'

'No,' I replied, 'that is not weird. That transcends simple weirdness and moves into surrealism. You're saying that you've put your career, your potentially high-earning career, into the hands of someone, and you don't even know what he looks like?'

'Oh, I know what he looks like, Auntie P,' he assured me. 'His photo's on his email heading and on his letterhead. He looks like a pleasant forty-something bloke.'

'As do conmen around the world, I'm sure. Where's he based?'

'Chicago. His mail goes to a post office box address in East Ontario Street.'

'Phone?'

'He has a mobile: US number.'

'Does he have a website?'

'No, he says he doesn't want one; he wants to choose his own clients, not have them approach him. But he's going to set one up for me, to give me a presence for potential sponsors.'

'Have you pressed him for a meeting?'

'I've suggested it, sure, more than once, but he says that he prefers to be reclusive and that anyway, he gets hay fever any time he goes near a golf course, which is where I should be spending all my time. Lena and Uche are my people on the ground, he says, and when we need to meet, we will.'

'Has Uche met him?'

'No.'

'Doesn't that concern him?'

'Why should it?' he countered, easily. 'He's my mate, I picked him, and I gave him a job that's going to help him get on tour.'

'How about Lena?'

'I've got no idea. I've never asked her. She works with me, not him.'

'What does your mum say about this? She told me Harvey checked him out, and came up with a different explanation for his nickname.'

'Hah!' he laughed. 'Yes, when I asked him about that he said it probably did fit him when he was younger, but that was a while ago. Harvey's fine about him; if he hadn't been I'd have told him to back off, but it didn't come to that. Grandpa would pester the man to death if I let him near him. And as for Mum, if Harvey's happy, so is she.'

I frowned. 'That's fine. But after a lifetime of odd relationships, I'm not so sure I am.' His smile didn't waver, but it occurred to me that I had overstepped the mark. 'I'm sorry,' I said. 'Forget that; it's got bugger all to do with me. We only met up again today for the first time in donkey's. What I think doesn't matter; I'm just your long-lost auntie.'

'No. You're a lot more than that already. I'm sure that Brush and I will have to meet some time soon. When we do, I'll make sure you're—'

'Hey!' He was interrupted by a shout from Tom. I looked at him to see him twisting in his seat, holding someone's wrist: male, white, with blue veins showing clearly. The hand to which it was attached was in the inside pocket of Patterson's jacket, which he had draped over the back of his seat. The rest of its owner was outside the fence that marked the boundary of the terrace restaurant.

The man reacted, instantly. He tore himself free from Tom's grasp, but my son had the presence of mind, and the youthful strength, to lock on to Patterson's wallet and rip it from the would-be thief's grip. Jonny was out of his chair in a second, brushing Shirley aside as he vaulted over the fence. He would have set off in pursuit, had it not been for Patterson's shout of 'No!' laced with an imperious authority that seemed totally alien to such a mild-mannered man . . . if you believed that's what he really was, of course.

Jonny stopped in his tracks, and turned, staring at him like a chastened schoolboy.

'It's not worth it,' he said, in a tone that was almost apologetic. All the people at the surrounding tables were staring at us, but he calmed them with palms-down gestures, until gradually their interest subsided. (Only Charlie was unaffected. Some bloody guard dog: he slept through the whole drama.) 'He didn't get anything,' he continued, looking at my nephew, 'and you never know with these guys. Thank you, Jonny, but if you'd caught him and he'd been carrying a knife . . .' He shook his head. 'No, it doesn't bear thinking about.' He smiled at Tom, who was holding out his wallet, like an offering. 'Well done, young man,' he murmured, as he accepted it, and slipped it into his trouser pocket. 'It's not like me to be so careless. It just goes to show; you should never take your surroundings for granted.'

'But here you can,' I protested. 'This is St Martí, not bloody

Barcelona. We don't have pickpockets and petty thieves here.' I was furious, partly because I'm very proud of my home village, but mostly, I'm sure, because my son had been involved in a situation way beyond his years. Later, after I'd gone to bed, I shed a few tears of pride over the way he'd handled it, but at that moment, all that registered was anger. 'I'm not having this,' I declared, digging out my mobile.

'What are you going to do?' Shirley asked.

'I'm going to call my pal Alex Guinart, and report the son of a bitch to the police.' He is one, a detective, based in Girona.

'And what are you going to tell him? To look out for a running man, and that's it? 'Cos I never saw him.'

'No, more than that; for a start he was . . . white,' I added, lamely, realising that I could offer little more than her by way of a description.

'He was wearing Lacoste pirate pants, and a Def Leppard T-shirt,' Jonny volunteered. 'Dark hair, skinny. Tom was able to get a good grip of his wrist, so it couldn't have been that thick. I think he'd a Mont Blanc wristwatch on the other . . . they're one of my sponsors, so I recognised it. And New Balance trainers . . . they aren't, but I had a pair in Arizona, so I know the logo.'

'He has blue eyes,' said Tom, firmly, 'a gold tooth, a scar on his chin,' he touched his own to demonstrate. 'He needs a shave and his hair's grey as well as dark. And he's not British,' he added, as a postscript, 'or Spanish, or French, or German ... and he's too short to be Dutch.'

Patterson frowned at him, curiosity engaged. 'How do you know that?'

70

'It's a game we play, Tom and me,' I explained. 'We reckon that seven times out of ten we can tell a punter's nationality just by looking at them, and at their body language, before we ever hear them speak. Apart from their clothing, and that's a big give-away, especially among the youngsters, we can tell the Dutch by their height, the Germans by their build, the French by their frowns . . . very serious people; always worried about something. We know the Spanish because they seem most at home here . . . and they're most likely to be smokers. Our lot, they're easiest of all. They might as well have "British" tattooed on their foreheads.'

'You're British yourself,' he pointed out, 'you and Tom. That must give you an advantage.'

'No,' I contradicted. 'Tom's lived hardly any of his life in Britain, yet he's better at the game than I am. I didn't get any sort of look at the guy, but if he says he isn't a Brit, then trust him; he isn't. Not that I'd expect it,' I added. 'That job that I had for a couple of years: I was based in the consulate general in Barcelona. I was in and out of there, but I still heard things. For example, I know that up to twenty people a week need passport replacements because theirs have been stolen. For example, I know that it's quite common for British youngsters to get themselves lifted by the Mossos d'Esquadra for drunkenness, brawling, and other loutish behaviour, but hardly ever for petty theft. And I have absolutely never heard of a British pickpocket, in his thirties, wearing designer gear and a thousand quid watch; not anywhere, and most certainly not here.'

I had a question in mind, begging for an answer. The restaurant was busy, and there were more than a dozen people seated against the fence. Most of them were as casual with their property as Shirl's new other half had been, yet none of them was panicking or screaming about a loss. Patterson was modestly dressed, in what looked like a Marks & Spencer shirt, and showed no obvious sign of wealth, yet the thief had gone straight to him, past a woman in a dress that was definitely not chain store, with dangly ruby and diamond earings, and a handbag slung so carelessly over the back of her seat that it was begging to be emptied. Why? Why him? *Because the guy was stupid,* I decided, *a man suddenly down on his luck, choosing a victim at random.*

I set the thought aside, and opened my phone. I was calling up the contact list, when someone tapped me on the shoulder. 'Excuse me, Primavera,' a man murmured, in Spanish. I turned; Cisco, the owner of the restaurant, and a good friend, was crouching beside me. He was agitated, even more so than usual. 'I saw what happened,' he said. 'I'm sorry, I'm so sorry. I don't want that sort of thing in my place. I've never known it before, not in St Martí.'

'It's not your fault,' I replied, in English, for the benefit of Patterson and Jonny . . . although during the day I had begun to realise that he understood quite a bit of Spanish. 'Anyway, there's no harm done. The guy didn't get anything and he's been scared off. He must feel a real idiot being caught by a ten-year-old. I'll report him to the Mossos; he'll probably be nicked the very next time he tries it.'

'I have something that might help them,' said Cisco, switching languages. 'A man at the table behind yours, he was taking pictures with his phone, and he has one of the guy, with Tom holding on to him.' He beamed at my son. 'Hey, amigo, well done. If I ever need a bouncer I give you a job.' Then he turned back to me. 'He says you can have it.'

I looked round and caught the eye of the diner in question. I recognised him at once; he was an ex-pat from L'Escala, called Stan something, at a table with his pretty blonde wife. He looked pleased with himself. 'Thanks,' I said. 'Can you message it to my phone?'

'Sure, love,' he replied. 'It'll cost you a beer, mind.'

'Cheap at half the price.' I gave him my number, he fiddled with his phone and a few seconds later, the image downloaded on to mine.

It was pretty sharp. I couldn't make out the gold tooth or the scar that Tom had described, but it showed the thwarted robber full on, well enough for a Spanish court to nail him when the time came. 'Brilliant,' I told the donor. 'Cisco, one beer on Señor Cowling's tab, please, and whatever Wendy's drinking.'

'Can I see it?' Patterson asked.

I passed my phone across to him, touching the dial to keep the image displayed. He peered at it, then took a closer look, focusing hard. As he did so, I could see his thumbs move. It was discreetly done, but I realised what he was up to: he was copying Stan's picture to his own mobile.

He handed mine back. I pulled up my directory once more, and was about to push the button on a call to Alex, when his eyes met mine. He shook his head, slowly. 'No,' he murmured, so quietly that I almost had to lip-read.

'Why not?' I asked. Our first courses were arriving, so the exchange wasn't picked up by the other three.

'It's not worth the trouble. This man's disappeared into the crowd already. He'll be out of town by now, well on the way to wherever he came from.'

'But the police can circulate his photo,' I protested.

'They're not going to do that, not for a robbery that never even took place. I'll grant you it's a good picture, but it is what it is, an image taken on a mobile from a few yards away. However good a friend this Alex is to you, he's not going to thank you for wasting his time, for that is all you'd be doing, I promise you.'

'I'll print it out,' I threatened. 'Cisco will post it in his window, and so will the other restaurants.'

He smiled. 'Wanted: five hundred euro, dead or alive? Would they really want to make this lovely place look like the Wild West?'

He had a point. 'Maybe not,' I conceded. 'Okay, have it your way. Let's call it a lucky escape and forget about it. It's your shout anyway, you were the intended victim.'

I put my mobile back in my pocket and turned my attention to what lay on the table before me. *Yes*, I thought, *let Patterson have his way*. After very little thought I was quite happy to do that, for I had a feeling that he could track down the scarred, greying, gold-toothed, thirty-something non-Brit with the Mont Blanc watch a hell of a lot quicker than the Mossos d'Esquadra ever could. And, given his surreptitious copy of Stan's picture, I had the even more distinct feeling that he might.

Four

Normally I'd have forgotten about the incident by next morning and got on with my life, but three things made it linger. First I was angry at the sheer effrontery of the guy, trying to whizz someone's wallet in broad daylight, and right at my front door into the bargain. Second, there was Tom's involvement. I was proud of the way he had handled himself, but a little scared by it too, for the same reason that Patterson had offered in talking Jonny out of pursuing the plonker. Third, there was my friendship with Alex Guinart.

I knew him well, better even than Shirley, and it didn't take me long to work out that he was more used to judging what was proper use of his time than we were. A bungled theft would not go to the top of his things to do list, no danger; nevertheless if there was a chancer on the loose and he had better luck second time around, Alex would be less than pleased if he ever learned that I'd known about him and hadn't bothered to tell him.

And so, as soon as I'd fed my boys and sent them off to face their different days, I called him, mobile to mobile, and filled him in on what had happened. I'd got it right; he was grateful for the tip, and he promised to spread the word among his patrol colleagues, and with it, as good a print as his people could manage from the picture that I forwarded to him, even as we were speaking.

'Who is this new man of Shirley's?' he asked me, when I'd done that and finished my step-by-step account of what had happened. 'What's his background, that he should be so considerate about my workload? Is he a cop?'

'No, he's a retired civil servant,' I replied, 'that's all. He worked in our Foreign Office at one point in his career, so he probably knows all about unsolved crime statistics and decided he didn't want to add to yours.'

'That's kind of him,' he growled. 'Maybe I should have a word with him and remind him he's in another country now. Maybe I'll take a run up to Shirley's. After all, by rights it should be him who's making the complaint.' He called it *denuncio*; although his English is okay and improving, Alex and I normally speak in either Castellano or Catalan.

'No, please,' I begged him. 'Don't do that. I'm sure he thought he was only doing what was best. If you want to be angry with someone, make it me, not him.'

He chuckled. 'Much good that would do me. Ah, what the hell! Thanks, Primavera, I'll circulate it but the truth is that Mr Cowling is almost certainly right. This clown will be long gone by now, well out of my area. Hopefully he'll think better of it next time he sees a pocket he thinks is unguarded. You tell Tom "Well done" from me; tell him I have the application forms in my drawer for him to join the Mossos when he's old enough.'

'If you ever take them out of there,' I warned him, more than half serious, 'you will be in big trouble.'

'Don't worry,' he said. 'I'm too cautious ever to recruit him. That one, he'd be in my job inside a year.'

I hung up and let him get on with his day, for I had things to do with mine. The first was to find a base for Uche, as I had promised Jonny I would. I hadn't anticipated too much difficulty and I didn't encounter any. In fact I was spoilt for choice. Several of the local resident families, the old-timers, in and around St Martí are multiple property owners, and if you know who to ask, you will usually find something available for medium-to long-term rent. I spent a couple of hours talking to a few people I knew and by the time I had finished I had three offers. Two of them were cottages on the outskirts of the village, while the third was right in its centre, facing our house across the square. There's a guy who has a number of studios kitted out for holiday rent, including a couple of very nice penthouses. He was used to their being booked for a few nights at a time, so when I asked him to come up with a weekly figure on the basis of an initial three-month lease he was taken by surprise. After a while, and after some deadpan negotiation . . . the Catalan poker face is only equalled by that of the Scots . . . he came up with a number that didn't seem to me to be beyond the means of the son of a Nigerian princeling.

That done, I headed for the golf course, to catch up with Jonny. When I got there, the car park was much busier than it had been twenty-four hours earlier. The place still wasn't exactly thronged with spectators, but the public catering was up and running, and most of the golf equipment and clothing stands in the main exhibition tent were open for business. I wasn't surprised to find Shirley there; she was studying the latest Barbour lines, while

Patterson was a few yards away, test-driving a Callaway driver with a head not much smaller than mine. I look at modern golf equipment and I find myself wondering what the likes of Bobby Jones would have done with it.

I put that very question to Jonny after I'd I caught up with him and Uche on the fifth fairway, and walked a couple of holes. He was in a four-ball with a couple of youngsters they knew from the college circuit, one Spanish, the other Korean, and with an Irish kid who, Uche explained to me quietly, was ranked in the world's top twenty, even though he was a couple of weeks younger than my nephew.

'Who knows?' was Jonny's reaction to my question. 'He'd have been on the same playing field as the rest of us. Courses have changed since his day.'

'He'd still have been pretty hot, though,' the Irish lad chipped in.

'No doubt, but maybe the real question should be, how would we get on with the equipment that Jones and Hagen and Sarazen used?'

'I won't be lookin' to find out at this year's Open, that's for sure,' the mophead declared.

I walked the course with the boys, doing what I could to be helpful. That wasn't much, other than acting as a runner for Uche, when he found that he'd underestimated the number of waterbottles he'd need, since they weren't stationed around the course as they would be when the tournament began. It took a long time, not unnaturally, since most of the competitors wanted to be out there, and particularly the newcomers, as Jonny explained, as we stood on the fourteenth tee, with one group waiting in front of us. 'There's a pro-am event tomorrow. I'm not in it, so this is the last chance I'll get to play here before we go out for real on Thursday afternoon.'

'Afternoon?' I repeated.

He nodded. 'Twenty past two, tenth tee. The very last group.'

'That's a bit tough,' I complained. 'You'll be out in the hottest part of the day, and the forecast's good for the rest of the week.'

'I'm the new boy, Auntie P; I'm lucky to be in the field, so I'm not complaining. You've got to earn the good starting times out here. Don't worry about the weather either; it's like this in February in Arizona.'

I was still narked, though. 'It's not fair,' I grumbled. 'This is the last proper golf you'll be able to play for two whole days!'

'She's got a point, boss,' Uche added. 'The dice are a little loaded.'

'Don't worry about it,' he said. 'We can always go and hit balls somewhere.'

The obvious caught up with me. 'We can play Pals,' I declared. 'I'm a member. I get priority there.'

'What's it like?'

'Nice. It's the oldest course in this part of Spain. They have played tournaments on it, but not for a while.'

'But is it similar to this course?'

'It's got trees,' I offered, lamely.

Uche laughed. 'That's all you need. You can practise missing them; that's going to be very important on Thursday.'

'Fuck off,' Jonny retorted, amiably, taking me aback, yet pleasing me at the same time, because it showed that he was genuinely relaxed in my company. Yes, you could say that he was treating me like one of the boys, but I didn't mind that. It's usually my position of choice.

We had barely finished before I had to leave. I didn't broach the subject of accommodation with Uche until we'd stepped off the eighteenth green and he'd finished tidying Jonny's bag. When I did, and told him what I'd lined up; he was pleased, and easy to please still further. 'Which would you choose?' he asked.

'The penthouse studio; no question. But don't you want to know what it'll cost?'

'No. I'll take it.'

'I'll tell the owner. You can probably move in whenever you like.'

'Sunday evening will be perfect; thank you very much, Auntie P.'

I wasn't sure how to take that. Uche was a very presentable young man; the realisation that he saw me as an aunt figure brought me up sharp.

So I ignored it. 'I'm sure we'll be able to book the one next door for your parents, if they want to come and visit you.'

His slightly cautious smile suggested a couple of things, either that if his parents did come to visit they'd be booking the best suite in the best hotel in town, if not a whole floor, or, that even if they were the chummy types, their son might prefer to keep them at a greater distance.

Business concluded, I headed on up the road, and made it home just before Tom. He has his own key now, but I don't yet feel comfortable about leaving him unminded too often, unless I'm within shouting distance. I'm much more relaxed about leaving Charlie, on guard in the garden, although he was pleased to see me, for he was running out of water. He needed exercise too, and so did Tom, having been cooped up in school all day, so they left for their usual run, along to Vaive and back, while I gave some thought to what I might lay on the table before my extended family.

I had just dug three steaks out of the fridge, and was starting to chop onions when the phone rang. 'Bugger,' I said as I picked it up with two fingers, trying not to smear it and leave it ponging for days.

'Thank you,' said Alex Guinart. 'I'll take that to be a term of endearment in English.'

'Sorry, Alex,' I replied. 'Awkward moment. And no, in case you get the wrong idea, I'm in the kitchen, not on the toilet. What can I do for you?'

'Nothing you haven't already done. I thought I should call to tell you that our specialists got a decent image from your phone picture. Just for fun I persuaded a friend of mine to feed it into the national computer, to see if we got a facial match. We didn't; not even close.'

'Did you try databases anywhere else?' I asked him. 'Although Tom was dead certain that he wasn't one of ours.'

'No, I didn't,' he laughed. 'I'm an inspector in a regional police force in Spain. I'd have had to go through our HQ in Barcelona for that sort of access, and I'm not about to do that. Look, Primavera, I've done as much as is reasonable, and a bit more. The photograph is out there, in Mossos stations across Catalunya, with a note that it came from a report by a concerned citizen. So thank you again. If we should happen to put a name to it, I'll let you know.'

As *if*, I thought as I hung up. I was still curious, though. I was flattered that Alex had gone that far, but I knew that it had been mostly PR. No, what I wondered was . . . had Patterson come up with anything?

Had it not been for the half-chopped onion, I might have called to ask him, but the onion took priority, and so I went back to the kitchen instead.

Five

Pals was quiet next day, so I didn't have to muscle my way into a starting time. In fact the club superintendent was very pleased to see us, even more so when Jonny showed him his European PGA membership card. These days pros are offered the courtesy of the course by most good golf clubs around the world; it's only a few, the nineteenth-century relics, the sort that still don't admit women as members, that won't allow them to play.

When I tee-ed off at the first, it was for the sake of appearance; I hadn't meant to play all the way round, but the boys insisted. As it turned out I'd have been bored if I hadn't, for Uche was meticulous in calculating the yardage for each shot, using the course guide and flag placement chart that the starter had given us, so that he could give Jonny the right club every time. I know the caddie is a team player, but I hadn't appreciated until then that it was a practice round for him as much as for his boss.

Although I'd watched Jonny hit a few hundred balls by that time, it wasn't until then, until I saw him in the context of my home course, that I realised how long he was. I'd played with his grandfather and his uncle often enough, and they could send it out a fair distance, especially Oz, but Jonny, he seemed to be knocking it into another province.

'It's not only about distance,' Uche replied, when I remarked upon this, as we set off down the long par five eighth after another rifling tee shot . . . Jonny's not mine; that one had gone a hundred and twenty metres. 'It's about hitting it the same distance every time with each club in the bag, and it's about accuracy.'

'And how good is Jonny at that?'

'He's up there with the best. The trouble is, there are a hell of a lot more of the best than there used to be.' He grinned. 'They're in for a shock this week, though. We've arrived.'

'You think he'll make the cut all right?'

'I know he will. I've been watching the other guys on the practice range. We weren't out of place there. We're going to make money.' He smiled. 'Ninety per cent to Jonny, ten per cent to me; I've got a real interest in giving him the right club every time.'

'Is that after this Brush character has taken his twenty per cent?'

Uche shook his head as we stopped at my ball. Jonny's was miles ahead; he was standing twenty metres away, engrossed in the yardage chart. 'Nope. Mr Donnelly isn't on the course, so he doesn't earn there. His commission comes from all the ancillary deals he does.'

I hit a fairway club in more or less the right direction; when it stopped it still hadn't caught up with my nephew's. I glanced at him, noting the logos on his clothing. The boy was a walking sales pitch.

'He's got some good sponsors,' I said. 'Do all young players turn pro with that sort of backing?'

'Some do. For example, there's a young American guy who was on the college circuit with us until a year ago. He looks like a rainbow on legs. But most of them? No, they need private money behind them, someone to stake them, and to carry the losses they're going to make . . . and quite possibly never recover them.'

'So why has Donnelly done so well for Jonny? Yes, he played in the Walker Cup, but so did quite a few other guys, and I haven't seen anyone else from our team lighting up the circuit. I know he's good, but I'm biased; I'm his aunt. Those badges he's wearing, they're all top companies. How did this man Brush get them on board when he hasn't even hit a shot yet, professionally?'

We'd reached my ball. I pulled out another club and clipped it forward again. A good one: another like that and I'd be on the green. As I set off towards my playing partner's tee shot . . . I read a distance marker on the fairway and worked out that he'd hit it two hundred and eighty-two metres . . . I sensed an unusual hesitancy in his caddie.

'Come on,' I insisted. 'No bullshit. How did he do it? Or is all this for show? Has Jonny just bought the gear?'

'Work it out,' Uche whispered. 'It's not just what he can do, it's who he is.' He left me gazing after him as he stepped towards his pro. 'Take a little off a three metal,' he called out, 'rather than a five. You want to hit it low. We're sheltered down here; you don't know for sure what the wind's doing above those trees. Watch for the bunker front right, otherwise it's a clear approach.'

'Just what I was thinking,' Jonny replied. 'I may need that shot a lot this week.'

As he took the club he was handed, and surveyed the distant flag, I lined up a few things myself, in my head. The fact that he was Oz Blackstone's nephew was, it seemed, still a highly sellable attribute. *And why shouldn't it be?* I realised. I, of all people, ought to have known that.

Oz might have been dead, but his career was still alive. He'd had three posthumous movie releases, all hits, including the one he'd been working on when he'd done that last fatal stunt. That, of course, had lent it added marketability, even if the last few scenes had been shot in shadow with a body double and his lines voiced over by an impersonator. Then there were DVDs; some of his films, most notably the cricket blockbuster *Red Leather*, had done huge business in that format, and sales showed no signs of slowing. On top of that the download market was just beginning to take off, and was being exploited very well by his near genius agent, Roscoe Brown. Yes, my late ex was still very big business, and consequently, anything to do with him just had to smell of money.

I knew all this, because I see the figures, twice a year. I didn't believe for a second that Oz foresaw his own early death, but he'd have been crazy not to have made a will, and he was more calculatingly sane than anyone I've ever known. Apart from individual bequests to his nephews, and a tithe that went to a small charitable foundation administered by Roscoe, his estate had been divided equally between his three children, Tom, and his two by Susie, Janet and 'wee Jonathan'. That split applied equally to all future income; ten per cent to the foundation, thirty per cent each to the three kids. The money was all tied up in trusts, a complicated structure put together by some very expensive accountants, and the will specified that the trustees should be 'the children's legal guardians'. I don't believe that he envisaged me being one of those when he signed off on it, but that's the way it had panned out: another reason why Susie and I should stay on good terms, whatever the rest of the Blackstone family thought of her.

For all that Tom and I go on about careers, the fact is that my son will never have to do a day's work in his life, unless he chooses. He doesn't know that, though; nor does anyone else outside our tight little family group. The last thing I want is for him to grow up complacent, or worse, under the constant eye of a bodyguard.

Jonny hit his three, with a little off. I couldn't see exactly where it finished, but the boys seemed satisfied. Their eyes were twenty years younger than mine, after all. We walked forward to my ball, I hit another fairway metal . . . Mac still calls them woods, for some reason . . . into the middle of the green, not too far from the pin. We took two putts each; birdie four for Jonny, bogey six for me, a result, since I was getting a shot at the par three holes, two at the par fours and three at the par fives. Eight holes played and I was only three down, not at all bad, since my 'opponent' was four under par at the time.

I must explain that I don't regard life as a competition. I've always hated being idle, and if I see something to be done I'll do it: for example, the tourist information service that I set up in my early days in St Martí. However, I've never felt the need to be better, only to be as good as I can. I was that way when I was nursing, to the extent that some people thought I was pushy. In truth the person I was really pushing was myself, but if I saw someone with a laissez-faire attitude to standards, I couldn't keep my mouth shut. As a mother, I don't care how Tom compares with the rest of his school class, only that he does his best. (*Mind you,* she added smugly, *that's pretty damn good.*)

All that changes when I step on to a golf course.

There I become the most competitive bitch you will ever see. Even Shirley says that my talons come out as soon as someone puts a score card in my hand, or as soon as a match-play opponent tees off. Not even my son is exempt from this. I don't swear or chuck clubs when he's around, but when we play for real, other than for fun, as we do more and more, the older he gets, I Do Not Let Him Win! (More often than not, he does anyway; if my evil side didn't dematerialise as soon as the last putt drops, or misses, as is often the case, he'd have gone to bed without any supper many a night.)

Buoyed by my win on the eighth, I headed for the next tee with undiminished determination and new hope. Three down, sure, but ten holes left and a generous shot concession coming my way, I wasn't out of it: par three at the next, win it with my shot and maybe Jonny would start to get rattled.

I was still thinking that way as we walked forward to red tees . . . okay, I was playing a shorter course than him, but he's a pro . . . despite him having knocked an eight iron to within a couple of metres of the target, when my phone vibrated in my pocket. (Any attempt to ban the things from courses in Spain will be doomed to failure.)

I dug it out, in case it was Tom: most of my calls and messages are from him. But it wasn't.

'Primavera.' Alex Guinart was using his 'all business' voice, one I'd heard very rarely. 'Where are you?'

I told him, in my own 'all business' voice. He isn't much of a golfer, but he and I play occasionally, so he knew what he was interrupting. I assumed that he'd ask me to call him back once I was finished, but I was wrong. 'I need you,' he said.

'Darling,' I replied archly, loudly enough for the guys' eyebrows to rise, 'many men have said that, but damn few have set me running.'

He wasn't in a joking mood. 'I'm not kidding. This is urgent.'

I felt a quick pulse of panic raced through me. 'Is something wrong with Tom?'

'No. Not at all. It's nothing like that, but I would appreciate your help.'

I sighed, out of frustration. 'I'm on the verge of something big here, chum; but for you . . . ahh, where are you?'

'I'm in L'Escala, almost. Do you know a street called Vall d'Aran?'

'Near Shirley's house? Yes.'

'That's the one. I want you to go there, right to the end to where the woods begin. One of our people will meet you there and bring you to me.'

'We're on the ninth, Alex. It'll take me the best part of an hour.'

'I appreciate that. As soon as you can, please.'

I was gutted; the hot blood of competition was still flowing through my veins. But when the cops, even the friendly ones, invite you seriously to help with their enquiries, it's best not to decline. When I told them I had to go, the boys assumed that their day was done too, but I told them to carry on. 'If I'm not back by the time you finish,' I said, 'wait for me in the clubhouse. Mine's a spritzer.'

'What's all this about?' Jonny asked.

'I have no idea,' I confessed. I hadn't bothered to ask. I knew that for my friend to call me in the way he did, it had to be as urgent as he'd said, but there was no point in fretting on the way there. I'd deal with it when I came face to face with whatever it was.

It took me a little less than that hour, thanks to a helpful course ranger, who gave me and my clubs a lift back to the car park in his buggy. I called Alex before I set out, with a new estimate of my arrival time. Sure enough, when I made my way up Carrer Bassegoda and along Vall d'Aran, I saw a Mossos vehicle at the road end, with a uniformed woman officer, a local that I recognised, leaning against it.

I parked behind her, a little way from the last house in the street; its presumptuous owner had tried to put a little distance between himself and the general public by constructing a makeshift barrier of stones and felled branches, but the cop had ignored it and driven her Nissan straight over it. The guy was glowering at her through the bars of his gate, but whatever he was thinking, he was smart enough to keep to himself.

'This way,' my escort instructed, making her way down a slope and taking a path that led into the woods, assuming that I would follow. Her name was Magda, and I read the fact that she didn't seem in the mood for chat as a further indication that Alex had not asked me along to show me a new species of mushroom that he'd discovered.

We hadn't gone more than a couple of hundred yards before we reached, and crossed, the unmarked track that is the boundary between the townships of L'Escala-Empuriès and Torroella de Montgri-L'Estartit, to give them their formal and imposing Catalan names. More cops, six of them, mingled in front of a derelict stone building. They were municipals; two from L'Escala and four from the other side, I reckoned from their badges. They didn't seem to be doing much, but I wondered as we passed them if a turf war was looming.

That seemed less likely the further we walked through the thickening woods, and the further we left L'Escala behind. My assumption was that they were there to keep the public away. But from what?

'How much further?' I asked Magda, but she still wasn't for chatting.

After half a mile or so, the track forked in two, and we bore left. I was becoming disorientated, glad I had company, and wondering how many people had wandered into those woods over the years, to become missing person statistics. Then, suddenly, we were in unfettered sunlight once again, in a wide circular clearing. There was a green signpost in the middle, with four route markers, each pointing at a different gap in the trees, including the one from which we had just emerged.

There was something else there too, a big, square, white tent.

Alex Guinart was waiting outside it; he was wearing a blue disposable crime scene one-piece. 'So, it's not the annual Mossos barbecue,' I said. 'And that isn't to keep the sun off the wine.'

'No.' It wasn't him who replied, but another man, identically dressed, who stepped out of the enclosure just as I spoke. I hadn't seen Intendant Hector Gomez, Alex's boss in the criminal investigation division, for a couple of years, not since he and I had stood on each other's toes in a very messy business that I'd been sucked into. My friend had assured me that everything was square between us, and that there were no hard feelings on the cop's side, but I'd never heard that from him.

'Good afternoon, Primavera.' So far so good; first-name terms. He didn't smile, but the environment wasn't exactly mirth-provoking, so I didn't hold that against him.

'And to you, Hector,' I replied. 'Now, will one of you guys please tell me why you hauled me off the golf course and brought me here?'

'We need you to look at something,' Gomez volunteered.

'Some-thing?' I repeated, with heavy verbal underlining.

'It is now,' Alex muttered, the first sign of anything approaching levity.

'Do I have an option here?'

'Of course you do,' the intendant insisted. 'We'd ask very few people to do this, only those we think have the stomach for it. But if you'd rather not, we'll understand.'

I held out a hand. 'Gimme,' I said.

'What?'

'One of those paper suits; I assume you want me to wear one.'

He smiled, for about half a second. 'Yes. Thank you.' He snapped his fingers, and pointed; Magda picked a fresh tunic from a pile on the ground and handed it to me. 'We're usually right about people,' he added. He hadn't been a couple of years before, but I let that go unsaid.

I got myself inside the garment, feeling like a Smurf as I fastened it and tucked my hair inside the hood. I'd worn sterile clothing often enough as a nurse to know that anything left uncovered can make the exercise effectively useless. 'Okay,' I said, 'lead on.'

Gomez glanced at Alex. 'You do it. I need a cigarette, to clear my nostrils.'

That didn't add to the party atmosphere either, but by that time I knew they had a real good one for me. A good what? Well, let me put it this way. It doesn't matter where you are, when the local criminal investigators arrive and put up a tent, you know pretty much what's inside it. The only matter in doubt is its condition.

The specimen they had summoned me there to view was in pretty bad nick. It was male, it was white, it was naked, it was dead, and it wasn't surprising that Gomez had wanted a Marlboro after spending some time with it. It wasn't easy to tell what had happened to the man, for animals had been at him, and maybe birds too, but my guess was that he had been shot, a couple of times, with a shotgun or something very like one, at close range. The abdomen had been ripped open, and most of the intestines had spilled out or had been torn out by predators. The face was a real mess too; in truth, there wasn't a hell of a lot left of it. There was so much blood and other matter in the hair that it was difficult to tell what colour it was. Whoever had killed him had taken everything from him, and not just his clothing. He wore no jewellery, but there was a very faint circle round his left wrist; he hadn't sported much of a suntan, but enough for a watch to have made the skin beneath it slightly paler than the rest.

'How long has he been there?' I asked.

'At least one full day, probably not two, the pathologist says, but he's still guessing at this stage.'

'Who found him?'

Alex winced. 'A group of schoolkids from Torroella, out on an orienteering day with their teachers.'

'Jeez! That'll be the talk of the playground for a while. I assume that they didn't take his clothes as souvenirs.'

'No. That's how he was found.'

'Why strip him?'

'Hector and I believe that it was to make him difficult to identify. It's no big task to trace someone through clothing labels and bar codes. He may have been shot in the face for the same reason.'

That pushed my scepticism button. 'So you don't know what he looked like and you don't know where he shopped. Whoever killed him left you his hands, though; you've got fingerprints.'

'Yes we have,' Alex agreed, 'but that could indicate that whoever killed him doesn't expect us to find anything that way. However, you say that we don't know what he looked like. That's why you're here. Parts of the face are still intact; we'd like you to take a look at them and tell us what you think.'

'Specifically?'

'The chin and the mouth.'

'Okay.' I crouched down beside the corpse, leaning forward, as close to it as I could get. The sun was high and clear above the tent and more than enough light came through its fabric for me to see clearly. I stared at the wreckage for a couple of minutes, puzzled, still with no idea why I was there or what I was supposed to find, until . . . I spotted a mark on the chin. It was blood-smeared, but it was clear to see, a small scar, crescent-shaped. And with it a memory returned and the connection was clear.

The top lip had been shredded and the teeth smashed, but enough remained to let me see that one of them had been gold.

'You think this is the man who tried to nick Patterson Cowling's wallet?' I asked, knowing the answer, but being unsure how to spell 'rhetorically'.

'What do you think? The image you gave me isn't good enough for us to confirm it, but Tom's description matches.'

'Fine, but I didn't see him that closely. I can't say "This is the man", not categorically.'

'Maybe not, but Tom . . .'

'No!' I snapped. 'A thousand times no. You are not asking Tom to look at that.'

He held up both hands, as if to fend me off. 'Primavera, Primavera! What do you take us for? I wouldn't dream of doing that, and neither would the boss. But we thought that if we showed him a sketch of the scar, a drawing, and he said that it matches, that would be enough for us to take to the prosecutor's office and get authority for a search that goes beyond criminal records.'

I considered the request for a while. 'Okay,' I agreed, eventually. 'You can do that. But you better come up with a cover story, a reason why you're asking him to do it, other than the real one. I don't want him even thinking about this mess.'

'Understood. I'll tell him that the man's been found, that's all, just found, and that rather than have Tom look at a line-up, all we need is for him to confirm that the scar matches what he saw.'

'I can live with that; technically, it's the truth, even if it does have holes in it. Get it under way and come to see us this evening.'

'Will do.'

I was still a wee bit doubtful. 'Alex,' I ventured, 'this wider search. It'll be pretty futile, won't it?'

'Not necessarily. We'll run the image against all Spanish nationals within a certain age group, looking for a match; also all the white male ex-pats we have on our criminal records. We won't rule any nationality out,' he chuckled, 'for all our boy's certainty that his man wasn't any of the usual. We'll also try immigration if we have to, in the hope that if he is foreign, he arrived in Spain by air. If so, our government will have a record of his passport information.'

'I have a vision of a whole stack of haystacks and a very small needle,' I told him, 'but good luck to you.'

'We are lucky sometimes.' Alex grinned, ruefully. 'Primavera, there's one other thing,' he continued. 'This friend of Shirley's, the man who asked you not to call us. We should speak to him; the only question is whether we should use discretion. What do you think?'

I stared at him. 'Why are you asking me?'

'Because I value your opinion.'

'That's flattering; it's also bullshit. Why should you want to speak to him at all?'

He shrugged. 'A man tried to rob him, failed, but got away. A couple of days later that man is found dead, killed in a cold and professional way. We have no reports of the guy trying to rob anyone else, so . . . Mr Cowling is of interest to us, it's clear.'

'What would you do normally?'

'I'd pick him up.'

'Then why do differently in his case?'

'That's what I'm asking you.'

I decided to be difficult; I was doing Alex a big favour, and I wasn't having him go all coy on me. 'Why?' I persisted.

He paused, as if he was having trouble explaining his motivation, even to himself. 'I suppose it's the fact that you went along, even for a little while, with his wish that you didn't report the incident. You're my close friend and you know that what he asked you was irregular. You hardly know this man, and yet he persuaded you to go against what I know to be your instincts. That makes me wonder whether there's more to him than it appears. So, do you know something about him?'

I was boxed in, firmly; I couldn't prevaricate any longer, even suppose it had been Hector Gomez who'd been quizzing me, rather than Alex. 'Honest answer, no,' I told him. 'He told me the first time we met that he's a retired British civil servant.'

'But . . . ?'

'No buts. That's what he is.'

He grinned at me. 'So you checked. I knew you would.' He paused. 'Come on, let's get out of here. I'll start smoking again myself if I have to spend much longer in this man's company.'

We slipped out of the tent, back into the clearing. Magda had gone, leaving only a couple of crime scene officers, who appeared to be searching the area, square centimetre by square centimetre, looking for … anything that didn't belong there, I supposed. I looked around and saw Hector Gomez, leaning against a tree, taking a long drag on what would not have been his first cigarette.

'So,' Alex continued, his tone questioning, once more, 'I can tell the boss we should pick up Mr Cowling and interview him formally? That's what you think?'

Bugger! was actually what I thought. Not what I said, though. 'I think that Patterson was a victim of an attempted crime,' I replied, a little testily. 'I don't see what you'd gain by interviewing him other than ticking a couple of boxes.'

'Oh, I dunno,' he countered. 'There is that connection between him and the victim, and Shirley's house is no more than a couple of kilometres from here.'

'For Christ's sake, Alex,' I exclaimed. 'That's ridiculous. Quite apart from being a pleasant, peaceable human being, the man is portly and pushing seventy. He's not Daniel bloody Craig or Jason bloody Statham.'

'You don't have to be, to rip someone open with a shotgun.'

'Oh, for fuck's sake!' I snapped in English, even more exasperated. 'Go ahead then, pick him up and clamp electrodes to his testicles, or whatever it is that you guys do. But you'll still get no more good from it than those same ticked boxes. On the other hand, you have no idea of the shit you might bring down on yourself!'

As soon as I'd said it, I knew that I'd underestimated my friend.

He didn't need to electrify people to get results. All he needed was quiet, indirect cross-examination for them to eventually tell him everything they knew . . . or in the case of me and Patterson Cowling, didn't know.

'Indeed?' he murmured. 'And where would that fall from?'

'Look, Alex,' I sighed. 'I'm not going to spell it out to you, because nobody spelled it out to me. You do what you believe you have to do, or whatever Hector orders you to do, but look out for yourself at the same time.'

'We will,' he promised. 'Hector doesn't even know about Mr Cowling's connection with the dead man. All I told him was that the scar and the gold tooth made me think of your report and Tom's description. From what you say, there'll be no harm done to anyone if I leave it that way.'

'Good.' I glanced at my watch. Time was getting tight; I had to pick Jonny up from Pals and get back to L'Escala for five. 'Can I go now?'

'Sure. Thanks for your help, for all of it. There's an artist I know who lives near here and isn't squeamish. I'll ask him to do a sketch from a photograph and bring it round for Tom to look at. We should go too; we need to get as much manpower as we can to organise a wider search of the area in case the dead man's clothing, and maybe even the murder weapon, was dumped somewhere near.'

'Do you think that's likely?'

'Not at all. But I need to get Hector out of here as well. He's not as tough as he pretends, and at the rate he's smoking, he's liable to set the forest on fire.'

Six

The boys were on the clubhouse terrace when I returned, each drinking what I hoped were only colas, and not Cuba Libres. Bacardi hangovers are not recommended on the morning of the biggest day of your life. I'd barely sat down before a spritzer arrived, in a tall glass, with ice and a slice of lemon. The barman there knows how I like them.

'How did you do?' I asked.

'I finished five under,' Jonny replied. He smiled. 'When you left, Auntie, you took my competitive edge with you.'

'Just as well I did,' I said, cheerfully. 'It wouldn't have done you any good, the day before a tournament, to have your ass whupped by a middle-aged woman.'

'Never happen,' he drawled, 'and you're not middle-aged.'

'Don't you believe it. Five years ago, you'd never have got to four up on me.'

His eyes gleamed, and I saw a flash of his uncle. 'Five years ago, I'd have been giving you a lot fewer shots.'

'There is that,' I conceded.

'What did the cops want?' Uche asked, boldly. For an instant,

I registered annoyance in Jonny's eyes, as if he'd known that I'd have told them in my own time, without being pushed . . . or not, if that was my choice.

'They had something they weren't quite sure about,' I said, carefully, 'and they thought that I might be able to help.'

'And were you?'

'Not really. All I did was confirm what they suspected already.' I didn't want to get into it, so I told him a lie that wasn't, not really, or the truth, but not quite. 'Alex Guinart, my cop friend, quite often asks me about things that concern the British community in St Martí and L'Escala. Everything's urgent to him, hence the summons.'

That seemed to satisfy his curiosity. We finished our drinks, Uche paid for them, then we went our separate ways, he back to the rented house and Lena's family, Jonny and I to St Martí.

We travelled in silence . . . if you don't count Norah Jones, and many people wouldn't . . . till we reached the bridge that leads into Torroella, across the River Ter. 'That was a load of crap, wasn't it?' Jonny said, just loudly enough to get my attention.

'What?'

'The way you fobbed Uche off.' He laughed softly. 'You have a way of telling people to mind their own business without them realising they've been told.'

'If I do, maybe it'll work on you.'

I must have spoken more sharply than I'd intended; I sensed rather than saw him frown beside me. 'Sorry,' he murmured, sounding just like Tom does when he's pushed his luck too far.

And making me realise that I couldn't treat the two of them in the same way.

'No,' I blurted out. 'I'm sorry, Jonny, I shouldn't have snapped at you. You're absolutely right, I did fob him off, but I shouldn't do the same with you. I'd be pissed off if you weren't open with me, so . . . They wanted me to look at a dead man.'

'Jesus!' he hissed. 'Why? Was he clutching a piece of paper with your name scrawled on it?'

'Written in his blood? No. They thought I might have seen him before. And they were right. So have you.' I told him who I'd seen, lying dead and desecrated in the suburban forest.

'Wow!' He whistled. 'What do you think; that he tried it on again but picked on the wrong bloke?'

An interesting assumption, I thought, and probably the basis of the continuing police investigation, once Alex rid himself of the irrelevant connection with Patterson. 'That's quite possible,' I agreed. 'Anyway, it's got nothing to do with us, at least it won't be once my friend shows Tom a sketch to confirm the identity as close to one hundred per cent as they can get. But what am I talking about?' I contradicted myself out loud. 'That won't, will it? They haven't the faintest idea who the guy is, and whatever Alex says, they've got a very slim chance of finding out, unless someone comes forward to report a missing person.'

'Ouch. Was it a mess?' he asked. His question was serious, not ghoulish. It sounded sympathetic, in a strangely literal way, but I don't imagine it's an experience we could have shared.

'That's why they're having to show Tom a sketch of the scar on his chin,' I replied. 'I couldn't look at the guy and say positively that it was him.'

'You shouldn't have had to,' he growled. 'Couldn't they have shown you a sketch too?'

'Don't worry about me, Jonny,' I assured him. 'I won't wake up screaming. I've seen worse.'

'Where, for Pete's sake?'

There were a couple of answers to that. I chose the safe one. 'I was a nurse, remember. I've been in operating theatres. I did anatomy as part of my training. And I worked for a while as a volunteer in an African war zone. But we won't go into any of that. All you need to understand is that Alex Guinart wouldn't have put me in a situation he didn't know I could handle.'

'A murder mystery, eh,' he said, as the CD changer moved Norah on and replaced her with the Drive-by Truckers; just at the right time, I reckoned, as a change of mood was called for. 'Right on our own doorstep. Or am I getting ahead of myself?' he added. 'Could it have been suicide?'

I chuckled, grimly. 'If it was, it was very definitely the assisted kind.'

The other band from Athens, Georgia, cranked up the volume at that point and so conversation was out for the rest of the journey, or rather until my car's Bluetooth cut it out automatically as it picked up a call. 'Yes,' I said, the simple command to accept it.

'Okay then.' Shirley Gash's voice, never subdued at any time, boomed out from the speakers. 'What the hell's up? There have been cops going up and down our road all day, and now one of my neighbours tells me she saw you heading in the same direction.

What's the story? I've asked a couple of the Mossos people, but they won't say a word.'

'Neither can I right now,' I told her. 'I'm driving and I've got a couple of roundabouts to negotiate.' I had been thinking, though. I might have talked Alex out of talking to Patterson Cowling, but that hadn't killed my own curiosity. I rather fancied a chat with the man myself. But it would be difficult to separate him from Shirley, in which case . . . tough on him.

'If I call you back in fifteen minutes on your landline, will you be in?' she persisted.

'Yes, but I'll be busy.'

'Meet us for supper?'

'No, I've got hungry lads to feed, but I could probably meet you somewhere later, for a coffee.' I glanced at Jonny, and managed to ask, just by raising an eyebrow, '*Will you stay in with Tom?*' He nodded.

'That'll have to do, then,' Shirley conceded. 'We're going to eat at La Clota.'

'Fine, I'll join you about nine-thirty; but don't get involved with anyone else, or my lips will stay sealed.'

'We'll ask for a private booth,' she said. I laughed: they don't have any.

I called in at a fish shop on the way home, and bought three monkfish, fairly small, as that species goes, but still well big enough for each of us. Jonny had never seen one before, not in its entire state. They're ferocious-looking bastards, all mouth and teeth, but they're fantastic when they're baked in the oven. The lady offered to take the heads off, but I declined. There are two thumb-sized pieces just behind the eyes; the best part of the fish, my son and I agree.

I'd just closed the oven door on them when Alex Guinart arrived, with a sketch, and with the Magda woman, still silent, looking as if she might have had other plans for the evening. I hadn't told Tom that he was coming. It wasn't only that I didn't want him asking me why, and dragging me into telling him about my trip to the woods, but also because I wanted him to have a clear mind when it came to look at the thing, his instant reactions always being the most reliable.

I'd have struggled to get his attention anyway; as soon as he arrived home, and had taken Charlie for his early evening run, he engaged Jonny in a detailed debrief of his round over Pals. Pros can remember every detail of every shot they play, and so it went on for some time. Indeed the last putt had only just fallen when the door buzzer sounded, a few seconds after the church bells had rung seven for the first time. Don't be confused when you come to St Martí; they always ring the hour again, at two minutes past, in case you missed it before, or lost count.

Alex told Tom what he wanted, not quite following the party line that we'd agreed, but safely enough. 'Remember the man you saw,' he said, 'the man who tried to rob Mr Cowling? The photo we have doesn't really show the scar on his chin. Take a look at this drawing and tell me, if you can: did it look like this?' He handed over the sketch; my son studied it for a few seconds and nodded.

'That's it,' he confirmed. 'Like a scimitar. Has he done something bad?'

'Stealing is bad, Tom,' Magda announced, stolidly. I winced.

Only the second time she'd opened her mouth in my presence all day, and she had to go and say something stupid. Nobody likes being patronised: there's an age at which kids recognise it and my lad had reached it at least a year before.

'I know that,' he replied, politely, then beat her at her own game. 'It's one of the Ten Commandments.' He might not believe in God, but he can cite him as evidence when necessary. 'But he didn't actually steal anything from Mr Cowling. I stopped him and he ran away.' He paused. 'Of course,' he added, as if he'd had a revelation, 'there's a Commandment against trying to steal too, the one about coveting.' Magda shifted from one foot to the other; they hadn't covered that in her training course.

'What I meant,' he went on relentlessly, looking at Alex once again, 'was, has he done something else? You haven't caught him, or you wouldn't be asking me to look at a drawing.'

The inspector shook his head, in confirmation. 'No, we haven't. But when we do find him, we have to be absolutely certain that we've got the right man. You understand?'

'Yes, Alex,' he replied. Of course he did: he understood that he was being spun a line, and Alex, being a family friend, probably realised that. But he knew also that if he told him the whole story, my wrath would fall upon him, and he didn't fancy that.

'Thank you, Tom,' he said. He was prepared to leave it at that, but my son wasn't, not quite.

'It's nothing. Will I have to be a witness if you do catch him?'

'I can't see that being necessary.' More carefully chosen words. He sniffed. 'Are you cooking fish, Primavera?'

I nodded. 'And tomatoes, chopped garlic, and some lightly sautéed potatoes.'

He smiled at my guys. 'Lucky you. It'll be a while before I get to eat. Come on, Magda,' he said, 'let's go. We've got what we came for.' He patted Tom on the shoulder. 'Thank you again, my friend.'

He almost headed for the door, but his cop's reflexes kicked in and stopped him. 'I'm sorry,' he said, offering his hand to Jonny. 'We haven't been introduced. Are you visiting Primavera?' he asked, as they shook.

I hoped that he wasn't wondering '*Toy boy?*' then realised that the Magda person almost certainly was. 'Tom's cousin,' I said, briskly, 'my nephew; Jonathan Sinclair. He's going to be living with us for a while, as he gets his new career off the ground. You've met their grandfather, Oz's dad.'

'Of course,' he exclaimed. 'It all fits now. I remember Mac mentioning you. You're a golfer, aren't you, which explains why . . .' he almost continued, '. . . why Primavera was so pissed off when I hauled her off the golf course,' but stopped himself just in time to leave that can of worms unopened. 'Alex Guinart. Primavera's my daughter's godmother; that makes us family, of a sort. Nice to meet you; see you around.'

He timed his exit perfectly, just as the oven alarm sounded. The monkfish was pretty damn good, I have to say. (I don't really have to, but I will.) I wish that I'd been in a better mood to enjoy it, though; as it was, my mind was running ahead, to my date later in the evening. Jonny offered to clean up after we were done, but I told him that his time would be better spent studying his yardage charts and getting his head right for day one of the Catalan Masters. So I packed the dishwasher, while Tom got on with his task. We have a ritual every time we eat baked monkfish. Afterwards, he boils the heads and bones in a big stock pot; it makes the basis of a great fish soup. Stinks the kitchen out, but it's worth it.

By the time I'd showered, using my most expensive body wash to ensure that I'd rid myself of the last vestiges of fishy smell, one of my pet hates, and prettied myself up, I was running slightly late, but only by Scottish standards. Fifteen minutes' slippage in L'Escala is still classed as being on time.

Shirley and Patterson were still on their dessert when I arrived. The restaurateur offered me a menu, but I declined . . . for a couple of minutes, then succumbed to a bowl of pistachio ice cream. The place was busy; the evening had turned cool, as it does quite often at the end of May, and so the diners had opted for inside tables rather than the terrace. Ours was in a corner by the window. It was the closest thing to a private booth that La Clota has . . . but when I surveyed the other customers I spotted an English lady, who knows both Shirley and me, and who is so relentlessly inquisitive that she makes Tomás de Torquemada seem like a chat show host.

'Let's move on for coffee,' I suggested. Patterson looked puzzled, but Shirl had done her own looking around and got the message. They paid the bill and we left. We didn't go far, only a few hundred metres, to a night bar called Octopuss; it tends not to get busy until later on and isn't a haunt of the British ex-pat chattering classes. It does have a corner table, and we took it, even though the place had just opened and we were its only customers.

'Well?' Shirley said, with an expansive beam, once a coffee and a large goblet of Bailey's had been placed in front of her. 'Out with it, Primavera. What was all that fuss about this afternoon? Someone told me after I'd spoken to you that they saw an ambulance driving away, and that the woods have all been closed off by cops, lots of them. But that's all I've heard.'

I ignored her and looked directly at Patterson. 'A body was found there this morning. A man. He was killed there, then stripped of all his clothing and possessions. But it wasn't a robbery, that wasn't what it was about. Whoever did it blew most of his face off too. You can guess why, can't you?' I asked. I hoped that I wasn't going to bring anyone's wrath down on the head of John Dale, but I had another friend to protect, and she was closer.

'Yes,' he replied, quietly. 'To prevent identification, or to hinder it as much as possible.'

Shirley looked at us from one to the other. 'Why're you asking him?' she murmured.

'Because he's got a passing interest in the stiff, a personal interest, even.' I switched my gaze back to him. 'It was the guy who tried to steal your wallet the other night.'

Patterson saw the complete picture, at once. 'And the police wanted you there to help them confirm that?' I nodded. 'Which means that you reported the incident after all?'

'Yes. I live here, mate; I have friends in the police. I couldn't let a thief run around here with a free hand. I'm sorry, that's not how I work. I gave them Tom's detailed description and Stan's mobile image . . . the same one I saw you copying on to your phone. They called me because the person who took a shotgun to his face left a couple of pieces intact. It was him; no question. They still don't know who he is, though. How about you? Have you managed to identify him?'

My friend laughed. 'How could he?' she gasped.

'Because he used to be a spook, Shirl. Is Patterson Cowling the name you were born with?' I challenged.

He sighed, then smiled. 'It's the name on my birth certificate, Primavera, I promise you.' He turned to Shirley. 'I'm afraid I've given you a slightly edited version of my past, dear. But it is my past,' he added, 'I promise you that. I am completely retired. I've moved on to a new life, even if I'll never be able to talk about the old one.' He looked back at me. 'I was warned that you've been asking about me, but they assured me that you'd be discreet.'

'As I have been,' I told him. 'So bloody discreet that I've even kept the cops from picking you up.'

He winced. 'For which I thank you.'

'Don't mention it. So? How did your trawl go? Do you know who the dead guy is?'

He shook his head. 'No, which means that he's probably nobody, other than what he seemed at the time, a rather inept pickpocket, Eastern European, maybe, rather than British, as Tom thought.'

'In that case,' I asked, 'why's he in a fucking morgue in Girona, with the shreds of his face that they picked off the trees in a box alongside him?'

'Probably for reasons completely unconnected with me,' he replied. 'I don't know why the hell whoever killed him didn't simply burn the body.'

'Because they'd have burned the woods down with him,' I

pointed out. 'The ground's covered in pine needles. They can spread fire as fast as you can run away from it, faster with a wind blowing. If they'd tried to cremate the poor bastard, the flames would have spread right up to Shirley's door.'

His partner was looking at him in the way that characters do at the end of a Poirot on television, as they look at the perpetrator of the crime of the week once he's been unmasked by the preening little Belgian. I guess they'd be having a conversation once she got him home, but I had a feeling they'd survive. Shirley's a very understanding lady, and she's been my friend for long enough to be able to take the unexpected in her stride.

'So,' I continued, 'you promise we can still call you Patterson?'

'Absolutely. That's my name; it's on my passport, on my bank accounts, attached to my National Insurance, NHS record, state and civil service, everything.'

'Hold on a minute,' Shirl intervened. 'I thought you guys were pretty much public figures these days.'

Patterson nodded. 'At the very top level, yes. The heads of the intelligence and security services aren't called by a single initial these days; they're publicly accountable to a parliamentary committee. But the rest of us, those of us lower down the ladder? Hell, no. We work in the dark.'

'Like the man in the woods?' I murmured.

'Not in the same way at all.'

'So you were management, rather than field level.'

'Senior management latterly, but always an office worker.'

'What did you do?' Shirley asked.

'I can't tell you any more than I have already, love, honestly.

And please, you can never talk about it to anyone else.' He looked at me, directly. 'Either of you. Are you all right with that?'

'I am,' I told him. 'I've already spoiled your scent for the police. As for this old trout here, I trust her with my secrets, and you can do the same. How's your Russian?' I added.

'Crumbled, through disuse. I can still understand some, but that's it.'

I pushed it a little further. 'And your Arabic?'

'Non-existent. It never existed. Now please, Primavera.'

'Okay,' I promised. 'I will probe no further, and I won't ask any more questions.'

He smiled. 'There would be no point. Your friend Mr Kravitz doesn't know about me. I've never appeared on his radar, and when I was active I never had occasion to make use of his skills and services.'

If he said that to shake me up, he succeeded. Mark Kravitz was a guy I'd known for years. Oz and I met him when he provided minder services for Miles on a movie project. After that he did some discreet stuff for Oz on occasion and he's been more than useful to me from time to time. For most of his career he'd styled himself a 'security consultant', a broad-brush picture of what he actually does. Mark was a fixer, and an intelligence gatherer; he operates on the edge of that community.

Patterson had meant to make a point by mentioning his name, and I took it. He was letting me know that when he'd been tipped off that I was checking up on him, he'd had the same job done on me, and that he was much better placed in that respect than I was.

'I never even thought of speaking to Mark,' I told him. 'He can't afford to go rattling cages in MI5. Besides, his MS limits him pretty badly these days.'

'So I understand.' He grinned. 'You have a limitation yourself, of course. When you accepted your attachment to HM Diplomatic Service, you signed the Official Secrets Act.'

'I don't have that job any longer,' I pointed out.

'It doesn't matter. That signature doesn't go away, and its meaning can be interpreted very widely.'

'Is that a threat?'

'God, no,' he protested. 'One of the things I was told about you was that threatening you would be a waste of time. Indeed it might even be counter-productive. But there are some people in my former walk of life who aren't as circumspect as me, and who have no sense of humour.'

'I know. About three years ago I met one of them, a woman who called herself Moira.'

He smiled. 'Yes, I believe that she did threaten you, and that a friend of yours made sure that it backfired on her. It's all on your MI5 file. You may be interested to know that she's now an administrator in GCHQ . . . and she hates Cheltenham with a passion, it's said. But there are others like her, only a lot more subtle; old guard who do not believe in freedom of information. So no, it's not a threat, just a word of caution.'

'I'll take it on board. You appreciate that all I was doing was looking out for Shirley's interests, just as she'd do for me. The last thing I want to do is compromise you.' I paused. 'Mind you,' I continued, 'I still think that for the dead guy to choose your pocket to pick, out of all the people in St Martí that night . . . that's a hell of a coincidence.'

'I couldn't agree more. That's why I'd still like to know who he was.'

'And who killed him?'

'Maybe I don't want to know that.'

'You don't think that you might have caused it, do you?'

'You don't mean that I might have ordered it, do you?'

'No,' I said, defensively; that had never occurred to me. 'But could someone in your old service have been . . . how do I put it . . . a wee bit over-protective?'

He shook his head. 'No, no; not for a second. I'm not that important, Primavera.' He smiled as he said it, but there was something in his eyes that suggested to me that he might not have been as convinced as he was trying to sound.

Seven

I'm not going to sit here and claim that by next morning I'd forgotten all about the man with no face; I'm probably as squeamish as you are. I've been able to hide it when necessary, but no kidding, my close-up view of that guy is still burned into my brain, and it always will be.

However I did have a diversion, to stop me from dwelling upon it. Jonny had to be fed, watered and got ready for the first day of his new professional life. His 'new boy' late starting time was something of a blessing, in that we didn't have to be up and about any earlier than was normal on a school day. In fact, Jonny might have been better staying in bed until Tom had left for school, for he was quizzed mercilessly over breakfast about his chances, so much that I could see faint cracks appearing in his super-confident image, and told my son, fairly sharply, to shut up and concentrate on his own forthcoming day at the office. I did give him one concession, though. I wanted to stay with Jonny right to the end of his round, and so I told Tom that he could take Charlie along to Vaive after school, and stay on the beach until seven, under the careful and caring eye of the xiringuita owners, friends of ours. After that, if I wasn't there when he got home, he could set the table for dinner.

Jonny left for the course at nine thirty; my plan was to go down around midday, meet Patterson and Shirley for lunch, and then with or without them, as they chose, be my nephew's gallery for the whole of his round . . . or until my presence started to make him nervous and he asked me to leave. (I'd made him promise that if that happened, he would.)

I busied myself with housework (a word you don't hear me use too often, but I'm not a slut, honest) for a couple of hours, did some preparation for the evening meal, then went down to the beach and swam for a while. I was ready to go, when the house phone rang.

'Primavera.' It was Alex. 'How're you doing? I thought I'd give you a call to let you know how badly we're doing. We can't find a trace of our murder victim, not anywhere. The post-mortem's been no help either. Other than the scar, the man had no distinguishing marks and no signs of any medical interventions during his lifetime, no surgical history to offer any leads. The only thing that's definitive is a report by a forensic dentist. Judging by his teeth, his opinion backs up Tom's, that the man wasn't British . . . or, to be more precise, that his dental work wasn't done there.'

'That's no help at all, is it,' I sighed 'if it means you can't identify him by his dental records.'

'There never was any chance of that,' he replied. 'Our expert didn't have a complete mouth to look at. He couldn't say where the guy's dental work had been done, only where it hadn't. Not Britain, not Russia, not Spain, but we're left with the rest of Europe as a possibility. No blame to him. The upper left jawbone was missing completely, and there was other damage. You saw that for yourself.'

'An unwelcome reminder,' I murmured. 'So what's next?'

'We're going with the little we have. We're going to ask all our Catalan newspapers and TV to publish the picture. With luck, that will be done over the next twenty-four hours.'

'Only in Catalunya?'

'Primavera, do you have any idea how many open murder cases there are in Spain with unidentified victims?'

'No,' I admitted. 'You realise what'll happen, even with that limited circulation? You'll have a thousand candidates; filtering them out will be a nightmare.'

'I know; but we're hoping that we'll be able to eliminate most of them immediately.'

I checked my watch; time to go. 'Poor Alex,' I sympathised. 'I'm sure you're doing all you can.'

'And one thing that I shouldn't have.' He paused. 'Well, not me; Hector.'

'What was that?'

'He called London and asked for a computer check on your friend Mr Cowling. Now I understand why you talked me out of picking him up. He had a call back; from our director general, no less. I didn't hear what he said, but Hector was very quiet for a while afterwards.'

'That doesn't surprise me.' I filled him in on my own inquiry, and John Dale's panicky phone call in response. 'I couldn't tell you before, Alex, not outright, but I hoped you'd got the message.'

'I had got it, but I neglected to pass it on to the boss. In the circumstances,' he chuckled, 'I'll be keeping that to myself.'

I didn't mention Gomez's embarrassment when I met Patterson and Shirley in the championship's tented village. Their relationship seemed undamaged by the grenade I'd lobbed into it the night before. Indeed, I sensed a little extra buzz about Shirl; I reckoned I'd spiced up her life even more.

That encounter came after I'd checked on Jonny in the practice ground. His swing looked absolutely grooved to me, and judging by the way Lena Mankell nodded after most of his shots, the most approval she ever seemed to show, she was happy too. The viewing stand wasn't full, but it was a lot busier than it had been three days earlier. Uche spotted me and gave me an expansive wave. Since he was probably the most eye-catching bloke on the range, it drew attention to me that I could have lived without.

'You family, then?' a fat, fifty-ish bloke asked. He was two seats along, dressed in shorts and a Lacoste shirt, and his beer gut shifted as he turned towards me.

'My nephew,' I replied, as modestly as I could.

'Who?' he retorted. 'The caddie? Bloody hell, love, your suntan's fading if you're his auntie.' He turned to his mate, seated just beyond him. 'D'you hear that, Nev?' he chortled. 'This lady's the black fella's auntie.'

A few other spectators looked around, at both of us. I sized him up. If I'd chosen, I could have kicked him solidly in the head before he'd even got one cheek of his ample arse off his seat. But that would have been a hell of a start to Jonny's round. More than that, it's not the way that disputes are handled in Spain. Still, I wasn't for letting the porky yob go unanswered.

Happily, neither was Clive, the practice ground manager, my Scots friend from Monday. While I was debating whether to poke the guy in the eye metaphorically or literally, he stepped over three rows of seats and plonked himself down, next to loudmouth. I couldn't hear what he said, but it worked. Tubby and Nev weren't inclined to have a bit of fun at his expense. They were out of there, without even a backward glance in my direction.

'Sorry about that,' Clive murmured as he made his way back to ground level. 'Bloody yobs from Benidorm; I can tell the kind a mile off. If they give you any more bother let me know and I'll have them banned from the course.'

'I'm more worried about them upsetting my nephew's caddie,' I confessed. 'Or deciding to heckle him and Jonny on the way round.'

'They won't go near them; be sure of that. I made it very clear to them that they shouldn't. Don't you worry,' he said. 'I'm looking out for young Mr Sinclair. I promised that I would.'

That puzzled me. 'Who did you promise?'

'His manager. Mr Donnelly. He called me, told me that he had a lad coming on tour and asked me if I'd make sure he got settled in all right.'

'You know him?'

The big Scot nodded. 'Aye, from way back. I played a couple of seasons on the PGA tour in my time. Brush was around then, on the edges of things, like. Crazy man, for all that he was a college graduate; all the Yanks are now, nearly all even in our day. The game's elitist over there; don't let anyone tell you different. He never amounted to anything on the tour. Plain truth, he just wasn't good enough, even without the drink. He lost his playing card, then dropped out of sight for a while, for a right few years, in fact. I'd heard he resurfaced . . . he got religion, so they say, but I was still surprised when I found out he's looking after your nephew. I'm doing him an injustice, maybe. Like I said, he was a bright enough guy, when he was sober and didn't have a golf club in his hand. Looking at the endorsements your lad's got, he's doing a pretty fair job for him; now it's up to Jonny to show whether he's good enough to wear all those badges.'

He had a gallery of seven when he hit his first shot as a tournament professional, at twenty minutes past two that afternoon. Shirley, Patterson, me and four others; like us, they were adherents of the other two players, one French, the other a Swede.

I know he was nervous, for he told me so afterwards. It couldn't have helped when one of his partners hooked his tee shot into the trees on the left, but it didn't affect him, as he hit a conservative three metal right into the middle of the fairway, short of the threatening bunker on the right.

I was standing well out of his eyeline but close enough to hear Uche tell him, 'Shot, boss. You can't win the tournament on the first tee, but it is possible to lose it.' It was the right thing to say; it calmed me down too, for in truth my heart had been hammering so loud that I'd been worried he'd hear it.

We set out after the group, following the cart path to the left of the fairway. The Stadium Course, as they call it, was built as a championship venue, and so the spectator vantage points were good, allowing us to get close enough but not too close. Jonny was away, furthest from the green after his cautious drive, but the perfect distance for his eight iron. They'd put the flag in the most difficult position, back left of the green, six paces on and near a bunker. Jonny's second shot landed just short of the target and rolled a little closer. A ten-foot putt later and he had his first birdie on the card.

The eleventh hole, his second, looked very scary indeed from the tee; it was less than two hundred yards long, a par three, but with a big bunker in front, and a water hazard the size of Lake Geneva at the back. The green was so small that I could hardly see it from where I stood, but my nephew must have had a good view for he nailed a six iron that would have hit the bull if he'd been aiming at a dartboard rather than a thirty-yard circle of grass. Two putts, and he'd made his first pro par.

The next was a par five on the card, but Jonny played it like a four. He whacked his drive further than I could see, close enough to find the green with a four iron, while his two partners each chose to play short. His putt was the best part of thirty feet and I knew that he was concentrating on leaving it close, but his line was good and he got lucky. He'd played his first three holes in nine shots, three under par. Shirley went as crazy as I felt; anyone else might have been embarrassed, but not her. My nephew didn't seem to notice her whoops; that's how far he was 'in the zone'.

The thirteenth was a beast, a par four of modest length but made difficult by a green that was mostly surrounded by water. The safe approach was to the left and that's where he played, putting his first four on his card.

By the time we reached the eighteenth, where he saved par after leaving his second shot in a bunker, he was five under. I looked up at the leader board behind the grandstand. The Irish kid was in the lead; he'd shot a sixty-five, seven under, one ahead of our Spanish pal with the ponytail and two ahead of Jonny and three others, all of them finished for the day and back in the clubhouse.

We had a little more company for the second nine. Word had got around and more spectators, English ex-pats in the main, came to join the party. So did a couple of journalists and a portly guy from a British TV station, microphone in hand, who seemed to be in hiding under a wide-brimmed Aussie hat. Nerves began to grip me again. They must have shown, for Uche saw me, smiled and gave me a large wink.

The second nine was tougher than the first had been. Jonny made his first mistake at the third, a par five, where there was no margin for error. He went for the green with his second, but tugged it slightly left. The ball took a hard bounce, into the water. The crowd groaned, and I felt like crying. He cheered me up with his next shot, his fourth after a penalty drop, a delicate chip that rolled up to the hole-side, seemed to pause as if to size up the drop, then fell in.

He played it ultra-safe after that, with his caddie's help, for I saw a few debates over club selection and guessed that Uche was urging caution where there was any doubt. Jonny played steady par golf from then on and was rewarded on the ninth, his last, when his long uphill putt made it all the way to the hole. He was seven under par: tied for the lead.

The first thing I did, as soon as he'd stepped off the green, was hug him. 'Extra big steak for you tonight, my boy,' I promised.

'Not too big, please, Auntie P,' he replied, with a smile. 'I have to talk to the press, so I'll be late getting back, and I don't want to be so full that I can't sleep.'

'Whatever you like. You're a star, now.' *Just like your uncle was.* The thought jumped into my brain but stayed unsaid. As well, for Jonny contradicted me.

'No, I'm not. I'm the first round co-leader and I'm surrounded by guys who are as good as me and who've been here many times before. I won't be a star for another three days.' He beamed, and gave me another hug. 'And then, I promise, we will have a party!'

The second thing I did, as he headed for the recorder's tent, to check, sign and register his score, was to call his mother, to give her the good news. It wasn't necessary. Ellie had been watching the coverage on the portly guy's TV station, and then keeping in touch with his score online when its live transmission had ended. She sounded a mess; elated, sure, but desperately sorry not to have been there. 'How is he?' she asked. 'Is he handling it okay?'

'He's as laid-back as his granddad,' I assured her. 'He's got loads of stuff to do here yet, but I'll tell Uche to make sure he calls you as soon as he's done.'

'He'd better not need bloody Uche to tell him,' she snorted, a welcome flash of the old Ellie. 'How's the Black Prince getting on anyway? That's what Harvey and I call him,' she added, as if explanation was needed.

'He's going fine. They're a good partnership.'

'That's what we thought. I'm glad it's working out. You know, I've got to say: the manager, the sponsors, the caddie . . . everything's almost too good to be true.'

Eight

I understood what Ellie had said, but it all made sense next morning, when I logged on to the main UK media websites, and found Jonny all over them. 'Tragic movie idol's nephew is new star on tour', was the headline on the *Telegraph* report, and a fair summary of all the other coverage.

One of two British writers had noted the connection in their advance pieces about the event, but they'd all been too cautious, or cynical, to go overboard on it. However, with a score on the board, everything had changed and for a day at least, he was the big headline. There was video footage as well, on the European Tour website, from the after-round briefing in the media tent. There wasn't much, but Jonny handled himself well, particularly when he was asked how his late uncle would have felt about his performance. 'He'd be trying to buy the movie rights,' he replied, with only the faintest smile.

My first instinct was that I'd like to have punched the questioner's lights out. Jonny was his own man and what he'd achieved had nothing to do with Oz. But then I thought of those endorsements and the fact that their relationship had been a help to his far distant manager in securing them. If the sponsors, or the tour publicists, had put it into the public domain, that was probably fair enough.

I didn't have a chance to discuss it with Jonny. Our alarms had been set for five thirty, and he had left for the course just after six, so that he could fit in a full practice session before his tee time, a more civilised nine forty. I'd decided that I wasn't going to go that day. 'Why not?' he asked, when I told him as he worked his way through breakfast, a mound of scrambled eggs on toast. (Tom was still sound asleep upstairs, so I'd delayed mine.)

'You'll have plenty of followers as the co-leader. I can't be there every day you're playing. Besides,' I added, 'you don't need me. You're so focused. You didn't look at me once yesterday and you didn't even hear Shirley screaming when you had that eagle. If I did go, you wouldn't even know I was there.'

'Maybe not, but Uche would. For all he's smooth, the guy's more African than you'd think. He's dead superstitious; you're his good luck charm, so he said after the round. If he doesn't see you he'll worry, and he might get his yardages wrong, give me a three metal instead of a three iron. You're a vital part of the team, Auntie P. Come on.' He paused. 'But hold on, I'm being selfish. I'm forgetting about Tom. He can't have packed lunches every day.'

'He'd be quite happy with that,' I assured him, 'and he would today, regardless. There's a class trip this morning, to the ruins at Ullastret; they're doing Iberian history.'

'Well . . .'

'Can I bring the dog?' I asked, mischievously. His face fell, but

I didn't let it hit the ground. 'It's all right,' I said. 'Kidding. Charlie'll be okay. Ben Simmers will pick him up if I ask him, and keep him with his two.' Ben's dogs and Charlie are from the same stable; they're family too.

I was easily persuaded in the end. Actually I'd been dead keen to go, but felt that I might be intruding. But if I was that important to the Black Prince, I could hardly refuse.

In the end, I was glad I'd let myself be persuaded. When I showed up on the first tee, the first people I saw were Patterson and Shirley. She'd found some tartan in her wardrobe and was dressed up like a bloody cheerleader. As I'd suspected, there was a proper gallery, up to a hundred people, but she was front and centre. Jonny had eyes for nothing but the fairway when he appeared, but Uche clocked her straight away. The look that he threw her suggested that if I was his good luck charm, then Shirl was a voodoo doll. Then he saw me, and brightened up.

Jonny started the way he'd finished the day before, with a steady straight drive, and once his partners, neither of whom had come close to breaking par in the first round, had played, we set off after them. 'Out of sight, and lip zipped,' I warned Shirley.

I'd thought that most of those who'd watched the start would have stayed in the stand, but I was wrong; they followed us around, as did a few journos, and a small contingent of photographers and radio correspondents. Television Man joined us too, at the sixth, keen to pick up on the story.

By that time Jonny was one under for his round, with two birdies and one bogey, a shot dropped after a pushed tee shot at the fourth finished close to a tree. 'No worries,' I heard Uche say as they left the green. 'You were bound to lose your cherry some time, and we're still on top of the leader board.'

That hadn't occurred to me, but he was, as I confirmed when I saw a board behind the fifth green. The Irish kid and the other early pacemakers were all out later in the day, and so, at eight under, Jonny was on top of the pile.

It got better over the next thirteen holes; four more birdies and one more dropped shot, after contributing another ball to the collection in the lake at the formidable thirteenth, and Jonny finished with a sixty-eight, eleven under for the tournament, and two clear of the ginger ponytail, who had reached the eighth by that time.

I'd managed to get rid of Shirley at the turn by telling her that she looked like one half of Fran and Anna, and that if she didn't want to figure in any embarrassing television clips on YouTube she'd be as well to lose the tartan or get out of sight. Since the former would have shown the world her underwear, she opted for a tactical withdrawal, using 'an early lunch, before it gets busy' as a tactical excuse.

I was waiting beside the last green once again as Jonny and Uche walked off. He took off his sunglasses, tipped back his logo-ed cap, lifted me up with those golfer-strong arms, gave me a great big hug and whispered, 'Glad you came, Auntie. Uche never put a foot wrong.'

I kissed him on the cheek and whispered back, 'Good for him. Now put me down; we're on telly.'

We were too; as I found out a few minutes later, his mother was watching the Sky coverage, along with a few million others. They included a couple of journalists at the scene. As Jonny and his caddie headed for the recorder's tent, one of them sidled . . . no other word could describe it; she approached me like a snake, side on . . . up to me.

She looked to be around thirty, blonde, dressed in loud golfer gear, red trousers and a yellow Ashworth shirt, and with make-up that was incongruously heavy, given where we were. She had a microphone in her hand, and she was smiling, but not with her eyes. They gave a different message; to me it read, 'Watch out.'

'Excuse me,' she began, in the sort of honey-soaked voice that answers the phone sometimes when you've called someone who wants to make you feel at home before they screw as much money out of you as they can.

I stared at her, and as I did I was aware of someone moving in on my right, a guy with a telly camera on his shoulder. 'Yes?' I replied.

'I'm Christy Mann,' she said, 'from Spotlight Television.' Her accent was Irish, I noticed.

I frowned. 'What the hell is Spotlight Television?'

'It's an independent station,' she volunteered. 'It broadcasts on the internet, and it supplies news footage to other stations.' Then she moved in a little closer, held the mike higher and got straight to the point. 'Can you tell me how delighted you are that Jonathan's leading his first event?'

I've heard questions asked in that form by broadcast journalists for as long as I've been shaving my armpits, and it's always struck me as lazy, or stupid, or both. My frown became a glare. 'How many degrees of delight are there?' I asked.

She giggled, then moved to Plan B; put words in the inter-viewee's mouth. 'Yes, you're over the moon. It's only natural that you would be, as Jonathan's Significant Other.'

'His what?' I bellowed. 'I'm his insignificant auntie, you idiot!' As I shouted, I caught a glimpse behind her of a tartan-clad figure, rocking on her heels with her hands over her mouth and her eyes full of tears. 'Have you been talking to that clown over there?' I challenged.

The reporter went all tight-lipped and serious on me. 'I'm afraid I can't discuss my sources, Miss . . .'

'Mrs,' I snarled, oblivious by then to the camera and its red light. 'Mrs Blackstone.'

She might have appeared to be a good imitation of an idiot, but she'd read her press coverage and she knew her two times table. A little light switched itself on in her deadpan eyes. 'Mrs Blackstone . . . and you're Jonathan's aunt. So that means you're Oz Blackstone's widow.'

I was where I didn't want to be. 'No it bloody doesn't,' I snapped. 'Oz and I divorced years ago.'

'But still,' she schmoozed on, 'you'll have a unique insight into Jonathan, and his motivation. They say he's the next big thing on tour. Do you know where he's living this week? With you?'

'That's none of your business.'

'But surely it is; he's a public figure.'

I went from annoyed to angry. 'He's a twenty-two-year-old kid starting out in a very competitive business. Look, if you're so interested in him, why are you wasting your time talking to me?

Why aren't you in the media tent with the rest of the press, talking to the man himself?'

For the first time, she backed off a little. 'We're not accredited for the tent,' she confessed. 'That's not what we do.'

'No,' I barked at her, not caring about the live camera, 'you hang around places like this looking for gossip. Which golfer's shagging which tennis player, stuff like that.'

She ignored my jibe. 'Is he living with you, Mrs Blackstone?' she continued. 'Or are you touring with him? Are you part of his entourage?'

'He doesn't have an entourage, woman, he has a caddie and a coach!'

'Where do you live, Mrs Blackstone? In Britain?'

'No.'

'In the US?'

'No.' I took a step to my right, ready to brush past her. I looked over her shoulder, but Shirley had made herself scarce, gone into hiding probably. I'd have set off in search of the silly cow, but the guy with the camera had stepped in front of me.

'So you live in Spain,' Christy Mann exclaimed, as if she'd exhausted all global alternatives. 'In that case we'd love an exclusive with you and Jonathan at home. The Blackstone saga goes on; it'll appeal to all of Oz's fans. They miss him so much; his memorial website has over a million hits a year, you know. And now that you and his nephew are together . . . The world needs to know that, Mrs Blackstone. It'll all be done in the best possible taste, I promise.'

I looked her in the eye. 'You know,' I said, 'if your brains were gunpowder and someone lit the fuse, the explosion wouldn't ruffle your hair. First, I repeat, Jonny and I are not together in the way you imply. Christ, I'm twice his age.'

She jumped in. 'That's no barrier these days.'

'It is for me. Okay? Now, second, if you harass me, or my nephew, or my son in any way, I'll have you arrested. If you don't believe I could do that, just try me.'

Her expression changed. Her eyes narrowed. I thought I'd put a stop to her, but I was wrong. All she was doing was thinking, a process that took a little time. 'Your son?' she murmured. 'You have a son? Would that be that Oz's child, Mrs Blackstone?'

There's this thing called Wikipedia. It's a self-building global internet encyclopaedia, and anyone with a little computer savvy can post an entry there. These days, you're nobody if you're not on it. I don't know who began Oz's bio page, but whoever did it researched his life very thoroughly. It lists his birthplace, his parents, the schools and university he attended, his career, step by step, and his three marriages. What you won't find there is any reference to his children. Susie and I monitor the content, and any attempt to post material about the kids, we delete. As far as we're concerned, they're off limits to any media.

We've found, over the years, that the legitimate press, even the red-tops, respect that, but Ms Christy Mann, her crude approach, and her intrusive camera didn't strike me as legitimate in any respect. I'll leave you to imagine what I wanted to do with her microphone, but I realised that however much we might both have enjoyed that, it wouldn't be very sensible. So I swept the red mist aside, took a deep breath and lowered my voice. 'Do you have a boss?' I asked her.

'That's irrelevant,' she said. 'Will you answer my question?'

'Not until you answer mine.'

'If you insist,' she sighed. 'Spotlight is owned by a company registered in London, and that's part of an international media group, American owned. Why do you need to know that?'

'I don't like to waste my time,' I replied. 'Now I'll tell you what you want to know. Yes, I have a son, Oz's son. But if you come within a country kilometre of him, I will use all the power and influence I have to have you crushed. If I have to do that, I'll go straight to source. And if you think that's a wild threat for a single Spanish parent to be making, you go and look me up on Wikipedia, sunshine. Primavera Phillips Blackstone; key that in and click the search button.'

She stared at me, and her painted smile turned incredulous. 'The camera's still running, Mrs Blackstone. Do you have any idea what you've done?'

I nodded. 'Yes. Now watch what I'm going to do.' I turned to the cameraman. I'd sized him up; he was a freelance, local. No way did this paparazzo chick travel with a regular TV crew. Her low-budget company hired them by the hour, wherever she and her like went. 'How much is she paying you for this gig?' I asked him in Catalan.

He switched off and lowered his weapon, a model that had been around for a while. 'Five hundred euro,' he answered, in the same language.

'In cash?'

'With her? Absolutely.'

'In that case, I'll buy your cassette for seven.'

He grinned. 'Deal.'

I always carry a reasonable float in old-fashioned money. Not secure, perhaps, but you never know when your car's going to break down, or when you're going to be in an accident and wind up somewhere where cash is king. That day I had just under a thousand on me. I took my wallet from my bag, stripped out fourteen fifties, and handed them to him. He ejected the cartridge and handed it over, thanked me, then turned and walked away.

'You can't do that!' Christy Mann screamed.

'We just did, honey,' I told her. 'Now fuck off.'

'Give me that tape back,' she insisted, 'or I'll get the police.'

'Go ahead.' I pointed along the pathway, towards the clubhouse. 'There's a cop.'

She followed the direction of my finger, towards the dark-haired man in uniform who was heading in our direction. 'Officer,' she wailed, 'this woman's stolen my tape.'

'And if I go after my friend Jaume,' Alex Guinart said as he reached us, 'who was your cameraman, will he tell me the same story? He works for us on occasion.' He looked at me. 'Has this woman been giving you trouble, Primavera?'

'None that I couldn't handle.'

'That's as well.' He frowned at the reporter. 'Papers, please,' he snapped.

'Papers? What papers?'

'Your press pass for this event. We'll start with that.'

'I don't have one,' she replied, still truculent. 'I'm general press.'

'Then you shouldn't be here. This is a closed event.' He held out a hand. 'Your passport, please.'

She frowned, sizing him up, then decided that further argument would not be a good idea. She delved into the vast shoulder bag that she was carrying and handed over a plum-coloured booklet. Alex opened it at the photographic page, studied the image, then looked at her.

'Christine McGuigan,' he murmured. 'Irish citizen, age twenty-seven.'

'She told me her name was Christy Mann,' I volunteered.

'That's my professional name.'

'Or I could class it as deception,' Alex growled. He returned her passport. 'Where are you living? Don't even think of lying to me.'

'In the Novotel at the airport,' she murmured, grudgingly.

'Then here's what you do. You go back there and you find some other way of going about your business. You do not come back here and you do not accost this lady again, or the families of any other golfers. You do, and I'll throw you in jail. Please leave, now.'

She did as she was told, albeit after throwing me one last malevolent glare, far removed from her earlier sugary approach.

'Thanks for that, Alex,' I said, as soon as she was out of earshot. 'Now would you like to tell me how you happened to be there, right on cue?'

He grinned. 'Shirley told me you were having trouble,' he explained.

'Shirley's the one who's in real fucking trouble,' I retorted. 'I reckon she set that cow on me. But that's not what I meant. What are you doing here, now, at this event? You're criminal investigation.'

'Why shouldn't I be here? I'm a golfer, even if I am shit at the game. This is a chance to see the top guys play, so why shouldn't I be here in my off-duty hours?'

'Because you're in uniform, Alex.'

'I'm grabbing a couple of hours off. I'm based in Girona; you know that. It wouldn't be practical for me to go home and change.'

I laughed. 'Hey, this is me you're talking to, remember, Primavera. She who knows that all you CI people keep a change of gear in the office in case you have to go plain clothes unexpectedly on an investigation. But you and Gomez have a murder investigation on your hands, a hot one. You don't have a couple of hours to spare. So, what are you doing here?'

'Nothing you need worry about,' he murmured.

'You're getting lamer by the minute. Has there been a robbery here? Is one of the players under threat?'

He shook his head. 'No, nothing like that.'

'Then . . .' No incident, and the dead man in the woods had to be at the head of his workload. 'Patterson Cowling,' I exclaimed. 'Are you here because of him?'

'Jesus, Primavera, let it go. I've just done you a favour with that television woman. You know as well as I do that I was bullshitting her. I couldn't have arrested her, not just for being pushy.'

'So? That's us square for the favour I did you in the woods. You're here because of Patterson, aren't you?'

135

He shrugged. 'If you say so.'

I pressed on. 'Is he a suspect after all?'

'No. Why should he be? I wanted a look at the man, that's all. I like to know who's who; to be able to put a face to every name. It's a cop thing. I know we were probably at the wine fair at the same time, but I have no recollection of seeing him there.'

'You've seen him now?'

'Yes.' He grinned. 'Unless Shirley has a different man with her today.'

'So you just happened to bump into them, accidentally like?'

'Actually Shirley bumped into me. I wasn't going to interrupt their day, but she saw me and called across to tell me you'd been waylaid by a pushy television reporter.'

'I see.' I paused, to let him think he was off the hook; but he wasn't. 'That only leaves one other question. How did you know they were here? I don't recall telling you anything about them coming to support Jonny.'

'I suppose I just assumed,' he said.

I laughed out loud. 'Cops don't travel twenty kilometres and join a crowd of a few thousand people, on assumptions. You knew he was here, Alex, because you're having him followed. Go on, admit it.'

He put his hands on my shoulders and looked down at me. He was smiling, but serious at the same time. 'Primavera, my dear friend, you must let me do my job without questioning me over every detail. Okay, I'm keeping Mr Cowling under observation, because he is a person of interest to me, or rather to us.'

'And Hector Gomez knows about it?'

'Of course he does. He's my boss.'

'But didn't you say he was warned off by his boss?'

'Yes,' He nodded. 'And he didn't take kindly to it. No investigator likes to be told that someone's off limits.'

'So you and he are ignoring your director general,' I murmured. 'Isn't that a bad career move, chum?'

'No, we're not ignoring him as such. We've been specifically ordered not to bring Mr Cowling in for interview, so we haven't done that. We were told to lay off him, and we have done, but I don't interpret that as forbidding us from keeping him under observation. That's all we're doing.'

'But why? He's just a retired bloke who didn't have his pocket picked.'

'By a man who wound up dead,' he reminded me. 'Look, your description of him is probably spot on. As far as we know, he's a newcomer to our town, and he doesn't know anyone here outside of Shirley's circle of friends. As far as we know,' he repeated. 'I'm prepared to take it as read that he couldn't have killed the man himself; Shirley would have noticed his absence and if she made a connection she wouldn't keep it from us. I trust her that much. All I want to do is be aware of the outside possibility that Mr Cowling might have an acquaintance locally that we don't know about, that's all, someone from a former life who's watching his back. That's why we're keeping an eye on him, just in case he makes contact with somebody we don't know about. Now, you're not going to tell him that, are you?'

'Of course not,' I snorted. 'Did Shirley introduce you?'

'Yes,' he admitted, 'she did, and I must say he seemed just as pleasant as you described him.'

'Fine. Let me tell you, now: from your casual presence here, Patterson will have assumed everything you've just told me. So if this comes back and bites your arse, don't assume that I've said anything to anyone. Not that it will,' I added. 'If by some miracle your outside possibility is on the mark, your big flat feet have just squashed any chance of any contact being made.' I looked him in the eye. 'I trust the guy, and I don't believe he has any involvement in that man's death . . .' I interrupted myself. 'You haven't identified him, I take it?'

'No, not yet.'

'No, I didn't think so. But listen, Alex, I'm serious, you have to assume that Patterson, if he chose, could run rings round you and Hector, so your surveillance is a waste of time, unless you bring in plain clothes people that he couldn't possibly know. So, how about laying off, and letting me keep an eye on him, as far as I'm able? If I'm wrong and he isn't as benevolent as he seems, then Shirley needs to be protected, but I'm probably better placed to do it than you in these circumstances.'

He frowned. 'I can't involve you in police work, Primavera.'

'Bollocks you can't!' I laughed derisively. 'You have done in the past when it suited your book. You did on Wednesday, as a matter of fact, when you hoiked me off the golf course. You let me look down this blind alley for you, and you can get on with the priority job of finding out whose body it is that you've got in your cooler.'

'I shouldn't.'

'But you will.'

'I'll ask Hector.'

'No, you'll tell Hector. If I do this, you'll be square with your director general, for no way will he ever find out.'

He gave in. 'Okay,' he conceded, 'but keep in touch. And if something unexpected does happen, don't expose yourself.'

'I'm not given to exposing myself, sir . . . not in public at any rate.'

'You know what I mean.'

'Sure.' I rose up on tiptoes and kissed him on the cheek. 'See you later, officer.' I left him and headed for the car park. I'd just reached my jeep when I spotted something buxom in tartan standing beside hers, a few rows away. I bore down on her.

'You!' I boomed as I approached. 'What the hell did you think you were doing, setting that twat on me?'

She held her hands up, as if she was warding me off. Beside her, Patterson exploded with laughter; I'd never seen him more animated. 'It was the tartan!' she protested. 'She spotted it and started to ask me about Jonathan. I told her you were the one she should talk to, that's all.'

'You should have stopped her,' I scolded Patterson.

'I'd made myself scarce,' he admitted. 'I run a mile from TV cameras, and you don't need to ask why.' I nodded. 'Go on, Shirley,' he chortled, 'tell her all of it.'

His 'Significant Other' turned a fetching shade of pink. 'I said he was your toy boy,' she confessed. 'But I was kidding, honest!'

'Jesus! And how exactly was she to know you were?'

'You sorted her out, though. So no damage done.'

I told her how I'd sorted her, digging the cassette from my bag and waving it in her face. 'Seven hundred euro that cost me!'

'Okay,' she sighed. 'I'll buy it off you.'

'Sure. And then you'd probably ask Tom how to put it on YouTube. No, I'll keep it. If she's daft enough to give me any more trouble it's evidence, of a sort.'

I can never stay mad at Shirley for long. In fact, she's usually a calming influence when I do get steamed up about something. Friends like her are to be cherished, not scolded. That's why I'd offered to keep an eye on Patterson for Alex; to keep the cops out of her hair, more than his. That, and also . . . I don't know for sure this far after the event, but I reckon I still had a small nagging doubt about him myself. That's probably why, on the spur of the moment, I invited Shirl and him to eat with the boys and me at Casa Blackstone that evening. He wasn't an enemy, but still, I felt that it would be no bad thing to follow the advice of General Sun Tzu (or Don Corleone, depending on which version of the phrase's origin that you believe) and keep him as close as I could.

Having done that I decided that I'd better tell Jonny of the arrangements, so I went back to the press area, and waylaid him as he left after finishing his round of interviews. By that time he was no longer the tournament leader. The Irish kid was six under par for his round in progress, two in front of Jonny, and the former US Open champion had moved up the board into second place. He wasn't worried, he assured me. 'I didn't expect to lead at minus eleven, not with a field of this quality.' He said that Uche was waiting for him on the range, but promised to be back home in time for dinner. 'I might even make room for a swim,' he added. 'Maybe Tom can show me the best place.'

I looked at him, at his serious Oz-like face, its expression older than his years, and found myself understanding why the Mann/McGuigan person had swallowed Shirley's line so eagerly. If I had been in the market for a toy boy, I could have done a lot worse. I focused on being maternal.

'How are you feeling?' I asked him.

'Solid,' he replied, firmly. 'I played a good round today, but that's it. Tomorrow's another challenge, and the course will be set up to be even harder. If I can shoot another sixty-eight, I'll be well placed.'

I left him to join his caddie on the practice ground, and headed back to the car park. When I got there my day took another downward turn. I hadn't noticed before, but the trusty old jeep seemed to be slightly off balance. I took a closer look and saw that my rear left-side tyre was flat. My reaction was multilingual and probably best not repeated.

I'm a member of the RACC, and my insurance covers me for roadside assistance, but there was no knowing how long help would take to arrive, so I decided to sort the mess out myself. Changing a wheel on a big heavy off-roader isn't particularly easy even on a flat, made-up road. When you have to do it in a field, it's all the more challenging. It took me a while to fit the jack and raise the vehicle up, and then even longer to undo the security bolts, but I was up to the job. My spare was unused, but fortunately I'd checked the pressures of all five wheels only a week before. I took the load off the jack, replaced it in its slot and was packing away the flat, when something caught my eye. The puncture wasn't hidden away inside the tread, as they usually are. It was in the side wall, a rip about an inch and a half long.

'Jesus,' I whispered, looking around, quickly, to see if anyone was watching me, but if there was, they were well out of sight. The guide books don't tell you this, but there are many car scams in our part of the world. Okay, most of them are targeted at rental vehicles or those with foreign plates, but not exclusively, and many involve putting a blade through a tyre. I was pretty certain that's what had been done to mine.

I checked the other wheels to make sure they were undamaged, then called Alex on my mobile, so that he could report it to tournament security. I was just about to climb in behind the wheel, when I noticed something else. The jeep has an aerial on its roof, a short stubby black thing that's removable, should it be put through a car wash. It was missing; a little added annoyance.

I was pretty sour all the way up the road, and when I dropped the wheel off at the Universal garage, for them to replace the tyre, but I'd managed to put it behind me by the time Tom came home from school. I was ready to bring him up to speed on Jonny's progress, but I didn't need to. He'd made his cousin promise to send him a text once he'd finished his round. By the same medium they'd also arranged to meet up at six, on the beach below our house, for a swim and possibly some windsurfing, although Jonny was doubtful about the latter, given that even a minor injury wasn't something he could risk. All that was fine by me, since I'd invited Shirley and Patterson for seven thirty, and I didn't need anyone under my feet when I was getting ready.

Great in theory, and almost in practice. By the time they arrived, a very acceptable five minutes past the appointed hour, I had put together a Catalan salad (dead easy; cold meats and various sausages), made a chicken curry, which was simmering quietly, with the rice under way in my Japanese steamer, and I'd chopped a couple of pineapples into cubes, mixed up with raspberries and blueberries. I'd also had a burst of femininity, which involved showering, a full hair and make-up job and a very sexy low-cut red dress that I hadn't worn for a while, and which I'd decided needed an airing. I knew that La Gash would come in all her finery, and for once I was prepared to rival her.

All that was lacking, to make my preparations complete, were my son and my nephew. Jonny had arrived just before six, as I was cooking, and had headed out at once, in swim gear. I'd assumed, rashly as it transpired, that they'd come back while I was in my bedroom, but when I called them, all was silence. 'Buggers,' I muttered. I sorted my guests out drinks, then headed out to fetch them.

I could have gone out through the garage, but that would have involved three flights of stairs, so I left by the front door, and walked round in front of the church. The evening was warm and there were a few diners in the cafes, but the Friday rush hadn't really begun, so I passed no one as I headed for the slope that leads down to the beach.

I saw the boys as soon as I reached the start of the descent. The church bells had just rung three times to signal the three-quarter hour. I suspected that Tom had interpreted it correctly as a signal that they were in the shit, for they were starting to head homewards;

he was carrying his sail and Jonny had the board slung on his shoulder. I stopped, and was waving to them to get a move on, when I heard a noise, on my right.

There's a little open area there in front of an old stone garage. It doesn't belong to anyone that I know of, and it offers an excellent view of the beach. Someone was in there leaning back into the corner by the garage, in the way that people do when they're foolish enough to think they can make themselves invisible. This one couldn't; her red jeans and yellow shirt were way too loud for that. I turned off the path and walked towards her, out of sight of the square, out of sight of anyone close by, and as I did she tried to stuff the object she had been holding into her enormous bag: it was a camera, with a long telephoto lens.

'How the hell did you get here?' I snapped.

'It's not a crime,' she retorted.

'How did you find out where I live?' I demanded.

'I'm a reporter,' she sneered, defiantly. 'I have skills.'

I took a guess at what they were. 'You followed me, you cow, didn't you? You watched me in the car park and you followed me up the road.' A further possibility occurred. 'Did you knife my tyre?' Her face flushed, her eyes shifted and I knew I was on the mark. 'And now,' I continued, 'you're here and . . .' The camera; her vantage point; the beach. 'You've been photographing my son!'

'And what if I have?' she challenged. 'He's Oz Blackstone's son too; there's money in these pictures, and you won't be buying them.'

'That's true,' I said, quietly.

I'd never punched a woman before. In fact I'd never punched anyone, apart from Oz a couple of times, when I was really angry with him. Until then nearly all my punching had been done in the gym and had been aimed at bags. I'd picked up the skill, though. I hit Christine McGuigan with a right-hander that her namesake Barry would have been proud to call his own. It caught her on the temple and knocked her on her red-trousered backside. I snatched up her bag, and pulled out the camera. It was a Nikon, like mine, and so I was able to find and extract the memory card in a couple of seconds. (As an added bonus, and proof of my theory if I'd needed it, I also found my missing aerial in there.)

'I'll call the . . .' she began, as she scrambled to her feet, but I didn't let her finish.

'No, honey, you won't,' I hissed. I went back in time. A version of Primavera that I'd thought I'd left way behind me showed all her claws. 'This is what you'll do. You'll get back into whatever brought you here and you'll fuck off. You'll put as many miles as you can between yourself and my boy.' I glared at her and saw her fear as clearly as I could see the lump rising on her head and the mark left by my heavy dress ring. 'If I ever find you anywhere near him again, I'll kill you. I'm not being figurative here, you understand; if I see you as a threat to his happy existence . . .'

'Auntie Primavera.' My nephew's calm voice came from behind me. 'Is everything all right?'

I looked over my shoulder; he was alone. 'It is now,' I told him. I nodded towards McGuigan. 'Jonny, if you ever see this woman again, anywhere near any of us, I want you to tell me. She thought she could make a couple of quid by selling pictures of Tom to the press. I've just been telling her that she can't.'

He took a few steps forward and stood beside me. He was still wet from the sea, and his muscles were hard and glistening in the last of the evening sun. He stared at the woman, unblinking. 'I'm sure she gets the message, Auntie,' he murmured. Then he took me by the elbow. 'Come on,' he said. 'You have guests waiting, don't you?'

I allowed myself to be led away, concentrating on calming myself down and becoming the nice Primavera once again, not the other woman. I'd frightened McGuigan, sure, but I'd frightened myself as well.

'Where's Tom?' I asked him, as we reached the house, although I could guess the answer.

'He's gone in through the garage to stow his board and sail,' he replied, pausing at the gate.

'He sent me up here to take the flak.' He laughed. 'He's a really good surfer, Auntie P.'

'So they tell me. You didn't try it, did you?'

He shook his head. 'No. Too big a risk. He'd have embarrassed me anyway. He's in a different league from me. Are they all beach boys around here?'

'Pretty much.'

He smiled. His back was to the sun as it went down behind the roof of the building behind him, and I had to shade my eyes to look at him. What I saw was a depth I hadn't appreciated before; I knew that there was more to Jonathan Sinclair than he allowed to show. At some time or another he'd been places that had left a mark on him, made him older than his years, and possibly a little wiser too.

'This is a great thing you're doing for him, you know,' he murmured.

'What thing?' I asked.

'Choosing to bring Tom up here, in this place. You're well off; you could live anywhere you wanted in the world, in any city: London, Edinburgh, Paris, New York . . .'

'I'm not sure the Americans would let me into the last of those, given my previous.'

'Don't kid me; you could fix it. I mean it, the world's your . . .'

'Mussel?' I suggested. 'There aren't any oysters around here.'

'Any shellfish you like,' he chuckled. 'But this is the one you've chosen, and it's fantastic for Tom. I thought I was lucky being brought up in St Andrews, but this, this is way beyond that. But . . . what's it doing for you?'

'Everything. It's my home; it's where I belong.'

'Because of Tom, yes; but one day soon, before you know it, it'll be time for him to go . . . and you'll want him to. I had that discussion with my mum and grandpa, four years ago. I'd have gone to Stirling University, happily, but the Arizona offer was there and they insisted that I take up the place. It'll be much the same with him, and then you won't be able to ignore the truth.'

'And what's that?' I whispered.

'That the part of you that isn't a mother, she's lonely.'

Suddenly, he seemed even more mature. 'Jonny, you're not making a play for me, are you?'

'God no!' he gasped. Then he added, 'No, I didn't mean it that way! I'm not saying you're not attractive . . . you are, very . . . and age doesn't mean nearly so much these days, but you're my auntie and he was my uncle and I couldn't ever look at you without seeing him. God,' he gulped, 'let's get inside. I'm sorry. I shouldn't have said any of that. I don't know what made me.'

'I don't know either,' I mused, 'but maybe it needed saying. A hell of a conversation to be having at your front gate with a half-naked young man, though. One night, next week, maybe, we'll have dinner, you and I, just the two of us, and carry it on.'

We went inside. I apologised once again to Shirl and Patterson for the hiatus, but they weren't bothered. In my absence they'd worked their way through most of a bottle of albarino. I killed the rest and opened another while we waited for Tom and Jonny to join us. As if he was following his cousin's lead, my nephew had thrown on a T-shirt and jeans, shedding the golfer gear for once, but that didn't get him out of a replay of his afternoon press briefing as my guests quizzed him about his round. I didn't let it go on for long. After a couple of minutes, I cried, 'Enough, you two. Jonny's had a hard couple of days, and he's got even tougher to come, so give him a break from the shop talk, please.'

Dinner, when I finally got round to serving it, with Tom's help, was pleasant. We talked about nothing more serious than the weather; the March snowstorm that had almost obliterated Catalunya the year before, and the searing summer that had followed. We relaunched the global warming debate (Tom was in favour, if it meant bigger waves on the beach) until Jonny ended it by saying that it was as real as the millennium bug. 'I went to college in Arizona, remember. It couldn't get any warmer there.'

As I looked at Patterson, eventually I remembered my undertaking to Alex, which had prompted my invitation, and I realised how preposterous the whole notion was, that he could have had something to do with the death of the stiff in the woods. Okay, his career had been in intelligence, but so what? I resolved to pay no more attention to the fantasies of the Mossos d'Esquadra. Their time would be better served freeing me from the attentions of the likes of Christine McGuigan, but with a hot murder inquiry under way, they'd hardly be doing that. As Alex had admitted, his dismissal of her that afternoon had been mostly bullshit, and, as it had turned out, pretty ineffective. Which was a nuisance. I'd thrown a scare into her outside, no question. But what if it wore off? I knew next to nothing about the woman, other than that she wasn't much good at martial arts, but did know how to blade a tyre. 'Bugger,' I whispered, as I realised I could have searched her bag further, for the knife; whispered to myself, I thought, but Patterson overheard me, and I realised that he'd been watching me a lot more closely than I'd been fixed on him, for all my earlier intentions.

Jonny broke the moment. 'If you'll all excuse me,' he said, 'I think I'll turn in. For all that I'm in the second last group tomorrow, I'll need to be on the course early. Uche will be up at sparrow fart checking on the pin positions, and I need to support him.'

That was it for Tom too; I'd noticed his eyelids beginning to droop. While he was too old for 'Time for bed, young man', there were still times when the suggestion had to be made, but that night wasn't one of them. He'd been putting on a show on his board for his cousin and it had tired him out. Or maybe he suspected I'd tell him to clear the table, and decided to forestall me.

That left the three seniors alone, for coffee and liqueurs on the terrace. Shirley was past her best by then, so Patterson had slowed up. He was seated between the two of us; on his left, Shirl was slumped back in her chair, with a goblet of amaretto in her cupped hands. When she began to snore lightly, he reached out, took it from her, with touching gentleness, and placed it on the table in front of them. She didn't stir; when someone can separate her from her drink, you know that she's asleep.

'You're a nice man, you know,' I told him. I was on amaretto too, but I had tonic and ice in mine, in a tall glass: my version of a highball.

'I like to think so,' he said.

'Have you always been?'

'Personally, I hope so. My daughters seem to think so.'

'Professionally?'

'You shouldn't ask me that.'

'I just did, though.'

He leaned back and closed his eyes. For a moment I thought he was taking refuge in sleep, like Shirley. But he wasn't; instead he was weighing up his answer. 'Without going into operational details,' he began, when he was ready, 'there were situations in which my service was required not to be very nice. But I was never part of those so I remained humane. Humanity is essential to a worthy society. Needless cruelty is inexcusable.'

'But what if captive terrorists won't tell the state what it wants to know?'

'That's their human right.'

'Even if people's lives depended on them talking?'

He sighed. 'At that point, people like us have to leave the room.'

'Is that a roundabout way of telling me that when cruelty is necessary, the state needs brutes?'

'I suppose it is. And you, Primavera,' he exclaimed. 'Have you always been nice?'

'No I have not,' I admitted, 'and I'll bet you knew that already.'

'I've given up on judging people. From what I've been told about you, I know you've been inside for foolishness more than malice, but I know also that you're an exemplary mother, and that the Foreign Office trusted you enough to give you a job quite recently, thanks in part to your connection with the former Home Secretary, which not a soul understands. Incidentally, it'll be kept open for you, should you wish to reconsider your resignation.'

'Are you sure you've retired?' I laughed.

'Oh yes, I have, I assure you. But the strings are still there, the access to information, for me to pull if I need to.'

'Could you pull them for me?' I asked him quietly.

'That wouldn't be proper, Primavera.'

'Neither was pulling them to run a complete background check on me.'

He smiled. 'Retaliation. You did it first, remember.'

'True,' I conceded, 'but in any event, I wasn't asking you to observe propriety. I was asking you to do me a favour.'

'Depends what it is. Shoot.'

I told him about my story, from my problem in the car park,

leading into my second encounter with Christine McGuigan, and about the way I'd dealt with her.

'Did anyone see this altercation?' he asked, hardly giving me time to finish.

'Jonny arrived right at the end of it. He backed me up, naturally.'

'Just as well. If you're right about her sabotaging your tyre, anyone who carries a knife as a matter of routine isn't to be trifled with.'

'Maybe I'm not either.'

He frowned. 'Primavera,' he said, 'I'm sure that the mortuaries of the world are full of people who thought that way.'

'Which is why I'd like to know a bit more about this woman. This afternoon she said she works for something called Spotlight Television, yet this evening I catch her taking telephoto shots of Tom on the beach. I mean what the hell is she?'

'She's probably what she says she is, a journalist. The world's moved on, Primavera. Fings ain't wot they used to be, as the old song goes. We've moved on from hot-metal presses and inky fingers. Nowadays, would-be reporters who can't sell their stuff to radio or television can set up their own blog sites then post whatever smears and libels and paparazzi pictures they choose, or they can shoot video and upload footage to abominations like YouTube. Nowadays, every wannabe, can be.'

'I'd still like to know for sure, though. Maybe I've scared her off, but maybe I haven't. What if she carries on stalking Tom?'

'What was the name on the passport she showed your friend?'

'Christine McGuigan, and it was an Irish passport. But she told me her name was Christy Mann.'

'And she said she worked for . . . ?'

'Spotlight Television.'

'Okay,' he murmured, as Shirley stirred beside him. 'Leave it with me. I'll see what I can do.'

'Thanks,' I said, but for the first time that night I doubted his sincerity. Instinct told me that I was asking him to wade into waters that he'd rather stayed untroubled.

'Do 'bout what?' his partner mumbled.

'About getting you home, my dear. Primavera has a busy weekend ahead of her.'

Nine

Was he ever right about that!

It began well enough; when I went down to the kitchen, still half asleep, I found breakfast on the table and tea in the pot. Jonny had gone, but Tom had got things moving as soon as he heard me moving about.

I'd done some pondering, as I showered, over whether or not I should tell him about Christine McGuigan and her interest in him. Finally I decided that if he was old enough to bake croissants from dough better than I can, he could handle that too, so I did.

His instant reaction? He laughed. 'Why would anyone want to take pictures of me? I'm not important.'

'To some people you might be,' I explained. 'Because of what he did in films, your dad had a lot of admirers. People loved him and want to know everything there is to know about him. And that means they want to know about you, and Janet and wee Jonathan. You know Conrad, the man who works for Susie Mum in Monaco?'

'Yes, of course I do. Conrad was Dad's assistant; I remember.'

Indeed, he'd been a lot more than that. 'Yes, that's right. Well now he does the same for Susie Mum, and part of his job is to protect the kids' privacy, and make sure they can grow up without being pestered by well-meaning fans, or by journalists who see them as a means of making money. That's what this woman is; she's one of those. We don't have a Conrad to look after you; I've always done that myself. Now you have to help me.' I described McGuigan, as best I could. 'If you notice anyone like her around in the next day or so, taking pictures of you, I want you to tell me. If I'm not there, suppose you see someone when you're at school, tell a teacher. If it happens when you're on the beach, at Vaive, say, tell Philippe or Teresa or anyone else you know.'

'What if she tries to speak to me and you're not around?'

'Ignore her and walk straight home.'

'What if she tries to stop me?'

I frowned, worried that I might be alarming him. 'Tom, don't be scared by this. She's not out to harm you; I don't believe that.'

'I'm not scared, Mum. Is she bigger than you?'

'No. A little bit smaller. She's not that much bigger than you are.'

An eyebrow rose. 'Did she scare you?' he asked.

'No,' I snorted. 'I'm careful about you, that's all. I won't have her or anyone else drawing attention to you, selling pictures to the press or posting them online.'

'Like you won't let me go on Facebook or on Myspace or on Twitter.'

'Exactly. Same reason. Your privacy's important, Tom.'

'Then don't worry, Mum. If she did try to stop me I wouldn't let her.' He chuckled. 'Neither would Charlie.' He had a point there;

Charlie might be a big oaf, but he's Tom's big oaf. If he turned serious, most people would pause for a moment of reflection. 'When are we going to the golf course?' he continued, dismissing Christine McGuigan from his thoughts.

'In time to see Jonny start his round.'

'Can we go sooner? He said I could watch him practise.'

And that's what we did. When we got to the range, just after eleven thirty, he was already there, just starting his practice routine. I had intended not to disturb him and go straight up to the viewing stand, but he spotted us and waved us across. Tom hadn't met Uche, so Jonny introduced them.

'Honoured, young sir,' the caddie said, at his most princely as they shook hands. 'The boss tells me you're a whizz on a sailboard,' he went on. 'I've tried it; I'm not. Sometimes on the golf course I can walk on water, but I can't float on it. I just sink.'

Tom frowned, wrinkling his nose. 'I float well enough,' he said, 'and I swim pretty well too, but I always wear a life jacket on my board.'

Jonny laughed. 'Uche would need at least two of those,' he said. 'He can swim, but like he says, only in one direction, straight down.'

As he spoke, Lena Mankell arrived, and the atmosphere changed, as if a cold wind had blown down from Sweden. Again Jonny introduced us. She acknowledged us, politely, and then ignored us completely. In other circumstances, I might have taken that badly, but we were in her workplace, so I didn't interpret it as rudeness, only professionalism. I left them to it and headed for the stand. I was going to take Tom with me, but Uche asked him to stay. 'You can be our runner,' he said. 'Fetch more balls when we need them. Otherwise that's my job.'

So he stayed with them on the range, he watched and he ran, whenever it was necessary. To his disappointment, though, he couldn't go inside the ropes when the round started. He had to stay in the crowd with me. Luckily, it wasn't vast; the main galleries were with the leading twosome, and with an all-Spanish pairing a couple of groups further back. Plus Jonny's playing partner was Thai, and there weren't a lot of them around to follow him. Because of that we saw every stroke, all sixty-eight of them, for Jonny shot another four under par round, taking him to fifteen under par for the tournament, still two shots behind the Irish kid in the lead but alone in second place. As soon as the last putt had dropped and I was able to switch on my phone, I found a voice message from Ellie asking me to call her back.

'How's he doing?' she demanded, as soon as I did. 'I won't be able to speak to him for another hour at least.'

'I haven't spoken to him myself yet.' I'd stayed clear of him as he left the eighteenth green, just in case Christine McGuigan was lurking somewhere, in disguise. 'But I did bump into Lena Mankell and she was smiling. Trust me, you can take that as a positive.'

'He's not getting too excited, is he?'

'Ellie, on an excitement scale of ten, I'd say he was just short of three. He's not going to choke tomorrow, I promise you. Tom was on the range with him this morning, acting as Uche's gofer; he says nobody else has got a chance.'

She laughed. 'Good lad; but what do you say?'

'You know what golf's like. Nothing's certain until all the scores are recorded, and the boy in the lead is a terrific player. But whether Jonny wins or not I'm sure he's going to do what he really came here to do and that's make a lot of money. He says that third place here would be enough to get him his tour card for next year . . . but that's not to say he's thinking of finishing third.'

I thought I heard a stifled sob on the other end of the line. 'To be honest,' Ellie admitted, 'he's done better already than I thought he would. I mean, he's just my wee boy. Remember him when you first met him? As wild as the purple heather, he was. He's calmed down a lot, but I still see him that way. Is he sleeping all right?'

'That is something I would not know for sure,' I reminded her. 'But he's eating well. I had a look in his bag on the range. Uche had more bananas in there than Tesco's fruit counter.'

'That Uche!' She let out a cracked chuckle. 'He's some boy. Maybe I'll get to meet his dad, one day, the aristocrat. If the son's anything to go by, he must be an interesting bloke.'

I've never known a Saturday evening like the one that followed. Jonny was so laid-back when he arrived home that I reckoned I'd placed him a point too high on that excitement scale. So was Tom; he could see only one outcome, so it didn't occur to him to be any more worried about the final round than he had been about the first three. No, it was me who was strung out.

I'd started putting a meal together, but only succeeded in slicing my finger instead of an onion. Jonny walked in on me as I was stopping the bleeding with a piece of kitchen roll. 'Auntie P,' he declared, 'I don't know what sort of sauce you were planning to make, but I don't fancy it. Anyway, you've cooked enough this week; I'm taking us all out.'

'You haven't won anything yet,' I pointed out.

'My credit card doesn't know that. Go on now; get dolled up.'

'Must I? I feel like jeans and a T-shirt.'

'Fine.' He smiled. 'Whatever makes you comfortable.'

In the end I settled for shorts and a check shirt, but with enough cleavage showing to make me feel, and I hope look, a little less like a middle-aged woman out with her two boys. Jonny let me choose where we'd eat; I surprised him by directing us out of St Martí, to Mike's, a simple German-owned waterside restaurant in L'Escala, where the menu never changes but is one hundred per cent reliable, and where they give you as many chips as you want. In Tom's case, that's usually a lot. In my nephew's too, as it turned out; he had a massive salad, followed by a schnitzel, then he and Tom each demolished the biggest, gaudiest ice cream on the list.

I left the talking to the lads. To my surprise much of it was about education. Tom was curious to know about schools in Scotland. (The obvious fact that he could have asked me, but hadn't, made me suppose that he thought I was too old to remember.) He was even more interested in Arizona, and the academic courses offered to promising athletes . . . not only golfers, for American colleges take most sport seriously. Jonny talked him through the lot. 'They don't do surfing, I'm afraid,' he said as he finished.

I had to laugh. 'Yes, sorry, Tom, you can't do surfing at university,' I told him.

He shot me down. 'You can, Mum. I've looked it up online. You can do a degree at Plymouth, in England.'

'You're kidding,' I gasped.

'I'm not,' he insisted. 'And you can do them in California. Isn't that right, Jonny?'

His cousin nodded agreement. 'Sorry, Auntie P, but it is. There are one or two.'

'Jesus,' I laughed. 'What next? Bungee-jumping?'

We didn't stay out late. As before, Jonny had to be up with the seagulls . . . you'll struggle to find a lark in St Martí, but those noisy bastards are omnipresent . . . to meet up with Uche. I had barely slept a wink, so I was able to send him off for the biggest day of his life with a mound of breakfast inside him.

I had hoped to spend a few calm hours before heading for the course myself, but I wasn't capable of calmness that morning. Neither was Tom, for once; he was impatient, itching to go. A year before he might have had other Sunday duties, as an altar boy in the church, a role he'd been given by Gerard, and latterly by the venerable Father Olivares. But after the old man's retirement, the new priest had taken the view that his assistants were required to have been baptised in the Catholic Church . . . and I suspect also, although he never spelled it out, that atheism was a definite bar to office.

So, as soon as Ben Simmers had opened his shop and could take charge of Charlie, we headed on down the road. As they had done since our first day, Shirley and Patterson were travelling independently. We hadn't made any formal arrangement to meet up; it was hardly necessary, because our Shirley would stand out in a full house at the Camp Nou football stadium. When we got to the course, the car park was busier than I'd seen it. The attendances had probably been in the hundreds on each of the first two days, and overwhelmingly ex-pat, but the weekend seemed to have lured a few more people out of the cities. Nonetheless, as Tom and I mingled with the crowds we heard as much English spoken as we heard Spanish or Catalan.

I was heading for the practice ground as usual, when Tom tugged at my elbow. 'Mum,' he said. 'There they are.' He pointed towards the clubhouse. Jonny and Uche were at the foot of the entrance steps. My nephew was in conversation with the telly guy I'd seen on the first day, the one with the Aussie hat, while his caddie was a few yards away, speaking, seriously, with another man, older, as black as he was, and entirely inappropriately dressed in a shiny suit that didn't look as if it had come off the peg. He had his back to me, but there was something in his body shape and in the way he stood that told me who he was. As I watched them I remembered what Ellie had said the evening before.

Uche saw me looking at them. It took a second or two for his smile to appear, but eventually it broke through and he beckoned us to join them. 'Primavera,' he exclaimed, at his most regal. 'Come and meet our new supporter.' He looked at him. 'Dad, this is my boss's aunt, Primavera Blackstone, and her son, Tom, Jonny's cousin.' Then back to me. 'Primavera, Tom, this is Kalu Wigwe, my father.'

The princeling turned, gave us a quick glance up and down, and said, 'How do you do,' in a voice that offered a preview of how Uche would sound once he had smoked a few hundred expensive cigars, like the one clenched between the first two fingers of his dad's left hand. He extended the right, first to Tom, and they shook formally.

'Very well, thank you,' he replied.

Wigwe senior turned to me, and as he did he swept off his wraparound Oakleys and fixed me with eyes that were vivid green, and more than a little bloodshot. I felt as if they were scanning me. The moment passed with a short courtly bow and another proffered handshake. 'And you, madam.' He beamed, showing all of his son's charm, but somehow with more substance to it. Close to, the suit was so sharp it was dangerous. The material was pale blue, with silk in it, I was sure, and the jacket was Mandarin style . . . my dad still calls it a Nehru collar. The eyes twinkled; I guessed he liked what he saw. (With all that red in there they made me think of traffic lights changing.)

Other than that, what I saw wasn't hard on the eye, either. Kalu Wigwe had the same oval-shaped face as his son, but his version was rendered more imposing by age, and it was adorned by a full, well-trimmed beard. His hair was cut to around the same length, and there were grey flecks through it all. He was a little thicker in the waist than junior, but for all that he still seemed well built and not gone to fat. Age? Given that Uche was a contemporary of Jonny, he was probably a little older than he looked, but surely no more than fifty. There was much about him to fancy, and yet . . . although one colour was missing from those traffic signal eyes, amber, they still managed to say 'Caution'.

'This is a surprise, Uche,' I said. 'You didn't say your father was going to turn up.'

'I rarely announce my arrival,' Kalu replied. 'I have an unpredictable schedule, and I can never be sure of being able to keep family appointments, so I tend not to make them. There is also the consideration that uncertainty keeps my sons on their toes.'

'You have more than one?'

'I have three; Uche is the oldest, then there's Oba and Solomon. Oba's nineteen and Solomon's seventeen.'

'And Mrs Wigwe? Is she with you?'

'Mrs Wigwe is with our Lord and Redeemer, Jesus Christ.' Behind him, Uche's eyes narrowed just a little as he spoke. 'I have a companion, but she didn't make the trip. It was, after all, short notice. I didn't decide to come until yesterday. When I saw that Jonathan was doing so well, I knew that I had to support the team. So I flew here.'

'I'm surprised you could get a flight so quickly.'

'I don't have that problem,' he replied, modestly. 'I have a Gulfstream jet, based at Lagos.'

'That's still a long trip,' I remarked, 'on the spur of the moment.'

'Around eight hours.' He shrugged, as if it was nothing. 'I landed around nine last night, at Girona, very close to here.' He smiled. 'It's a very comfortable aircraft; and it's always ready to take off. I'd be happy to show you around. Perhaps you and Tom would like to take a flight with me.'

'You don't fly it yourself, do you?'

'My goodness no, Mrs Blackstone,' he laughed. 'It's not built for pleasure flights. I employ a crew; previously they were with Air New Zealand. They're the best, I'm told.'

The last time I flew on a private aircraft it came down a lot harder than the pilot had intended. I walked away, but nobody else did. As a result, I've stuck to scheduled services ever since. 'That may be,' I said, politely, 'but I think I'll pass on that, thank you. And it's Primavera, please.'

'Anywhere you like?'

'I like it here. Thanks all the same.'

'Dad,' Uche growled. 'Stop being a flash arsehole.'

His father looked at me, his expression pained. 'You hear that, Primavera? The money I've invested my son's education and that is the result.'

'But he does have a fine, cultured accent, Mr Wigwe,' Jonny pointed out. He'd finished his chat with the telly guy and come over to join us. 'They called him the Count at ASU. It went down very well with the cheerleaders.'

'So did they,' his caddie murmured. 'Very well.' I shot him a warning glower; Tom was within earshot, and I didn't want to have to explain the remark . . . or maybe I hoped that he didn't understand it.

But as it happened, he seemed to be in conference with Jonny. 'Can I?' I heard him exclaim.

'It's all fixed up,' his cousin replied. He looked at me. 'Our board boy's called in sick,' he told me. 'You know, the kid who follows us round with the sign that shows our scores. The tournament director told me in the clubhouse, and I've volunteered Tom for the job.'

'Is he big enough?'

'Mum! I've grown two centimetres in the last month. I'm a hundred and fifty-two now.'

Or five feet tall, expressed another way; and still short of eleven years old. I found a chart online a couple of years ago, and I've been plotting his growth ever since. It says that he's on course to be around six three.

'He's well big enough, Auntie P,' Jonny assured me. He looked at Tom's feet. 'He might be better in golf shoes than those trainers, though.' He punched him lightly on the shoulder. 'Come on. Let's go and see the FootJoy guys. They might just have a pair your size. Then I'll introduce you to the guy who runs the board boys.'

'Shouldn't you be practising?' I asked.

He checked his watch; his large, multi-buttoned sponsored watch. 'I'm not due on range for another fifteen minutes,' he said. He glanced at Uche. 'See you there, mate, okay?'

He and Tom left, and I found myself alone with two generations of Wigwes. I recalled the serious discussion they'd been having when I'd arrived and thought it best to let them resume it. 'See you later, guys,' I chirped.

'Please don't go, Primavera,' Kalu exclaimed. 'I hoped we might have lunch.'

'Sorry,' I lied, sort of. 'I have to meet friends.' He was an interesting man, no question, but he was radiating interest in me as well. He wasn't unattractive, a bit more than that indeed, but I thought of the absent 'companion' and decided that if he was advertising a temporary vacancy, it wasn't one I saw myself filling.

I headed for the retail tent hoping that Shirley was in shopping mode, but if she was she was doing it somewhere else. Still I killed a quarter of an hour looking for her, then headed for the practice ground. When I got there, Jonny and Tom were waiting, alongside

Lena Mankell, looking not her usual frosty, but downright glacial. I could guess why: no sign of Uche. As for my boy, he was wearing a nice new pair of shoes, with cotton liners that didn't quite qualify as socks, and he was carrying a bag that I guessed contained his trainers.

Shirley and Patterson were in the stand, watching the action. I didn't think that Lena was nice to be near at that moment, so I headed towards them. I passed close enough to hear Tom ask, 'Would you like me to go and find him?'

Jonny started to nod, then stopped, frowning over Tom's head. I followed his eyes, and there was Uche, toting the massive bag and smiling, probably as close to apologetically as he could manage. Kalu was following behind him, on his way to join us in the bleachers, or so I thought until he stopped, said something to his son, and stepped back out through the entrance to the arena. I carried on, and settled myself down beside my chums.

Shirley pointed in the direction from which I had come. 'Who was that?' she asked. 'The black guy in the Savile Row suit?'

'Uche's dad,' I replied. 'He flew in for the big day; on his own jet, no less.'

She whistled. 'Bit of all right,' she pronounced. 'And Uche's mum?'

'She's in the arms of another; our Lord and Redeemer Jesus Christ, to be specific.'

'What a shame. Uche never said his mother was dead.' *No, he hadn't,* I thought. 'Leaves a clear field, though.' She winked, lasciviously.

'Which I will not be cultivating,' I declared.

'No?' she exclaimed. 'And him with a private jet? Could be your chance to join the mile-high club, and you probably wouldn't even have to do it in the toilet.'

I frowned at her, severely. 'No thank you very much. Anyway, I am a member, several times over.'

Her eyes widened. 'You are?' she gasped. 'You dirty little bitch. Come on, spill the beans.'

'Aspen, Colorado,' I revealed. 'Oz and I went on holiday there once, oh, must be twelve, thirteen years ago. That's well over a mile high.'

'Gawd! You must have been out of breath.'

'Not once, my dear, not once. We weren't in any rush.' I smiled as some very vivid memories came back. 'You should try it,' I advised her.

'You hear that,' she said, turning to Patterson. But he wasn't there; nature must have called while we were talking, or he'd had a severe case of the munchies. While Shirley had been wheedling my sexual exploits out of me, he'd slipped out, without either of us noticing.

Below us, Uche was on station and Jonny's practice was under way. Lena's expression had gone back to mildly severe, so she must have been content that his swing hadn't altered overnight. The Irish kid and the other main contenders were lined up on either side of him, each with his own distinctive technique, each one hitting the ball straight and true, as if they were combining to show the new lad . . . and me, for that matter . . . what he was up against. But the new lad wasn't watching; he was concentrating entirely on his own game. 'Your best is all you can be, Auntie P,' he'd said to me the night before. 'The trick is to make that a little bit better every day.'

Still . . . I won't say that my faith in him was waning, but young Irish really did look unbeatable.

I was in danger of succumbing to nerves and maybe even despondency, when my phone vibrated in my pocket. I couldn't answer it on the stand, so I whispered an apology to Shirley, and slipped down from the stand. There was a 'missed call' message on the screen by the time I was able to take it out: Alex Guinart.

'Shit,' I muttered. 'What now?' I remembered my undertaking. 'He's not expecting daily reports on Patterson's movements, surely?'

I considered, quite seriously, deleting the call from the list, and acting the daft lassie (self-explanatory Scottish saying) if Alex asked me about it. Probably that's what I would have done, if it hadn't started to tremble again as I held it in my hand. I looked at the screen: him again. I tutted, impatiently, as I pressed the green button. 'Yes, Inspector Guinart?' I said. 'Don't you normally have Sundays off?'

'Normally, yes,' he conceded. 'But normal went out the fucking window a few days ago. Where are you, Primavera?'

'You must know where I am, surely. I'm at the golf tournament, waiting for my nephew's big moment.'

'Of course,' he sighed. 'I'd forgotten.'

He sounded so out of kilter that I began to worry about him. 'What is it?' I asked him.

'Forget it,' he replied, but without any sincerity. 'I don't need to involve you. Not yet anyway.'

'But you will, at some point?'

'Possibly.'

I persisted. 'Do you need me?'

'No, but . . .' He hesitated. 'I'd appreciate it.'

'Will it take all day?'

'No, just a couple of hours.'

I knew from experience that Alex never said too much over the phone, but I could work things out. It was indeed Sunday, and he sounded very different from his normally phlegmatic self. A friend in need . . . I completed the old, ambiguous, saying, then added in the fact that the needy friend was a cop. 'Okay, where are you?'

'Are you sure about this?'

'No I'm not, so out with it quickly. Where do I find you?'

'You don't need to,' he said. 'We have people where you are. I'll have one of our cars bring you. It'll be faster that way; we can do it under blue lights. What are you wearing?' I told him, leaving out the black thong and the pop-up bra.

'Then go to the clubhouse and wait by the steps. I'll have a car there inside five minutes.'

'And will there be one to bring me back?' I asked, pointedly.

He chuckled. 'Unless I arrest you.'

I headed for the meeting place and beat the car there by about thirty seconds. Just one officer, the driver, unsmiling behind his shades, but courteous; he opened the back door for me, and didn't put his hand on my head when I got in, as you see them do on the news and in the movies.

We left the course at normal speed, then headed north, my first clue to our destination. As soon as we were on the main road, the lights went on and the foot went down. I didn't speak to my driver at all . . . at that speed, I didn't reckon it was a good idea to distract him . . . just watched the road and ticked off each exit as we passed it. We left the motorway just north of Girona, then took a quiet road, one I use often when I go to the city. That made me assume that we were going back to L'Escala, or even St Martí. I carried on thinking that until we went past the turn that would have taken us there and instead drove on towards Torroella de Montgri.

The options were lessening; in the small town, we turned off the central roundabout, headed down the leafy ramblas and eventually crossed the River Ter. *Pals?* I wondered, until the driver made a left turn, into a narrow road that I'd driven past a few hundred times, but never along. I wasn't sure where it led, other than eventually to the sea, but there were a couple of restaurant signs at the beginning, so I knew that it wasn't entirely uninhabited territory.

We drove on for maybe a kilometre, through absolutely flat land, before we took another turn, into a camino, a track rather than a proper made-up road. A few hundred metres ahead, I saw cars; three of them and, ominously, a dark, unmarked van. I'd seen it, or its brother, before, and I knew what it was for.

Until that very moment, I hadn't attempted to guess why Alex wanted me. He'd been his usual cautious self on the phone, I knew it couldn't be a family crisis, nothing wrong with Gloria or Marte, for he'd used police transport, and if anything had gone wrong at my place I'd have had a call from my alarm monitoring service well before he'd know about it. I certainly hadn't considered, not for one second, that he'd want me to look at another stiff.

That must have been written all over my face as I stepped out of the car, for he came towards me, in another paper tunic, with hands outstretched as if to ward me off. In the background, I could see the obligatory white tent; until then it had been hidden behind the mortuary wagon. 'Alex,' I said as he reached me, 'the last time was once too often.'

'I know,' he admitted, 'and I'm deeply grateful. You'll never have another speeding ticket in Catalunya, I promise.'

'I want Hector's signature on that one as well,' I told him. 'Where is he, by the way? Intendants don't have their Sundays interrupted, is that it?'

'He's off sick.' Alex's reply was barely more than a whisper. 'He had chest pains in the office on Friday, late in the afternoon. I took him to the Trueta, and they kept him in, for investigation. He's still there; they think he's going to need bypass surgery. It's not generally known, but it will be very soon.'

At the rate Gomes had been smoking when I'd seen him last, that news didn't surprise me too much. He was in a good place though; the 'Trueta', named after a Catalan nationalist doctor who was exiled in Britain during the civil war, and became a professor in Oxford, is a teaching hospital, Girona's biggest and, by general agreement, its best.

'That'll be bad news for Marlboro,' I ventured. 'I hope he'll be all right soon.'

Alex nodded. 'He will be . . . unlike the patient we've got here. Again, Primavera, thank you for coming.'

'Okay, but why did you want me?'

He smiled. 'Honestly? I don't know, for sure. I just did, given the circumstances.'

'What circumstances? What have you got here?'

'Come and see, if you want.'

'I don't, but that's why I'm here, isn't it?'

I put on a sterile suit and boots and went with him, into the tent. It was bigger than the one in the woods, but it had to be, for there was a thorn bush taking up a lot of the space inside. A body lay at its base, a white woman, naked, stripped of all clothing and adornments, and with no face. 'Jesus!' I whispered. 'The same.'

'As our victim outside L'Escala,' he added. 'Stripped and mutilated, I assume, for the same reason: to make identification as difficult as possible. It's very effective too, for we still are no nearer knowing who the other one is.'

I crouched beside the body as he spoke and leaned forward for a better look. Whoever had used the shotgun had done an even better job second time around. Most of the head was missing . . . actually it wasn't, but it was scattered all around, and all the king's horses and all the king's men could try all they liked, but Ms Humpty was fucked, permanently. I peered at the part that remained, the left side, from the jaw to just above the temple. And as I did, a shudder ran through me.

'Our pathologist believes that she was strangled first,' Alex was saying, above me, 'and that she was dead when the gun was put to her head.' He sighed. 'What a mess. I suppose I wanted you here because you were at the other scene, and so I hoped that you might see something that I don't, something that connects in some way.

It's not very professional of me, I know, and not very kind either. Stupid also, because why the hell should you? I'm the bloody detective. What could have I expected you to tell me?'

I could have kept my mouth shut. Indeed, if there had been anyone else in that tent, even the photographer who had stepped outside to give us room, I might have, for that moment at least. But there wasn't, it was just Alex and me, and I'd held his daughter at her baptism. So I said, 'How about if I tell you who she is, or was, if you're feeling pedantic?'

'Eh?' he gasped.

'That's the woman you threatened to run out of town on Friday, at the golf course, the TV reporter with the Irish passport. That's Christine McGuigan.'

'You're kidding me,' he croaked.

'I wish I was.'

'But how can you possibly know, from . . . from that?'

I beckoned him, and he joined me, crouching. When he was in position I reached out and pointed. 'See that mark?' I asked. 'There on her temple. That abrasion.'

He nodded. 'Yes. The pathologist said she must have struggled with her killer, got it then.'

'Then your pathologist is wrong.' I pushed myself to my feet, paper tunic rustling, and he followed suit. 'You know that big dress ring I have, the one with the red gemstones that look like rubies but aren't, in a gold setting?'

'Yes,' he murmured, cautiously, as if he wasn't sure that was the right answer.

'I think you'll find it matches that bruise. You didn't scare her as much as you thought. Alex. She wasn't going to give up that easily.'

I told him about my confrontation with Christine, about me catching her in the act of taking long-lens pictures of Tom, for sale to the highest bidder, and about me knocking her bow-legged.

'Oh my,' he whispered, when I'd finished. 'When I said earlier, about arresting you, I was joking. But now . . . Why the hell did you have to go and tell me that?'

'Because you're my mate and you know I'm not a bloodthirsty killer.' I paused. 'But just in case you have to convince anyone else, what time was she killed?'

'The pathologist says between ten and midnight last night. But not necessarily at this place; the mutilation was done here, clearly as you can see, but he believes that it must have happened some time after death, because of the absence of blood.'

'In that case,' I said, 'you can take me off your suspect list. I was in Mike's Restaurant with Jonny and Tom and quite a few other people until just before ten. From there I went home and phoned my dad. When we were done, I went online and wrote an email to my sister, telling her all about my week, and my new family member. I finished and sent it at ten minutes to twelve, and then I went to bed. The transmission time will be logged into my computer and there'll be a record of the call on my phone.'

'Thank you,' he said, sincerely. 'We're both off the hook.'

'So what have you got to go on?' I asked, as we left the tent.

'Nothing, other than I'm certain that the murderer is local.'

I frowned. 'Why?'

'Because he's left the bodies in two remote areas. It was pure luck that they were found so quickly. This one was discovered by the chef in one of the restaurants along there, walking his dog. Only a local has that sort of knowledge.'

'Tell me you're kidding,' I exclaimed. 'Haven't you heard of Google Earth? That will take you anywhere, and usually show you nice pictures as well. For example, you're in your front garden in Google Earth's street view.'

'Yes, I've heard of it, but . . .' His eyes widened. 'They can't do that, Christ; I'm a cop.'

'It's okay,' I assured him. 'They pixelate all the faces, and car registration numbers. But what it means is that everyone's a local, everywhere, when it comes to knowing the lie of the land.'

He ran his fingers through his hair. 'Thanks,' he moaned. 'Now I have nothing to go on. Are you sure you wouldn't like to be a suspect after all?'

'I'd rather not, if it's all the same to you.' He looked really down, and so I did my best to raise his spirits. 'Come on; it's not all that black. You know who this victim is. The two were both killed in more or less the same way, by the same person.'

'I can't prove that,' he muttered, gloomily.

'Spoken like a defence lawyer.'

He shook his head. 'No, spoken like our new prosecutor. She's a hard woman to please.'

'Then don't go to her until you have to. What I'm saying is that when you look into Christine McGuigan's background, she might point you at the identity of the first victim. They have to be connected; they must be. Fuck it, they are! They have a murderer

175

in common. So it could well be that they knew each other and that when you look into McGuigan's life you'll find the first victim. And when you do, the next step is to find who else they had in common.'

He peered at me, from under his frowning eyebrows. 'Since when were you a detective?' he chuckled, if a little grudgingly.

'You're forgetting,' I retorted. 'I was once. There was a period in our lives, when Oz and I lived together in Glasgow, when we ran a private inquiry agency.'

'You wouldn't like to take it up again, would you? I'm up against it. With Hector on the sick list for God knows how long . . . and maybe tied to a desk for the rest of his career . . . I'm acting intendant, with two murders on my hands, and bosses in Barcelona who don't listen to excuses.'

'They'll give you help, though, an extra pair of hands.'

'They have done already. Magda's been pushing for a move to criminal investigations; I've been told to use her, for now.'

'Magda,' I repeated. The sullen woman from the woods, the one who had tried to talk down to Tom, the Mystery of the Missing Personality.

'Exactly,' he murmured.

I looked around the crime scene, in vain. 'So where the hell is she?'

'She has a little girl. She couldn't come at short notice, she told me.'

'So have you, and you did.'

'Yes, but I'm a man; I don't have a choice.' He nodded in the direction of another officer in paper clothing. 'Neither did

Jorge over there; it's his wife's birthday and he's had to cancel a family lunch.'

'Bloody nonsense!' I exclaimed. 'She's at it.'

'Maybe so, but they don't know that in Barcelona. I'm stuck with her, which is only a little better than being on my own.'

I felt heart sorry for him; and a little worried. A job like his generates stress at the best of times, and when there's someone in a small team who isn't bearing her share of the load, it makes it worse. 'So, tomorrow,' I suggested, 'give her a nice desk in your office. That one next to the toilets should suit her. Then gather up all your petty stuff, all your open burglary investigations and the like, and tell her to get to work on those.'

'I can't. All that has to be on the back burner till I make progress on these murders.'

'In that case, give her a phone and a computer and tell her to find out all she can about Christine McGuigan.'

'Fine, but I'll have to tell her where to start looking.' He paused. 'The Novotel.'

'Pardon?'

'That's where she said she was staying, remember. The hotel at the airport.' He waved at his sidekick. 'Jorge,' he called out. 'Let's leave this to the technicians. Primavera's given us a lead. You and I will take her back to her golf tournament, and then we will follow it up.'

Ten

It didn't happen quite as smoothly as that, though. On the way south, Alex explained, politely but firmly, that certain things had to be done by the book, to keep the sharp-eyed, sharp-tongued prosecutor happy, and that it would be necessary for us to stop off at his office in Girona, for me to put everything I had told him on the record.

I was keen to get back to the action, but I didn't argue. He had enough on his plate without me turning awkward. Back at the 'Yard', they went as fast as they could, but the clerical staff didn't work Sundays and so Jorge had to transcribe the story I told to the tape, and that wasn't his strong suit. It took him the best part of an hour before Alex was satisfied, but finally, I was able to sign it.

The final round was well under way by the time they dropped me at the course. The early starters, the also-rans who were playing for as many euro as they could pick up, were completing their week's work, but only their families and managers were interested in them and so the stand by the eighteenth green was almost empty. Behind it, the main leader-board told me three things: the last match was playing the fifteenth hole, the closest challengers to the leaders were six shots adrift, and Jonny was eighteen under par, one shot behind the Irish kid, who had just birdied the fourteenth.

They were a fair distance from the clubhouse, and I was making my way against the flow of the crowds, so it took me a little while to reach them. Just as I did, I heard a roar; by that time my ear was attuned to gallery sounds so I knew that someone had just holed a putt for a birdie at least. I eased my way greenside, just in time to see young Irish pick his ball out of the hole, with an even wider smile than usual splitting his face in two. As he did so, his caddie handed the flag to Uche; a good sign, possibly, since it meant that Jonny had still to putt. I looked around for Tom, and saw him a few yards to my right. His face was expressionless, as he changed one of the numbers on his board, replacing the red nineteen with twenty.

The cheer had subsided as quickly as it had erupted, but I doubt that Jonny would have heard anything as he lined up the shot that faced him, five or six metres I judged, across a slope, downhill at the finish, virtually impossible to leave short yet impossible to stop once it had passed the hole. If his opponent had been allowed to place it, that's the spot he'd have chosen. Jonny waved Uche to join him; they surveyed the line together, then the caddie backed off. By that time, I'd seen enough of Jonny in competition mode to know that when he made up his mind about a shot, he didn't hang about. That's how it was then: step up, line up, steady, stroke.

I was sure he'd missed it on the right, dead certain; and so was he, I reckoned, for he started to walk after it, a sure sign of golfer resignation.

The impossible never happens. Sometimes you think it has, but it's only an optical illusion. The hole doesn't really move sideways into the path of the ball. In reality there's a borrow, an extra slope so slight that no one can see it, until it takes effect. That's how it was, but it really did look as if Jonny's Titleist had been gulped down and swallowed, rather than simply falling into the cup.

The roar exploded again. (I must record that the Irish cheered as loudly as everyone else. The most admirable thing about European golf galleries is that they appreciate the shot regardless of who plays it, of whom they may be supporting and of how they may be betting.) If anything it was louder than before, and not just because I was yelling too. I looked at Tom, and felt a surge of overwhelming love for the way that he wasn't quite able to stay professionally neutral, but managed nonetheless to control himself far better than I did as he peered into his bag and changed Jonny's score, not to the red nineteen I'd been expecting, but to a twenty, tying for the lead. Of course, I'd forgotten; the fifteen was a par five on the card, so his putt must have been for a three.

It might not have been as busy as the Old Course at St Andrews but I was swallowed up by the crowd nonetheless, and swept towards the next tee in what I can best describe as a human tidal flow. I didn't fancy that, so I broke free; since the sixteenth is a par three I headed straight for the green, and found a spot behind the flag, up against the rope. It was a perfect vantage point. I had a clear view of both tee shots; the hole was dangerously close to trouble and neither player took the risk of shooting at it, leaving themselves putts that were no more than outside birdie chances.

Tom saw me as he approached the green; he gave me a discreet wave with his free hand, but otherwise kept his game face on. He looked more determined than anxious. Jonny looked at me too. He was frowning when our eyes met, and for a second or two I was worried that I'd broken his concentration, until he winked at me, flashed me his uncle's smile, then held out his hand to Uche, for the putter that the caddie had taken from his bag.

As he surveyed the green, studying the slopes and borrows, I looked around the gallery. Suddenly I felt sorry for him, and a little angry too. The crowd was predominantly green; the shamrock seemed to be everywhere. The navy blue of Scotland and the thistle were conspicuous by their absence. And so, it seemed, were three other people. I looked right, left, and all around, yet saw neither hide nor hair of Shirley Gash, and since there is a lot of both, if she'd been there I would have. And Patterson Cowling would have been easy to spot too, because he'd have been stood right alongside her. I took another look around, acknowledging the possibility that Shirl might have gone in search of a comfort station, but still I couldn't spot him. If he'd been there, even without Shirley as a marker buoy, he'd still have been obvious, since there were no other double-breasted blazers with gold buttons in sight. Not surprisingly, there were no other tailored, pale-blue, silk blend, Nehru-jacketed suits either . . . not even the original.

For Kalu Wigwe was missing too. There was no question about it, for even if he'd nipped back to his plane and changed in my absence, and he'd had time to do so, I wouldn't have missed him, for his would have been the only black African face on my side of the rope. To me, that was strangest of all. Neither Shirley nor Patterson were in the first flush of youth and eighteen holes around a golf course on foot, on a warm Spanish day, is quite a hike. If they had bailed out or had decided to sit and wait for the finish at the eighteenth green, I had no problem understanding that; indeed that was my assumption. But Kalu? The guy . . . the middle-aged, fit-looking guy . . . had flown for eight hours, on impulse, to 'support the team' as he'd put it. I guessed that he'd gone for lunch, maybe even found someone else to entertain, and had decided that the live TV feed in the dining room was a better way of supporting than being out there mingling and jostling with the crowd. After all, the guy was a princeling.

I dismissed him from my thoughts and concentrated on Jonny and on staying with him to the end, however it worked out, even though I didn't have a Scottish flag to wave.

And so I was there, on that great day. I was there as the Irish kid's putt just lipped out on the sixteenth, matching my nephew's more cautious par. I was there as they negotiated the tricky seventeenth, playing short of the fairway bunkers, taking the safe line into the green and settling for four each. I was there as they came to the final hole . . . although, possibly, it wasn't, as there would be a sudden death play-off in the event of a tie.

Jonny had the honour; he drove first. His body must have been pumping adrenaline, for he carried the bunkers that were meant to catch the careless. Unfortunately, he carried the fairway as well and his ball settled down in the rough. His opponent had been in last-day combat before; he knew to take a deep breath and to hit a three metal rather than a driver, arcing the ball into the centre of the fairway, and giving himself the advantage of playing first to the green from a perfect lie. I looked at Tom; his mouth was set in a tight line and I could feel that mine was too. Jonny? He was smiling as he reached his ball, but his eyes looked like steel.

Half of Ireland seemed to hold its breath as the kid . . . did I tell you his name was Cormac Toibin? . . . took out an eight iron. (No, I wasn't close enough to read the number, but I caught the finger signal his caddie sent to Telly Man.) I'd seen him hit that club a few dozen times by then; I knew how good he was with it. Nine times out of ten he'd have knocked it in close, but the tenth is usually the one where the big money is on the line. That's how it was. His ball flew beyond the flag, took a hard bounce and disappeared into the back left bunker.

'Come on, Jonny!' I wanted to shout it out loud, but my tongue was sticking to the roof of my mouth, so I willed the thought to him.

I got as close to his ball as I could, close enough to see that it wasn't lying too well, close enough to hear him ask Uche what he thought.

'Strong wedge and fucking murder it,' the caddie replied, loud enough to make Telly Man wince under the Aussie hat. He was standing just in front of me, on the other side of the rope; I guessed that his microphone was live and that the prissy director would be making the prissy commentator apologise for the language lapse.

Jonny took the advice to heart; he did indeed fucking murder it, so effectively that his ball flew clean over the flag and disappeared into the same bunker as his opponent's.

The crowd scrambled towards the green, rushing to fill the last few seats in the stand or to get as close to the action as they could. I left them to it; instead, when I got there I found a marshal and flashed the 'Competitor's family' badge that Jonny had given me at the start of the tournament and that I'd never had to use. I found a vantage point in front of the stand, beside a couple of guys I'd seen on the range and knew to be Cormac's dad and older brother. Senior pointed to Jonny. 'Mum?' he asked. 'Aunt,' I replied.

'Good luck,' he murmured. 'Your lad's done really well, regardless.'

For a moment I wondered whether he was being patronising, but he wasn't, just kind. 'Yours too,' I whispered. As I did I looked up and into the stand, in search of Shirley and Patterson, but there was no sign. *Bugger them*, I thought. *Serves them right.*

It took a referee to decide who was to play first. After some deliberation, Cormac got the nod, as Jonny would have had to stand on his ball to play. I'd picked up some stats in the course of the week. Among them was the fact that the kid was number one in sand saves on the US PGA Tour.

The shot that faced him was over a couple of metres of fringe then on to a slope down to the flag. I couldn't see how he could stop it anywhere near the hole, but he did, angel-feathering the ball in a shimmer of sand and leaving it about a foot short for a dead certain nailed-down four. He walked up and marked it with a golden coin.

Standing behind the bunker, Uche reached into the bag, took out a club and held it out for Jonny. He shook his head. 'No,' he said firmly. 'Not the sand iron. Lob wedge.'

'You could leave it in the bunker,' the caddie protested.

184

'But I won't. I see the shot.' He snapped his fingers. 'Gimme.'

I looked at Tom as he stepped up to the ball. He was gripping the pole of his board with both hands and his knuckles were white. I might have kept on looking at him, but I found the strength to overcome my nerves and turned back to my other boy.

As always he didn't waste any time. His backswing was long and steep and he drove into the sand so hard that I sensed disaster . . . which tells you how much I know.

The ball flew high, much higher than Cormac's had, but remarkably seemed to land even more softly, at the very start of the slope. For a second or two, I thought that backspin would keep it there, leaving him the mother of all difficult putts to stay alive in the tournament, but then it moved very slightly, and started to roll very gently, picking up pace, but not too much. I was sure it was going to miss on the left; indeed it might have, had it not, as countless high-definition TV close-up replays showed later, clipped the edge of Cormac's marker and changed course, very slightly but enough to leave it perched on the edge of the hole, until gravity gave it one last shove and it fell in. The winner and Catalan Masters champion, Jonathan Sinclair, Scotland.

There followed one of those moments beloved of moviemakers, when time seemed to stand still and all the players in the drama were frozen as if encased in plastic . . . until it was broken by the sound of a board hitting the ground and of its bearer, as he jumped high, punching the air and yelling, 'Yes!!!!'

Everyone went crazy after that, including, to their eternal credit, the Irish, who love a miracle above all else. In the mayhem that followed, Jonny and Uche embraced, then he and Cormac shook hands formally and hugged a little less so. I couldn't hear the kid, but I'm a good lip-reader, so I could follow when he said, 'Welcome to the European Tour, Jonathan. Are you really that good, or was that shot just plain crazy?'

I couldn't see the reply properly, for the two older Toibins seized my hands and offered congratulations that were both genuine and generous; also my eyes were starting to tear up, as I saw my nephew turning towards me.

If you're a regular watcher of golf on television, especially the American style, you'll know that it is de rigueur for the nearest and dearest of the combatants to be greenside as the drama concludes. Great for the winner's family, tough shit on the loser when it's a razor-edge finish. I'd always found that staged emotion more than a little sick-making; until then, for, without a thought for the prying cameras, without caring that I was making a tit of myself live on air, I rushed on to the green and jumped into Jonny's arms.

'You did it, you did it, you did it,' I murmured, as I cried on his shoulder.

'Yeah,' he replied. 'I owe you the finest dinner in town.'

Uche left us alone for a little while, before reminding Jonny . . . after I'd hugged him too . . . that the job wasn't done until his score was recorded. 'God, yes,' I said. 'Get that done, properly . . . then I can study the menu.'

As they walked towards the recorder's caravan, my phone vibrated in my pocket. I didn't even look at caller ID; I didn't have to. 'Yes, Ellie,' I said, as I answered, 'you didn't dream it.'

'The wee beauty,' she exclaimed, in the snuffly voice of someone who doesn't know whether to laugh or cry and winds up doing both. 'I thought you were going to eat him there, woman,' she added. 'You should have seen yourself. But I don't blame you. Christ knows what I'd have been like. Who'd have thought it, eh? My wee boy, champion. Believe it or not, I had a phone call from his father last night; he was too busy to go to Girona, of course, but he asked me to pass on his good wishes. Hey,' she chuckled, 'maybe the roles will be reversed now, and Jonny can send him a cheque for his birthday. Make sure you tell him to call me once he's collected his cup . . . and his winnings, of course.'

'I won't have to tell him, you daft bat. Have you heard from Mac yet?'

'No,' she replied, 'the old eedjit's sailing back to Singapore, cut off from all communication. I'm going to ask the shipping line if they can get a message to him. If only that wife of his hadn't insisted on dragging him off on a cruise. He'll be shitting rattlesnakes when he finds out what he's missed.'

She left me with that vision in mind. It might have stayed there for a while, if it hadn't been for Lena Mankell. She bore down on me from the crowd that was gathering in front of the television backdrop, the one with the sponsors' logos, where the interview and presentation would take place. Her fists were clenched above her head . . . and she was almost smiling.

Lars followed her, with a toddler in the crook of his left arm and an older child holding his right hand. He'd played on Thursday and Friday, on an invitation. He had missed the cut by eight shots; it did seem that the best of his career was well behind him, but equally he didn't seem too worried about it. It made me wonder what a swing coach earns, if he was happy to follow his wife around and able to afford to. There are many ways for pros in decline to make money, but as far as I could see he wasn't bothered.

'I knew he would win,' Lena exclaimed.

'Even when he was in the sand,' I challenged, 'and Cormac was stone dead next to the hole?'

'Jonny was number one in sand saves,' Lars informed me, 'and he played the eighteenth better than Toibin all week. Even if he had not holed out, there would have been a play-off, on that hole, as often as it took, and he would have won.'

It hadn't come to that so I could afford to be sceptical. 'Golf isn't all about statistics,' I argued.

'It creates them,' Lars countered, sombrely, in his accented English. He seemed more solemn in his wife's presence. I wondered if they were all serious people in their household, kids included. 'And they all add up,' he continued. 'There was a player last year who was best in Europe, if you look at the greens hit in regulation. But then if you looked at the money he earned, he is not in the top one hundred. Link those together and you didn't even need to look at the putting stats to know he was damn near enough worst putter on the tour.'

'But Jonny doesn't have any stats. This was his first tournament.'

Lena took me surprise by laughing; a light, pleasant tinkling sound. 'And so he has stats. From his very first round, he has stats; everything is measured in golf. In this tournament he is number three in greens in regulation and number one in putting. Those are the two that matter; the others not so much. For example, driving distance doesn't tell you whether the players hit driver off the tee, only how far the ball went.' She nodded backwards at her husband. 'Lars, here, he hits three metal off the tee mostly, because he's lousy with driver. It still goes two eighty-seven yards, but stats say he's weak.'

Her master class might have taken in every club in the bag, had not Tom arrived, looking flushed and triumphant. 'Were you fired?' I asked him. 'You went crazy when Jonny won.'

He beamed at me. 'So did you. So did the referee; that made it all right. But Uche's going to be fined, one of the Tour guys says.'

'What for?'

'Swearing on TV. It's not allowed.'

'But he didn't know he was on air,' I protested.

'That doesn't matter; he's supposed to assume that he can be heard.' He shrugged. 'But it's all right. Jonny said it's the best advice he's given him all week so he's going to pay it.'

That seemed fair to me; and to Uche, it seemed, for he was well happy as he came out of the recording area, although he looked exhausted. His 'boss' followed him, and was ushered towards the presentation area by a man in a green jacket.

The enormous trophy, and the enormous cardboard cheque (purely symbolic, I learned later; the money hits the bank through electronic channels) were presented by a distinguished man whom I recognised as the President of the Catalan government. His office didn't earn him a speaking part though, for Telly Man in the Aussie hat moved straight in on Jonny and began an interview. He asked him about his last shot. 'Most guys would have played it the way Cormac did,' he said.

Jonny nodded. 'I know, and so would I if I'd seen it that way. But I didn't. As it turned out, I caught it just right, spot on, and I got the other fifty per cent, luck.'

A few more questions followed, but I could tell that they weren't the ones he wanted to answer. Finally, just as Aussie hat was ready to hand back to the commentary box, he leaned forward and said, 'Before I go I'd like to thank everyone who's helped me this week; Uche, Lena, Brush, my Auntie Primavera, and my cousin Tom, who knows more about surfing than I do about golf. But most of all I'd like to thank three people. For various reasons, none of them could be here this week, but they're the people who gave me the confidence to come out here and play and they're all the bedrock of my support team: my mum, my Grandpa Mac, and my Uncle Oz.'

At the mention of the last name, Tom squeezed my hand. Me? I had to smile through the tears, for I saw that my nephew was a natural. He knows what a headline is and he'd just given them one.

Green blazer wanted to take him straight to the press tent as I approached. 'Have you . . .' I began.

He grinned, and nodded. 'I called her as soon as my card was registered.'

'What about your father?' I ventured.

For an instant his eyes went hard. 'I just thanked him,' he murmured. 'He was the closest thing to a dad I ever had.'

'And Brush?' I asked, moving on quickly. 'What about him?'

'He called me just before I came outside. We'll speak again tomorrow, to organise my schedule. I've got a tour card now, so everything changes. I'll be home in a couple of hours. We'll talk about it over dinner.'

Yes, I thought as he left, *I'd like to talk a lot more about the reclusive Mr Donnelly.* We would have too, if something hadn't happened that knocked him right off my 'things to do' list.

Eleven

For most people, the day that the circus leaves town is a metaphor for anti-climax. Not for Tom and me, though, not that day. We were high as kites, both of us. He'd shown the courage to be certain of the outcome. I hadn't: for all the confidence I'd expressed to Ellie after the third round, the closer Jonny had come to the finish, the more scared I'd become, the more fatalistic, anticipating the moment when his luck would change or he'd overreach himself and we'd all waken from the dream. Yes, I had been weak in my faith. But maybe it wasn't as simple as that: maybe I'd simply been conditioned to assume that the worst would happen by too many not-so-happy endings in my life.

When it didn't, when the fan stayed shit-free, I was more elated than I'd been in almost eleven years, since the day that Tom was born. Finally, something had worked out the way it was meant to.

I slung an arm around my son's ever-rising, ever-thickening, shoulders. 'Home, kid?' I suggested.

He nodded. 'Yeah. There's a Barca game on TV tonight. Jonny was going to take me to dinner with you, but I told him I want to watch it in Esculapi. Is that all right?' Six months before

I'd probably have told him no, that he had to come with us. But his pals would be there, and his faithful hound, and I'd already decided that however big a cheque Jonny was banking, I'd bypass elBulli in favour of Can Roura, in the square. There was something else too; while he was young and while I was filling in for his mum in a way, Jonny was nonetheless a man, and it was a couple of years since I'd been out with one of those on a twosome.

'Sure,' I said, and then the thought of Can Roura reminded me of something else. 'Hey, what about Uche?' I exclaimed. 'Isn't he supposed to be moving into his studio tonight?'

'No,' Tom replied. 'He asked me to tell you to let Joan know that he's going to leave it until tomorrow. He's going to have dinner with his dad tonight.'

'That's nice for them. Hey,' I chuckled, nudging him, 'I wonder if he really is a prince.'

Before he could react, my mobile sounded again; I imagined that it would be a PS from Ellie, so I didn't even glance at the screen. If I had done I'd have known that it was Susie calling, the official widow Blackstone. 'I've just seen you on telly,' she exclaimed, without preamble. 'Imagine, our Jonny the champ. He's turned into a good-lookin' boy, Primavera. And was that Tom, carrying his board?'

'Yes to all of that,' I declared. 'Fantastic, isn't it?'

'Absolutely. Is his mum not there? I assumed she'd be basking in it.' Her tone suggested that Ellie's feelings for Susie were reciprocated. I didn't remark upon it, though; I simply explained the reasons for her absence.

'Poor cow,' she muttered. 'I know . . .' she continued, then stopped.

'What?' I demanded.

'Nothing.'

'Don't bullshit me, Susie,' I warned. 'What were you going to say?'

She sighed. 'That I know how she feels. I've got a wee health issue myself.'

I turned away from Tom so he couldn't see my frown. 'How wee?'

'It's nothing,' she assured me. 'I'm off my food, that's all. My doctor took a blood sample; now he's sending me for tests. He's muttering about pernicious anaemia.'

I switched to nurse mode. 'Don't worry about it,' I said. 'That used to be serious, but it's easily treated nowadays. Keep your chin up.'

'I am. Don't have any choice with Janet and wee Jonathan running my life.'

'What about your love interest?' Susie had acquired a new man a year or so before, a hedge fund dealer that she'd come across in the casino. I'd met him briefly, when I'd delivered Tom for his annual bonding visit with his half-siblings, and had been well under-impressed. I hadn't told her that, though, and so her response took me by surprise.

'Duncan? History. He was starting to behave as if he was the kids' dad, and I wasn't having that. So you'll be pleased to hear that I've binned him.' I was about to protest, insincerely, but she cut me off. 'No, don't deny it,' she went on. 'I could tell from your eyes that you didn't like him. You've never learned to fake anything, my dear. Maybe that's why you're still single.' She paused. 'Or . . . what about Father G?'

'Now Brother G, and staying in Ireland.'

'And are you devastated?'

'Who? Me? No.'

'Fine. You'll find him, eventually.'

'Find who?'

'The man of your dreams. I had one of my own about you the other night; you were fixed up in it.'

I listened for sounds of suppressed chuckles, but heard none. 'Do tell. What was he like?'

'Big bloke, greying hair, grey beard. I didn't really get a good look at him.'

'Was he wearing a red suit and driving a sleigh pulled by reindeer?'

'Hah! Mock me if you will, but I'm becoming fey in my middle age. That's why . . .' She stopped, again.

'What?'

'Nothing, and this time I really mean it. Love to Tom, and Jonny. I'm off.'

I stared at my silent phone as if I expected a Santa Claus lookalike to appear on the screen. But he didn't, only my wallpaper, an image of Charlie on the beach. I turned back to my son. 'Sorry,' I told him. 'Susie Mum sends her love.'

'That's nice. He's an emir,' he declared, solemnly.

'Who is?' Susie's fey dream had erased our previous conversation.

'Uche's dad,' he said, patiently. 'Uche says that's the same as a prince. He doesn't have a palace, though, just a big house in Lagos. He's very rich. He has an oil company, and he exports tobacco and clothes and all sorts of stuff.'

'Does he now? It's a pity about Uche's mother. Does Uche talk about her?'

'No. I asked him about her, but he said she's dead, that's all. I don't think he likes to talk about her. I understand that.'

That surprised me. 'You like to talk about your dad,' I pointed out.

'Only to people I know really well. I never talk about him with anybody else.'

I hadn't appreciated that; or maybe I simply hadn't noticed it. With me, the subject is usually off limits, absolutely when Tom's around, and all my friends know that. All my friends, including Shirley Gash. She was bearing down on us, coming from the general direction of the clubhouse. And she wasn't smiling.

'What have you done with him?' she demanded.

'Done with who?' I replied, ungrammatically.

'Patterson,' she barked. 'Who else? Where the fuck did the two of you go?'

This was not Shirley-like behaviour and Tom did not take to it at all. I felt his shoulders tense under my arm, and he seemed to grow an inch or so taller. I gave him a little squeeze, to restrain him; the lioness and her cub, roles reversed.

Not that I was best pleased either; astonished, and instantly irked. 'Would you calm down, woman,' I told her sternly. 'And don't use that language around my son. Now what are you talking about? Why should I have done anything with him?'

'You went off together, didn't you?' she challenged, her chin stuck out.

I stared at her. 'Don't be bloody daft,' I exclaimed, barely stopping myself from shouting, and forgetting my own interdict about language.

'Come on! We were up on that stand, the three of us; I turned round and you two had buggered off!'

As soon as I recalled the scene, I could see where she was coming from. 'Yes,' I countered, fiercely, 'but not together. I had a phone call; I got down from the stand to take it, then I had to leave in a hurry. But Patterson had gone by that time. You were so wrapped up in ogling golfers that you didn't notice, so don't get on to me if you can't keep track of your bloke. Okay!'

I knew that it was anxiety as much as anger that had made her snap at me, so I wasn't surprised when her face crumpled and she seemed to fold in on herself. It wasn't a pretty sight; I'd never seen her looking so old.

'Hey,' I said, friend and counsellor once more, 'what's this? Don't panic, Shirl; everything has an explanation. Have you looked for him?'

I had to wait for her to blow her nose on a tissue before she answered. 'I've been looking for both of you ever since. I thought . . . I thought all sorts of things, but mostly that you'd gone off to follow the golf on your own, 'cos I would have held you back, being old and slow. I looked for you all over the bloody course, then when Jonny started I went back to his match, but you weren't there . . .'

'That's right,' Tom confirmed. 'She asked me from across the rope, at the third hole, if I'd seen you. I told her I hadn't. I was worried too, Mum,' he added. I hadn't considered that possibility: bad mother.

'I'm sorry, love,' I said contritely. 'I should have taken time to tell you before I left.'

'Why did you go?' The question came in stereo, from him and Shirley, simultaneously.

'Someone needed my help,' I told them, 'but that's not important. Tell me where else you've looked.'

'In the clubhouse,' Shirl replied, 'in the tent with all the clothing and golf club stands, in the bars, everywhere save the gents' bogs. I looked in the car park too, and when I couldn't see your jeep anywhere, I thought . . . Well, I won't tell you what went through my mind.'

No, you'd bloody well better not, the guy's twenty-five years older than me, went through mine, but I let it stay there.

'You didn't look hard enough,' I retorted. 'My jeep never left. Your imagination was probably running so wild by then, you didn't want to see it.' Actually I'd parked it alongside a big Callaway truck to catch some shade through the day, so it wasn't a surprise that she'd missed it. 'What about your car?' I asked, although I was sure that I'd seen it when Alex and Jorge had dropped me off.

'Still there,' she confirmed. 'I looked for that too.'

'Then on the face of it, he should still be here. Phone him,' I instructed.

She took out her mobile and obeyed. I watched, and saw hope go quickly from her eyes. 'Straight to voicemail,' she murmured.

198

I frowned, then turned to my son. 'Tom, I want you to do something for me. Go to the emergency medical centre. You know where that is?'

'Sure, beside the bar tent.'

'Good. When you get there, ask whether they've treated an English gentleman for anything. You know Mr Cowling, so describe him, and say that he was wearing grey trousers and a blue blazer with gold buttons. Then meet us back at the clubhouse, in front.'

'Why are we going there?' Shirl asked.

'To check the gents' toilets, or have them checked for us.'

We did, courtesy of the club manager, who despatched a bag boy to look for a locked cubicle with an unresponsive customer inside, but came up blank.

'He's gone,' Shirley wailed, as Tom reappeared, shaking his head.

'Come on, girl,' I cajoled her, 'hold yourself together.'

'How can I? He's fucked off and left me. He's been taking the piss, Primavera, all this time.'

I had to admit, if only to myself, that the same possibility was beginning to gain ground in my list of possible causes for Patterson's absence. 'If he has gone,' I asked nobody in particular, 'how has he done it? Let's assume that he isn't hiding among the trees waiting for it to get dark.'

'But what if he is? What if he's had an accident? There are snakes here, Primavera.' My robust pal was verging on hysteria. I didn't want to call out the National Guard, but . . .

'He was wearing nice sensible shoes, so forget the vipers,' I said. 'Let's try to answer my last question.'

'He could have got a taxi,' Tom pointed out.

'Are there taxis here?'

'A lot. Some of the players and most of the caddies use them to get back to their hotels, and the crowd do as well.'

'Then let's see if we can find some.'

'I'll show you where they are.'

He led us to a compound, alongside the spectator car park. I hadn't noticed it until that moment. Most of the crowd had gone, but there were still plenty of people around, tournament staff, media and as Tom had said, competitors and their aides. There were a dozen cabs in a line waiting to be picked up. As we approached I saw Lena, Lars and their kids sliding into one, then being driven off.

The lead driver in the rank beamed at me expectantly as we approached. 'Sorry,' I said, wiping the smile away with a word. 'I need your help,' I continued, in Castellano, then switched to Catalan, knowing that Shirley doesn't speak a word. 'My friend here may have been robbed. Earlier on today she met an Englishman, a middle-aged man, in the shopping tent. He said he was on his own, like her, and a fan of golf as she is. He was very nice, very plausible, they talked and they had a drink together, on the clubhouse terrace. After a while, he asked her if she would like to have lunch with him. She said she would, he went to book a table and he never came back. It was some time before she looked in her bag, but when she did she found that her money was gone, and her credit cards and some very valuable rings that she had taken off because her fingers were puffy in the heat. We've spoken to the police; they said "Tough" as they do. Our only hope is that he might have used a cab to get away. Can you help us. Did he?'

The further I got into my story the darker the driver's expression grew. Why did I lay it on? Simples, as that meerkat used to say. If I'd told him that Shirley's boyfriend had done a runner, had second thoughts and buggered off, there was a better than even chance, no, much better than even, that I'd have run into the male solidarity thing. But show him a woman robbed, rather than a woman wronged, and by an Englishman at that . . .

Perhaps I'm doing the man an injustice; perhaps he'd have helped us anyway, but I've lived in Spain for long enough to know that for those of a certain age, as he was, it's still a male-dominated society. I described Patterson in detail, from his immaculate brown coiffeur to his sensible shoes.

'Hold on,' he growled. 'I'll ask around.' He waved his fellow drivers to him and they went into conference. When they were done, he turned back to me, and shook his head. 'None of us picked him up,' he said. National Guard it is, then, I was thinking, when he added, 'But hold on, I'll get on the radio and check the other guys.'

He got into his cab. I watched him reach for a small hand mike on a wire and speak into it, then wait. Within no more than half a minute he was speaking again, then nodding, his eyes brighter and more alert. When his CB exchange was over, he climbed out. 'Yes,' he announced. 'The guy who left a minute or two ago, with a couple and their kids, he says he picked up a man just like that, five, maybe six hours ago. Is that time about right?'

'Spot on. Does he remember where he dropped him?'

'Sure. The airport; Girona Airport. He thought it was unusual, because the guy had no luggage at all, not even a small bag.'

I whistled. 'So he's well gone.'

'For sure. Your friend will never see her rings again, and she'd better cancel her cards.' He looked at Shirley. 'I'm sorry, lady,' he said, in English. 'You've been done.'

The same thought had occurred to her, even without the elaboration of my cover story, for she burst into tears.

I gave the guy a twenty; he refused at first, but I insisted. It was only right, since I'd deceived him a little. I hustled Shirley away, waiting until she'd composed herself before giving her the full story.

'The airport,' she repeated. 'But that's crazy. He didn't bring his passport. I know that for sure, I saw it on the dressing table this morning. I said he should put it in my safe, and he said he would when we got back. I know he left it. But why else would he go there, if not to catch a flight?'

'To catch the Barcelona bus,' Tom pointed out. Of course, he'd heard the entire discussion with the cabbie, and his Catalan is better than mine.

'There's that,' I agreed, 'or maybe to hire a car. Shirl, do you know whether he had his driving licence on him?'

She nodded. 'Yes, I told him he should carry it all the time, in case he was ever asked for ID with a credit card. But only the plastic bit, not the paper licence, and you need both to hire a car, don't you?'

'Technically,' I agreed, 'but they don't usually bother with the counterpart here.' I considered our tactics. 'You go home,' I said eventually, 'just in case there's a bizarre but innocent explanation for all this and he's sitting there waiting for you. He does have a key, doesn't he?'

'Of course.' She gasped. 'And he knows the safe combination. What if—'

'Stop it!' I commanded. 'We're miles away from there yet. He was a nice man at breakfast-time and chances are he still is. I repeat, you go home; we'll head for the airport and check out the car rental desks.'

'And the ticket office for the buses,' Tom added, helpfully.

'That's right,' I nodded. 'There too, if we have to. We'll call you if we have anything to report.'

Shirley was still badly shaken, but I judged . . . or maybe I hoped . . . that she was fit to drive. She was okay at least as far as the airport exit on the autopista, for I followed her there, before I turned off. The terminal building at Girona Airport has almost disappeared within a small city of multi-storey car parks. Local knowledge led me to pick the oldest, even if the walk was a little further. As we entered the concourse, it occurred to me that I might have a wait on my hands, but we struck it lucky. There was an early evening lull in flight arrivals and there were no queues at any of the car hire windows.

Judging that the staff might not part with customer information just for the asking, I had another cover story worked out. My father, Mr Patterson Cowling, had been due to arrive that afternoon and had planned to hire a car for a business trip. He was a sales representative, so I had no clear idea of his route; a family emergency had arisen, his mobile was down and I had to get in touch with him. Had they supplied him with a car and, if so, what was the drop-off point? If I knew that, I might be able to contact him there.

I spun them the yarn, wearing my most anxious expression. Hertz were sympathetic, but hadn't rented a car to anyone of that name. Avis tried even harder, but neither had they. Nor had Europcar. It was only when I got to the last window, that of a local outfit called Bettamotos, that I ran into a spirit of total non-cooperation.

The guy at the desk was forty-something, with bad skin, bad breath and a bad attitude. He must have been practising obduracy all his life. He let me finish my tale and then shook his head, very slowly. 'No,' he said, with a virtual line drawn under it.

'No he didn't, or no you can't tell me?'

'We do not give customer information.'

'But it's an emergency,' I pleaded, not altogether a lie.

'We do not give customer information.'

'Does that mean that he is your customer, but you're not going to tell me?'

'I'm not saying that at all. We don't give customer information, is all.'

I gave him my best blonde smile. 'Not even to me?'

'No chance.'

I withdrew the smile. 'One last chance,' I offered instead.

'Or you'll do what?' he sneered.

'This.' I took out my mobile, and held it up for him to see. 'Call me Aladdin,' I said, 'and consider this a magic lamp. I am now going to summon the genie.' Beside me, Tom chuckled.

I keyed Alex's number. He answered straight away. 'Primavera, I was—'

That could wait. 'Where are you?'

'At the Novotel, in Christine McGuigan's room.'

'Good. I've got a problem, and now I need your help. With everything else that's on your plate I didn't want to bother you, but I have no choice. Remember a couple of days ago, I promised to keep an eye on Patterson Cowling and let you know if anything odd happened around him?'

'Yes, although we both knew you didn't really mean it.'

'Maybe so, but this is my first report. He's disappeared.'

'What?'

'From the golf tournament, in broad daylight, without a word to Shirley, or me. So far I've established that he took a taxi to the airport; that's where I am now. I know he couldn't have caught a flight . . . no passport—'

It was his turn to cut me off. 'Could he have been taken?'

'It's not likely. He was alone in the taxi. I'm trying to find out whether he hired a car, but there's a difficulty. There's a roadblock at a thing called Bettamotos.'

'Wait there.' The line went dead. I waited for a minute or so, then stepped back to the desk.

'Where's your genie, Aladdin?' the clerk chuckled. 'Your lamp not working?'

'It takes a few minutes to heat up. Oh, I should have warned you; he's very bad-tempered after I've wakened him.'

He looked at me as if I was nuts. I let him go on believing that for a little longer, until a Mossos d'Esquadra vehicle pulled up in the bus bay outside.

'That's him,' I said.

Alex came through the door, nodded to Tom and me and leaned over the desk. 'I know you, don't I?' he murmured. 'Antonio Santos, ex Guardia Civil, Figueras.' The man nodded. 'Okay, Antonio: did you rent a car today to an English gentleman, Mr Cowling?'

He didn't yield at once; instead he folded his arms, and repeated his mantra. 'We do not give—'

'Sure, I know,' Alex snapped. 'Customer information is confidential. But not from me. This is now a police matter. Yes, you could make me get a court order, but I don't need one to pull every one of your company's cars off the road for inspection, and you know how long that can take. Piss me about on this and that will happen. If it does I'll make sure your bosses know why.'

Antonio sighed. He also shot me a look full of bluster and 'If I ever see you on a dark night' threats. Alex saw it too. 'Friend,' he said quietly, 'this lady works for me, undercover. If she says I should arrest you, I'll do it in a heartbeat.'

'Yes,' the clerk snapped. 'Okay, he did, this man. I rented him a Seat Ibiza, white, just before one o'clock.' He scribbled on a scrap of paper and handed it to Alex. 'That's the number.'

'How long was the hire?'

'A week.'

'Where's the drop-off? Which of your depots?'

Antonio shook his head. 'This one. He'll bring it back here.'

'And you believed that?' Alex snorted. 'Let me see the paperwork.' The man stared at his desk. 'The paperwork!' he repeated.

'There is none,' he murmured. 'Cash deal.'

'Jesus!' He looked at the number. 'This car's at least four years old,' he pointed out. 'I'll bet it's a piece of shit, the oldest on your lot, the one that never gets rented out.' He smiled. 'I get it. You pocket the money, he brings it back and nobody's ever the wiser. Or possibly he doesn't bring it back. Do you care if he doesn't? No. You report it stolen from the lot, and the company collects the insurance, more than the thing is worth.' He looked up at the sign. 'Who owns this outfit?' he asked. 'Tell me, now; don't make me find out.'

'My brother-in-law.' It was a whisper, as if he feared being overheard.

Alex laughed. 'Then you give him a piece of advice from me, and you take it too, ex-cop. From now on, you drive straight. Understood?'

'Yes. Okay; now let me alone, huh?'

Alex turned away, and Tom and I followed, leaving Antonio to enjoy what was left of his day.

'He's in the wind, your mysterious friend,' he murmured. 'You know that, don't you? They'll never see that car again. Why would he do that, Primavera, why?'

'I have no idea,' I told him, honestly. 'I can't imagine that it had anything to do with Shirley, but who knows for sure.'

'So where do I start looking?'

'Why should you?' I asked. 'He hasn't broken any laws. You have no grounds for starting a manhunt. Alex, you're under enough pressure as it is without piling more on to yourself.'

'The dead man in the forest connects to him,' he pointed out.

'So what? Not nearly as much as he connects to Christine McGuigan, and she and Patterson don't relate at all.'

'True,' he conceded. 'So you're saying that I should simply forget about him?'

'Yes.' I paused. 'But I'm not saying that I will. He's left my friend in the lurch, knocked ten bells out of her emotionally, and I don't take kindly to that. For her sake, okay and for my own curiosity, I'd like to find him and ask what the hell he's playing at.'

'That brings me back to my question, more or less. Where do you start looking?'

'Close to home: his, that is. The only thing that he told me about himself, directly, is that he has two daughters, so that's where I'll begin.'

'Okay,' he said. 'You do that, if you want. You're right, of course; if I were to make his disappearance an official matter I'd be carrying even more heat, and I'm in danger of melting as it is. One condition, though; if you turn up anything that makes it my business, you tell me, straight away.'

'Sure.' I grinned at him. 'I know I'm not really working undercover.'

'I wish you were; I could use you. I suppose you want to know about McGuigan.'

I glanced, quickly, in my son's direction. 'Not at this moment, no.'

He took my meaning. 'Then maybe I'll call you tomorrow. You get on home now. So long, Tom.'

We did as he suggested, but with a detour along the way. I knew it might delay my dinner date, but I felt that I had to do it. Rather than drive up to Shirley's place and press the buzzer, I called her as we approached and the big jail-sized gate was open when we arrived for us to drive in.

'I'll stay in the car, Mum,' Tom said as I unbuckled my belt.

I smiled, for I knew what he was doing: giving Shirl and me room for frank girl talk, but also making sure I didn't stay too long. Game time was looming and he was clock-watching.

She was waiting for me at the front door. She'd been crying, again: I felt sorry for her and, simultaneously, angry for her, and furious with the guy who was giving her such grief. 'He's been here,' she said, as we walked through to her living area. 'He's packed his things, or most of them, taken his passport and he's gone.'

'Have you checked the safe?' I asked, sharply.

'Yes, nothing missing apart from a box of bonds he kept in there. It's a bugger; I felt guilty doing it.'

'YOU felt guilty?' I exclaimed. 'You poor love. When I find him he'll know what bloody guilt is.'

She slumped into an armchair, round-shouldered, make-up smeared, looking worn and defeated. 'Find him?' she repeated. 'No point in that, Primavera. He's voted with his feet, hasn't he, and who can blame him? Look at me, a self-indulgent old woman throwing myself at him.'

I gasped. 'You know, you do talk a load of old bollocks sometimes. You are Shirley Gash, the queen of L'Escala, the strongest woman I know, and one of the most attractive. Snap out of it and put this thing in perspective. If this man has run away from you, it's not because he's rejecting you, that's for bloody sure.'

'But he left me a note,' she wailed. She pointed to her massive oak dining table. 'And the house keys.' I looked; they were lying there, a big bunch that included the zapper for the electrically opened gate.

'Was it open when you arrived?' I asked.

'No, he must have used the back entrance. The door there's on a Yale, remember.'

I did. I've used it myself. I went across and picked up the note. It had been scrawled on the back of an old restaurant bill, by a man in a rush, possibly in a panic, not the neat, meticulous Patterson Cowling that I'd come to know. 'Sorry,' I read aloud. 'I'd hoped it would work out between us. Love, Patterson.'

'You see? I've been dumped; chucked. That's never happened to me in my life before.'

'And it hasn't happened now. This man's running away from his own inadequacies, not any of yours. Come on, 'fess up. Is he any good in bed?'

She shot me a quick, girl-to-girl look. 'I can see why you left Tom in the car.' Her chuckle was a promising sign. 'He's all right, I suppose. A bit quick, maybe.'

'Always missionary, I suppose. Car ferry sex.'

She stared at me. 'Whatever are you talking about?'

'You know. Roll on, roll off.'

She laughed. 'That's a fair description.'

'And you put up with that?'

'Not always,' she murmured, coyly. 'Sometimes I had to take things into my own hands, so to speak. Gawd, listen to me, Primavera, staring seventy in the face and here are you telling me that I'm a nympho.'

'I'm telling you no such bloody thing. I'm reminding you that women are entitled to expect as much from sex as men are. If Patterson's done a runner because he couldn't handle you getting on top, that reflects on him, not you. And by the way, you are not staring seventy in the face, you can barely see it in the distance; you're still looking over your shoulder at sixty. Nice man, but if that's the way he was, write him off to experience and find yourself someone with a bit more energy.'

'A bit more stay up and go?' she tittered.

'You get my drift.'

'A bit younger?'

'No reason why not.'

'Even someone half my age?' I'd seen that cunning gleam in her eye before. I knew then that she was turning back into Shirley, even if I wasn't going to where she was leading me.

'That would be pushing it,' I said, firmly. 'But that does remind me; I'm having a celebration dinner with my nephew . . .'

'Oz's nephew.'

'Our nephew, my son's cousin.'

'Tongues are wagging already, you know.'

'Any that wag within my hearing will be torn out, and you can feed that to the chattering class. Now, are you going to be all right?'

She nodded, square-shouldered normality once again. 'Yeah. No harm done, eh. Nobody died.'

Considering what I'd seen earlier that afternoon, she could have chosen a better phrase. I shuddered, slightly, but she didn't notice.

'You're not really going to try and find him are you?' she continued.

'Yes, I am. To satisfy my own curiosity, if nothing else. You probably did shag the poor man out of town, but you know me, Bloodhound Blackstone; when I get a scent in my nostrils, I have to follow.'

'I know,' she conceded. 'Even if it gets you into terrible bloody bother as it has done often enough. Did you find anything out at the airport?'

'Yup. He did hire a car, and we know now that he used it to come here and pick up his stuff. There's every chance that as we speak he's back at Girona, or some other airport, about to board a flight, or he's driving north, from whence he came. As soon as I know for sure, I'll be happy.'

'And what will you do then?'

I hadn't thought that far ahead, but the answer wasn't hard to find. 'If I can, I'll speak to him, or if not, I'll get a message to him suggesting that he owes you a better apology than what's in that bloody note.'

'Fair enough.' She stood up, straight-backed, clear-eyed and smiling. 'Go on then, woman; off home and doll yourself up for your date with Oz's dishy nephew, and don't be having him for dessert.'

Twelve

Jonny was home by the time we got there, and he was fretting, poor boy.

'Please, Auntie P,' he exclaimed, as soon as we'd climbed the stairs from the garage, 'please don't do that to me again. I've been worried sick. I thought you'd been in a smash or something. Your friend Ben just dropped the dog off. When he said he didn't know where you were, I'd decided to call the police.' He held up a book, my English-Spanish dictionary. 'I wasn't sure of the words for "traffic accident". Then you walked in.'

I was hit by an immediate guilt wave; the biggest day of the lad's life, and I'd put a damper on it. 'Sorry, Jonny,' I pleaded. 'Something came up and I had to deal with it.'

'Mr Cowling's run away from Shirley,' Tom volunteered.

'No he hasn't,' I contradicted him. 'He's . . .' Then I stopped, for he was right.

My nephew's frown melted into a grin. 'Not up to the job, eh?' he chuckled.

'Nothing like that,' I replied. 'I'm sure he had his reasons.' *And I'm going to find out what they are*, I added, mentally.

'Then good luck to him,' Jonny said, dismissively. 'Where do you want to eat?'

I told him. 'Can Roura, in the square. Tom's going to watch Barcelona in Esculapi; we'll be next door.' I checked my watch; it showed seven fifty-five. 'You go across there and book a table on the terrace, and I'll begin the ever more laborious business of getting ready.'

I ran up the stairs to my room, heading for the shower, but with a call to make before I got there. I kept in touch with Mark Kravitz, as you did with an old friend, but we hadn't spoken for a few months. When Patterson had dropped his name into conversation a few days before, he'd been making a point of saying that their orbits had never cut across each other. I'd been a little dubious about that at the time, since there are damn few people in the intelligence community that Mark didn't know about, but it hadn't occurred to me to check it out.

I don't make Skype video calls very often, but I used it with Mark, because I liked to see for myself how he was doing. He'd been an MS sufferer for at least three years, but the disease was still in the primary stage, with lapses and then periods of remission. He put himself forward as a guinea pig for new treatments as they were developed, and they seemed to be giving him extended periods of stability, but if he was in a wheelchair when I called him on camera, I knew he was having a relapse. When he came on screen I was pleased to see that he looked okay, a little greyer, but no worse than he has done for the last couple of years.

'Hey, girl,' he greeted me, with a smile. 'How's your life?'

'Interesting. How's yours?'

'Better than it's been for a while. I'm on a new drug combination and it's working. I'm more mobile than I've been in three years.'

'That's great,' I said.

'For now; they're warning me that in six months or so the disease may have worked out a way round it and I'll be back in my chair. But I'll deal with that when it happens. What about you? Are you calling with the good news that your ex-priest's coming back from Ireland to sweep you off your feet?'

'No, the good news is that he isn't. I'd gone off him anyway, and Tom's made it clear that he isn't desperate for a new dad.'

'But he does accept that the original isn't coming back, yes?'

'Oh yes. He's reconciled to it. But we do have a new man about the house.'

'Ah,' he laughed. 'I thought you were even twinklier than usual.'

That was news to me. 'Not in that way,' I told him, firmly, then explained about Jonny's arrival.

I'd bounced some serious stuff off Mark, in the course of our acquaintance, but I'd never seen him surprised before. 'You're kidding!' he exclaimed. 'I watched him win a golf tournament this afternoon; I'd no idea he was Oz's nephew.'

'Then you must have switched off before the presentation; he gave him a namecheck at the end of it. But he's just one of the things that have happened to me in the last week.'

He winced; at first I thought it was a spasm of pain, but I was wrong. 'Oh dear,' he lamented. 'I knew your life had been too quiet of late. What the hell's up?'

'Lots of stuff; my friend Alex, the Mossos d'Esquadra detective, is in charge of a very nasty double murder investigation, and I've been helping him, sort of. I was able to identify his victims, but that's as far as I expect to be involved. No, it's not my crisis this time; it's my friend Shirley who's been upset. She's been led up the garden path by someone I thought was a gentleman, and I'm not about to let him get away with it.'

'Then God help him,' Mark said, cheerfully. 'Who is he?'

'Does the name Patterson Cowling mean anything to you?'

'Should it? Is he the wrong-doer, the love rat?'

'That's him.'

'Then I'm sorry; can't help. Never heard of him. But what made you think I would have?'

I told him about my call to John Dale, and about his emphatic 'Do not disturb!' warning.

'In which case,' he said, slowly, 'don't you think you should take it to heart?'

'The hell I will! Shirley's hurt. The guy got up and left her, without a word, right in the middle of the golf tournament. He went back to her place, packed his gear, and walked out, leaving her nothing but a pathetic little note. I'm not going to let him get away with that; I'm going to find him and make him apologise properly.'

'Are you sure you're only annoyed for your friend?' A shrewd question, by someone who knew me well.

'Maybe not,' I conceded. 'I liked the man, Mark. I feel like he's made a fool of me as well.'

He frowned, and scratched his chin. I noticed that his hand trembled a little. 'Be that as it may, Primavera. This man seems to be a retired spook, and you've been warned off by his masters. How are you planning to find him? I tell you now, I will be of limited help; security service records ain't covered by Freedom of Information.'

'He has two daughters,' I said. 'One's called Ivy; she's married with a couple of kids and I don't know what her new name is. But the other's an army surgeon, Major Cowling, first name Fleur. She shouldn't be at all hard to find, so I was wondering . . .'

'No, she shouldn't be,' he agreed. 'I have contacts in the Ministry of Defence who can tell me whether she's UK-based or in Afghanistan. But suppose I do find her for you? What are you going to do after that?'

'I'll get in touch with her and tell her I'm looking for her dad, and why. She should know what a shit he's been.'

Mark smiled into his webcam. 'If this was anyone but you, I wouldn't touch it with a very long bargepole, but what the hell? From the sound of things Mr Cowling deserves what's coming to him. Give me a day or so.'

We said our farewells, and I headed for my long-overdue appointment with the shower, and with my slinkiest black dress, some very expensive cosmetics, and the kind of jewellery I keep in the safe. Half an hour later, I judged myself not half bad, and went downstairs to meet my date. His eyebrows rose, and I realised with not a little satisfaction that he shared my opinion. I have to say that Jonny looked pretty sharp too, in Lacoste jeans, a muscle-tight white vest and a soft black leather jerkin. He was freshly shaved, and he looked as if somehow he'd managed to fit in a visit to the haircut shop at some point during the week. He looked different, fulfilled, as if his afternoon triumph was sitting easily on him and had moved him on to a new level of maturity. He might have been only twenty-two years old, but he was a dish. Yup, I reckoned, if the chattering classes were out and about . . . and in St Martí, it only takes one . . . the rumour mill would have some new material to grind. About time too, I thought wickedly; a couple of years had gone by since the main topic of British conversation was Primavera Blackstone shagging the priest . . . not that she ever did, I declare emphatically.

'Where's Tom?' I asked.

'One of his pals came to fetch him,' Jonny told me. 'The teams were lining up, he said.'

'Damn, I meant to give him some money. Never mind, we'll look in there on the way.'

'No need, Auntie P. Board boys get paid; he's flush.'

'Who pays them?'

'The tournament director.'

'Nice to know they're not being exploited . . . even though Tom would probably have paid himself to do the job. Now, one other thing. How about you stop calling me Auntie P . . . just for tonight if that's what you want? I do not get dolled up in my Dolce and Gabbana number and my Jimmy Choo shoes to be made to feel middle-aged.'

He smiled, his perfect teeth befitting the grandson of a dentist. 'If it makes you happy, Primavera. God, that sounds funny.' He stopped, raising an eyebrow. 'But no way do you look middle-aged.'

I took his arm as we walked through the square, taking our time over the fifty metres from my front door to the restaurant, if only because the pathway isn't paved there, and I had to be cautious in the designer shoes. Even in that short way, I discovered that my nephew was famous; word of his profession had spread through the village since he'd moved in with me, and news of his victory had travelled even faster. St Martí has never boasted a resident celebrity; that night, as people called out congratulations to him, mostly in English but one or two in Castellano, it seemed to have found one.

The interior terrace was empty when we arrived; nine o'clock is seen there as an early booking, but there was a reserved sign on a table for four. I chose the one furthest away from it. 'Champagne?' Jonny asked.

'On this special occasion,' I told him, 'I reckon you're entitled.' I wasn't certain that any would be available in cava country, but it was, Lanson Black Label, which was fair enough by me. 'I'm surprised you don't fizz it around the place like a racing driver,' I said, as the waiter opened it.

'I'm my mother's son,' he laughed. 'Every time she sees that done on telly she goes on about the waste.'

'Are you going home to see her?' I asked. 'I know she's gutted that she couldn't be here.'

'She couldn't be here for that very reason,' he pointed out, with a smile. 'They say that hysterectomy isn't as severe surgically as it used to be, but it's still pretty radical. I saw her after she had the op, before Brush got me a sponsor's invitation to Girona. Depending on how my schedule works out now, I might wait till she's fit to travel and then take her for a convalescent trip somewhere. Maybe she could come with me to a tournament.'

'That would be nice,' I agreed. 'How many tournaments will you get into for the rest of the year?'

'All of them; automatically, as a tour winner. I need to decide which ones I'm actually going to play. Brush and I need to talk that through, and we will tomorrow.'

I looked him in the eye, over my glass. 'You know, I still think the set-up's weird, having a manager you've never met, but I'll say this for the guy: he's done a brilliant job for you simply by getting you this chance to prove yourself. At the same time, though,' I added, 'you've done the job for him, by taking it. What you've achieved this weekend, it's just beginning to sink in. To win your first event; it's fantastic.'

I reached out and squeezed his hand. He held on to mine for a while, gently. I felt a tingle, in my fingertips. 'It is, isn't it,' he whispered. 'Fuck! When I think of that last shot I played . . . I'll bet you thought I was crazy, Primavera. But did you know that I was actually trying to hole it?'

'My darling boy,' I replied, 'I was too busy trying not to pee my pants to be aware of much of the detail of the moment. But now you mention it, no, you didn't seem to show any doubt at all.'

'I didn't feel any, honestly. Like I said to Uche, I could see it in my mind; play the parachute shot, land it softer than Cormac did his, from higher, and let it take the slope as slow as possible. The only thing I didn't plan for was getting a nick off his marker.'

He raised his glass and grinned. 'Thank you, Mr Toibin,' he chuckled. 'I'm sure you'll do it to me many a time in the future.' He winked at me. 'Truth is, he's a better player than me, by a street; I do what I can do, nothing more, every shot is the one with the best percentage chance of success. I'm good, but I know my limitations, and this week I was mentally strong enough to play within them. Cormac's a genius; I don't think he has any limits. He'll be the number one player in the world for years; I never will.'

'Jonny,' I protested, 'don't sell yourself short. You've just beaten him.'

'By playing what will probably turn out, when my career's over, to have been the shot of my life.'

'Come on, you're twenty-two,' I reminded him. 'Stop sounding as if this is the pinnacle. Be excited, dream some dreams, be a kid for a bit longer.'

He shook his head. 'No, I'll be a realist; it doesn't hurt as much. You should know that.'

His remark took me by surprise. 'What do you mean?' I asked him.

'Nothing,' he said, too quickly.

'No, not nothing; go on,' I insisted.

'No, this is supposed to be a celebration. I don't want to upset you.'

'There is no chance of that. Now please, tell me what I should know.'

He sighed, deeply. 'Okay, if you insist. My Uncle Oz was the greatest man in the world. When I was young, mid-teens, I got myself into a bad situation, way over my head. It could have ruined my life, finished it even, but he made it all go away, and then he looked after me until I understood fully that although what I'd done was bad, it wasn't evil, and that I should spend the rest of my life atoning for it by making the most of the second chance I'd been given.'

I couldn't say a word, I couldn't show any expression, for I knew what Jonny had done; close to the end, when the badness between us was over and Oz and I became lovers again, we were closer than ever before, and we kept no secrets from each other.

'It was him that made me a pro golfer. Mum wanted me to be a lawyer like Harvey; I might have too, and with him behind me my career would have been assured. But Uncle Oz knew what I really wanted. He made me admit it, and when I did I was embarrassed. He saw that and asked why. I told him that I didn't imagine I was anywhere near good enough. He just laughed, and said, "Son, I'm not the best actor in the fucking world either, but I know what I can do and I know what I can't, and that's how I play every part. You're at least as good a golfer as I am an actor, so what's to hold you back?" Then he went to see Mum and he talked her into believing in me. When she was onside he fixed the place at Arizona for me. And he had no sooner done that than he upped and fucking died.' He had to pause for a few seconds; I was glad of it. 'I had this dream, Primavera, that he'd be greenside at my first event, at my first win, the first time I made the cut in a major and so on. But he isn't, and he never will be. So I don't dream any more; I try to control my feelings for others. I wall myself up within my comfort zone, my safety zone, and I keep myself mentally strong enough to do what I can within it, and never ever to expose myself to hurt or disappointment again.' He looked into my eyes, and suddenly I had the wildest feeling that through him, someone else, a ghost, was speaking to me. 'And that's what you've done too, Primavera; you've built a fortress here for you and Tom. You'll probably keep him in it for as long as you can, and you'll never leave it yourself. Sure, you took that job in the consulate . . . Grandpa Blackstone was dead chuffed when you did, by the way . . . but how long did that last? A couple of years and you withdrew again. But I'm not blaming you, understand; I'm saying you're right. Don't expose yourself to the unexpected and it's less likely to find you and bite you on the arse.' He refilled my glass: I hadn't realised that it was empty. 'If I'm wrong and that's not true, I apologise, but if it is, then good luck to you.'

I smiled at him, at least I think I did. 'I've never thought of it that way,' I whispered. 'But I can't argue with your analysis. I can feel sorry for you, though, since Oz's death has affected you that badly.'

'I don't think it has. I reckon it's made me stronger.'

'And sad, and lonely.'

'Like you . . . or at least like the part of you that isn't a parent.'

'A consolation which you do not have,' I observed, 'and won't, if you continue to isolate yourself. Yes, I'll always mourn, but you, you shouldn't and I won't let you. Come here,' I murmured, drawing him towards me and meeting him halfway. I kissed him, full on, for quite some time, flicking his teeth apart with my tongue and probing further.

Then, while I still could, I broke off, smoothed his hair and stroked his cheek, and said to him, 'That is how you should be celebrating tonight, with a hot and loving girlfriend, not by sharing a sombre conversation with a woman twice your age. If I thought it would have any long-term benefit for either of us, I'd happily take you home right now and fuck your brains out, but even though I'm sure it would be a fine, energetic shag, and for you probably educational, I'd feel monstrously guilty afterwards and so would most of you. The part that didn't, the part that isn't connected to your brain, would want to do it again, and since that couldn't be, pretty soon you'd move out. I wouldn't want that to happen because Tom and I really do like having you around, so I won't put it at risk, especially . . . and this is why you and I are not the same . . . since there has only ever been one person I've wanted to sleep with, and it ain't you, Jonny boy.'

He looked at the tabletop for a few seconds; when his eyes came up to meet mine once more, they were twinkling. 'Know any women, then?' he laughed.

'Only their mothers and even their grandmothers, I fear. Uche's a better source than me, I'm sure.'

'Jesus,' he snorted. 'Auntie Primavera . . . I'm going back to calling you that 'cos it's safer . . . I would not go near a girl he recommended. Quality control is not Uche's strong point; he can line up my putts, but nothing else.'

'What about Kalu? Maybe he could help. He seems like a smoooooth individual.'

'I wouldn't know. I'd never met the man before today, and Uche hardly ever talks about him.'

'What happened to his wife, Uche's mother?'

'Again, I don't know. The only time I ever asked him about her, he said, "She's not around any more." I didn't press further.'

'Poor boy,' I said. 'Here, now that you're a full tour member and don't need those sponsor invitations, maybe Brush could pass them on to him.'

'That's not quite how it works. I had a track record as an amateur, Uche doesn't. The fact is, Auntie P, he's got no chance of making the Tour. He's a decent golfer, but that's all. He didn't get to Arizona on a scholarship; he paid his own way, or his father did. He said he was a track athlete, a sprinter, when we were freshmen, but he had a knee injury that stopped him competing, so he'd switched to golf. But he didn't get near the college team. I'm helping him as much as I can, and Lena's given him all the swing advice she has, but it isn't working. He'll never make it, and he knows it. He hasn't even entered the first stage of Q school.'

'So he's just a spoiled rich kid, eh. Did he graduate?'

'He did enough, that was all. He missed enough classes to get any other guy cut, but he always seemed to get away with it, and he squeezed through in the end. Mostly he studied the football cheerleaders, or any skanky tart that looked in his direction; that's his specialist subject, not business administration.'

'So what's he going to do with his life? Caddie for you permanently?'

'Brush isn't too keen on that idea. Neither is Clive Tate; he collared me this afternoon and told me that I need to replace him with someone who actually knows the courses I'll be playing on from now on. I won't rush into anything, though. In fact I'm hoping that his dad and he are having a heart-to-heart about career options over dinner tonight. Kalu has all sorts of businesses: oil, manufacturing, import-export. He's bound to want Uche to get involved at some point.'

The arrival of the waiter to take our orders slipped a natural break into our conversation. When he'd gone, I changed the subject. 'Going back to what you said before, there's one thing I must put you right about. It's impossible to hide from the unexpected. Even here my arse has been well bitten, I can tell you. Huh,' I snorted. 'Never more so than today, as you were having your finest hour.'

'How?' He paused. 'Ah, Shirley's man doing a runner.'

'That's the least of it. Remember last Wednesday, when I was called away from Pals by my policeman friend Alex?'

'Yeah.' He nodded. 'He came and showed Tom a drawing later; it was the man who tried to pick Patterson's pocket. Nasty. Have they identified him? Is that's what's bitten you?'

'No, but fast forward to the scene you walked in on the next day: me dealing with Christine McGuigan, that sneaky woman I caught trying to take pictures of Tom. She was found dead this morning. Alex asked me to look at her as well.'

'Bloody hell! Why did he do that?'

'Because she was killed in much the same way as him, her face blown away with a shotgun.'

He stared at me. 'My God,' he exclaimed. 'What do the police think?'

'The assumption is that they were killed by the same person, but that's as far as it goes.'

'What? Even with ... Auntie P, there's an obvious connection.'

'Sure, me! Happily I was able to alibi myself for the times of both killings.'

'That's not what I meant,' he countered. 'Think back, did you actually catch the woman taking pictures of Tom?'

I did as he asked. 'No,' I admitted. 'Not exactly. But she didn't deny it, and anyway, what else could she have been doing? What are you getting at, Jonny?'

'Who else had just arrived at your house?' he asked. 'You went out there to give Tom and me the hurry-up because we were late.'

'Patterson and Shirley.'

'Correct. The first victim, the guy, he tried to steal Patterson's wallet but he failed. What if this McGuigan woman wasn't interested in Tom at all? Isn't it just as likely that Patterson was her target?'

'Then why did she target me with her video camera at the course?'

He frowned. 'Good question.' As he thought about it our starters arrived. I was adding croutons to my vichyssoise when he came up with an answer. 'You'd been speaking to them earlier, hadn't you?'

'Yes.' I had a vivid recollection. 'And I said to them they should be at my place at seven thirty.'

'Then that ties it. She had no reason to approach them in her journalist guise, had she?'

'But she did,' I exclaimed as I remembered what Shirley had said. 'Only Patterson didn't want to be on camera, so he avoided her. Then Shirl got rid of her by turning her loose on me.'

Jonny nodded, his thinking confirmed. 'And that gave her an excuse to find out who you were, and in the process to lead you up the garden path by winding you up about Tom. To get to Patterson through you. Doesn't that fit?'

I was on his wavelength. 'She was probably trying to find out where I lived, when Alex intervened and told her to bugger off.'

'Right, so she went to Plan B and followed you home, so she could be waiting there when Patterson and Shirley arrived.'

'She was photographing someone, that's for sure. If only . . .' And then I surprised him by laughing. 'But I do! I do know who it was. After I decked her I took the memory card from her camera. I've still got it. When I got home, I stuck it in my purse, then forgot all about it.' My bag was at my feet, and my purse was in it. I dug it out and found the tiny card. 'There you are,' I said, soundly pleased with myself.

Jonny held out a hand. 'Let me see it.' I gave it to him. He took a small camera from a pocket in his jerkin, removed an identical device from its slot, and replaced it with mine. He pressed a couple of buttons, then grinned. 'Look,' he said. He turned the camera so that I could see its tiny LCD screen and ran through its contents.

The first seven photographs were all of Patterson, but he was hidden by Shirl in four of them. Those in which he was recognisable had him in profile, none of them full face. Those had all been taken as he and Shirley approached my house, but as Jonny scrolled back I saw that she'd taken a couple at the golf course as well. They'd been shot from a distance, probably with a different lens, and he was in them all as well, in the stand at the practice ground. Patterson's mother wouldn't have known him in those . . . but given the life he'd led maybe she wouldn't have recognised him anywhere any more.

'There's your link, Auntie P,' Jonny declared. 'The pickpocket was sent to steal Patterson's wallet. He failed, and he's dead. Christine McGuigan was sent to photograph him. She failed and now she's dead too. "Sorry, I tried my best" doesn't cut any ice with whoever sent them. What I don't understand is why they wanted to identify him. What's that all about?'

'A blast from the past,' I murmured.

'Eh?'

'Mr Cowling wasn't your run-of-the-mill public servant,' I told him. 'As I understand it he was the sort who might have made a few enemies in his career. He's been rumbled by someone, that's for sure. That's why he got off his mark; no cover story for Shirl, no tearful farewell. He just waited until she turned her back on him, literally, and he ran for it.'

'Bloody hell!'

'Indeed. I had him down as a man who'd lost his bottle. I was planning to find him and give him a piece of my mind for messing up my pal's life. But this connection that you've made, that changes everything.' It occurred to me at that point that I should call Mark, to tell him not to bother tracing Major Fleur, but I decided that could wait till morning. He wouldn't do anything until then anyway, and my vichyssoise was getting warm.

Thirteen

Alex called me early next morning, just as Tom was leaving for school and Jonny was heading down to the beach with a mat, a towel and a book, a story called *The Loner* that I'd just read and thought he might enjoy. He couldn't begin his schedule-planning with Brush until America woke up, but the European Tour press officer had warned him that he might have quite a busy day dealing with media, and so he decided that he'd better grab some relaxation time while he could. We'd spent the rest of our dinner date walking through old memories, some of them mutual, others confessions of a sort. The most surprising to me was Jonny's revelation that he'd got a girl pregnant in his second year at college, a psychology major who hadn't been as clever as she'd thought. She'd insisted on a termination, and he hadn't argued. He'd felt guilty ever since; another reason for his self-imposed emotional isolation.

'Don't,' I told him. 'Her choice, not yours. That's a moral maze and you were too young to get lost in it.'

'When you found you were pregnant with Tom,' he ventured,

'after you and Uncle Oz had split up, did you ever consider having an abortion?'

'Not for one micro-second,' I replied. 'Oh, I made a very bad choice in keeping him secret, but I was always going to have him. You see, the difference between your girl and me . . . I loved his dad.' I looked him in the eye. 'That's why you're screwed up about women, Jonny, isn't it? It's got fuck all to do with concentrating on your career.'

'True. There are whispers already that I'm gay. Even on the amateur circuit, if you don't have a girl in tow you're looked on as odd. Among the pros . . . look no further than at the Ryder Cup. A guy gets divorced and there's paper talk that the other players' wives will freeze him out. They shouldn't even be there! It's a golf match, for fuck's sake!'

His outrage made me laugh. 'If you make the team next year,' I suggested, 'and you don't have a girlfriend, you may find that your mother doesn't share that view.'

I was still smiling as I picked up the phone next morning. 'Can I come up for coffee?' my friend asked.

'And croissants, if you play your cards right. I've fed my guys, but I haven't had my own yet. But shouldn't you be heading in the other direction, for your office?'

'You're forgetting,' he chuckled, 'I'm acting boss. I decide where I go. Anyway, this is business of a sort.'

'You're not wrong,' I agreed. 'I have something to tell you as well.'

By the time he arrived, just over half an hour later, I was showered and dressed, out of the house dress that I normally throw on when I get out of bed, and into denim cut-offs and a baggy T-shirt with a Gaudi motif, that I'd bought in Barcelona. By that time also, I'd phoned Shirley.

Her voice sounded bleary, and I guessed her eyes matched. 'Sleepless night?' I asked her.

'Pretty much.'

'I take it he hasn't been in touch.'

'No, not a cheep; not a phone call, not a text, nothing. He's a son of a bitch; that's the long and short of it.'

'Maybe not,' I said. 'Maybe there was a good reason for him going, one that he couldn't tell you about.'

'Huh,' she snorted. 'That doesn't wash with me. My idea of a partnership is that you don't keep secrets from each other.'

She was quoting me back at myself. I'd said the same to her, word for word, not long after I'd moved back to St Martí and we'd renewed our friendship. 'Yes,' I conceded, 'but remember this. We know that the man worked in a culture of secrecy. It's his way; the sort of lifetime habit that can be hard to break.'

'Are you trying to tell me you know something?'

'No,' I replied, truthfully. 'I'm not trying to tell you anything. I'm asking how you are, that's all.' I heard the gate creak. 'Look, I'll come up and see you later. Bye for now.'

Alex reached the door just as I opened it. I let him in and told him he should go to the first-floor terrace, unless he didn't want to be seen with me that early in the morning.

'People will talk, you mean?' he laughed. 'Let them, I'll be in good company. People talk about you all the time, Primavera. For example, did you enjoy dinner last night? Are you sure the boy's your nephew?'

'How the hell did you know that?' I demanded. 'Have you got a spy in the village?'

'Only you, my dear, I assure you. No, I called the office before I came here, and the sullen Magda was very quick to tell me about you. She and her boyfriend had dinner at Can Coll last night. She saw you walk past and go into Can Roura with, as she described him, your young lover. She added that a little later, when they were leaving, she looked in, through the open door and saw you kissing him.'

I felt myself flush up. 'Yes, platonically. Alex . . .'

'Hey,' he said, in his soothing voice, 'I believe you. But even if your tongue was down his throat like she said, it's your business, not mine. Most certainly it's not Magda's. She is not going to enjoy the job I'm going to give her when I get to Girona. I'm only telling you because I don't want you to hear the story first from anyone else. For all I know, she's phoned a newspaper by now. For her sake, I hope not; I'll end the career of anyone I catch spreading gossip from my office. Now,' he said, briskly, 'come on, girl, what about these croissants?'

I served them up on a tray, on the terrace, five minutes later. He'd finished the first of his before he said anything more. When he did, he began, 'Jorge's done some good work for me. He's established that Christine McGuigan was what she said she was, a freelance journalist and photographer who used the name Christy Mann because it looked better on by-lines.'

'It'll look good on her tombstone too,' I said, a little cruelly, I concede.

'She was, as we knew already, twenty-seven years old,' he continued, 'born in Cork, Ireland, where her widowed father still lives. The Irish embassy in Madrid came up with her life story pretty quickly. She trained as a photographer on an evening paper in Dublin, then had a spell as a sports reporter with a satellite television station that's no longer in existence.' He paused. 'She moved to Spain just over a year ago; that's when she decided to become Christy Mann apparently. Since then she's operated mostly on the Costa del Sol, but in other areas whenever she was given a specific commission. Most of her video work was for websites, but she did contribute photography to newspapers in Britain, Ireland and in Spain; all of it was as Christy. As Christine, she was a member of the National Union of Journalists of the UK and Ireland, but that lapsed. She never resigned formally; just stopped paying her subscription.'

'What brought her to the golf tournament?' I asked. 'Did you find any lead in her room to who it was who hired her? She told me she was from an internet station that she called Spotlight Television, but given what became of her I don't believe that any more.'

He picked up his second croissant. 'Primavera, we didn't find anything. She was in the Novotel, right enough; she checked in on Thursday afternoon; as Christine McGuigan, incident- ally, even though there's no evidence of her having used that name in Spain before. She had a lime-green suitcase, the clerk recalled. There was no sign of it, or anything else, in her room; it had been stripped bare. There was nothing left, not so much as a toothbrush.'

'Bugger,' I murmured. 'Her killer really didn't want her identified, did he?'

'Clearly not,' Alex agreed, 'as he's shown by removing every clue to her identity, including her face, as he did with his first victim. I'm sure he didn't expect her to be traced to the Novotel, but he covered that base just in case. But this time, we've been lucky, thanks to your run-in with her. And to me asking for her passport,' he added. 'Jorge's established that she's used the name Christy Mann since arriving in Spain. It's on her tax identification document, on her bank accounts, in the telephone directory, everywhere we've looked.'

'Then why did she have her Christine passport on her when you asked her for it?'

'Because it's the only photo ID she had, and the airline she flew in on insist on that. She had to book her flight under her real name. Incidentally, she did that only on Wednesday, proving that she got a short-notice summons from whoever hired her.' He grinned. 'All that subterfuge overcome by a couple of pieces of blind luck. Without them, I doubt that we'd ever have identified the body. But we have, and that gives us an advantage. The murderer thinks he's free and clear, but he's not. Hopefully, just knowing who she is will lead us to him.'

His voice was more confident than his eyes. 'But you're no nearer to knowing what links her to the man in the woods, are you?' I observed. 'Or to understanding what got them killed.'

He shook his head, ruefully.

'Then let me make your day,' I said. From under the breakfast tray I took the large envelope I'd left there, and handed it to him.

He opened it and withdrew a series of photographs, prints that I'd made, using my own camera as an interface with my computer, of the images on Christine McGuigan's memory card.

He stared at them, one by one. 'What the hell are these?' he hissed.

I told him, and explained how I'd come by them. 'She had no interest in selling photographs of Tom,' I said. 'The connection between your two bodies is what, or rather who, you suspected it was after the first murder. It's Patterson Cowling, and it seems bloody clear from his reaction that he knows it too. Yes, Alex, his disappearance is your business after all.'

He looked at the images, in silence, over and over again. He finished his second croissant, and his coffee. I poured him a refill.

Finally, he turned to me. 'Primavera, you are a remarkable woman, and I'm proud that you're my friend. But in the real world, little lady detectives don't exist. As the last few days have shown you, close up, the real world is a very dangerous place. I thank you for giving this to me. Now I tell you in all seriousness: whatever it is you think you might do from now on, forget it. Every aspect of this, including Mr Cowling's disappearance, is now a police investigation.'

'But I could help more,' I protested. 'As for danger, I've known more in my life than you have, mate.'

He nodded. 'I'm sure you have, in the days when you didn't have a son.'

He had a point there, but I wasn't giving in that easily. 'Man, I'm not suggesting that I go chasing people with guns. But—'

'No.'

'You're not even going to ask why he might be—'

'Yes, but I'm not going to ask you. Primavera, I'm adamant. Up till now in this, I've humoured you, and yes, you've been very useful. But no more. Come on, don't you have other work to do? Aren't you going to get involved in your brother-in-law's wine business?'

He had a second point. I had indeed promised Miles that I'd go there that very week for a tour of inspection by the manager.

I added a third. *So what?* From any viewpoint, Shirley had had a narrow escape. Whether he was only running from her voracity, or whether from real or perceived danger, he was not the kind, manly, uncomplicated, loving companion she thought she'd found and as far as I was concerned she was well shot of him. If he was out in the jungle with man-eating tigers on his tail, that was his problem . . . as long as my friend wasn't on the menu herself.

'You'll look after Shirley?' I asked. No, the way it came out it was a demand, not a question.

'I will,' he promised, getting my point, that someone might imagine she knew where Patterson was headed. 'I'll have her house watched, round the clock.'

'You'll only need to cover the back entrance,' I said, 'in Plaça Puig Sec. I've seen prisons with walls and gates that are smaller than she has at the front.'

'I know,' he agreed. 'But just to be sure I can put movement sensors in her garden.'

'I think you'll find that she has them. Anything bigger than a cat going through there sets off her alarm. You don't need to tell her about this, do you? At the moment she doesn't realise that Patterson's in danger.'

'I must. If there's any sort of a threat to her, however slight, I have a duty to make her aware of it.'

'In that case I could—'

He smiled. 'No, Primavera. Credit me with a little diplomacy. She does know about the work he did, I take it?'

'Yes.'

'That makes it easier.'

'And raises another question. Do you report this to your own . . .' I paused, knowing nothing about Spanish security services. 'Who exactly could you report it to?'

He frowned. 'I might be an acting intendant, Primavera, but I'm still only a regional cop. I'll tell the directorate in Barcelona about this new development and what I'm doing about it. They can take it from there. I imagine they'll talk to the British. Indeed, it may be that Mr Cowling has done that himself, by now, and that they've pulled him out. It's the best part of a day since he dropped out of sight; he could be in London by now.'

'If he caught a flight, you'll trace it, yes?'

'Yes, but if he caught a train, from Perpignan for example, across the border in France, then we couldn't.'

'Unless he bought his ticket with a credit card.'

'True, but . . .' He broke off, laughing. 'Woman, would you stop doing my thinking for me! However hard you try to make yourself invaluable, you are not involved in this. Go on, be a mother, be a champion golfer's secretary, sell wine. Be whatever you want, but please don't try to be an investigator.'

My croissant . . . they are in essence lumps of baked carbohydrate waiting to be turned into body fat, so I eat only one at a time . . . still lay untouched on the plate. I snatched it up, withdrawing from further argument.

'That's a good girl,' Alex chuckled, really chancing his arm. If I'd had access to his soft bits, they'd have been at risk.

But I did no more than grunt, and gaze ahead, from the terrace across the square, where the cafes, other than Meson del Conde, which was closed, were readying themselves for what would be inevitably a quiet Monday, since May still had a couple of days to run. As I did, a newcomer to the village appeared, with a bag slung over his shoulder, and distinctive, by his bewilderment and by the colour of his skin.

I stood, and waved. 'Uche!' I called out, unnecessarily, for he had seen me. 'Jonny's caddie,' I explained. 'He's moving into one of the apartments above Can Roura. Come on up,' I instructed him.

The two men passed in the doorway, with brief introductions and a quick handshake. Most people are slightly disconcerted when they meet a uniformed cop, but Uche simply gave a brief courtly bow, managing to suggest that the honour was all Alex's. I led him into the kitchen, stuck another couple of croissants under the grill, and offered him coffee. He opted for water, but scoffed the rolls as if he hadn't eaten in days.

'Is your father still here?' I asked him.

'Yes, until tomorrow. He's given his crew a forty-eight-hour stopover in Barcelona.'

'Ah, so his offer of a flight was bullshit.'

'Possibly not; he's a qualified pilot himself, and I'm sure he could have found someone locally who was qualified to sit in the other seat.' He frowned. 'However, you were right to turn him down; when he invites a lady to fly with him, he usually has more than travel in mind.'

I shrugged. 'That's not a crime. He's a single man, isn't he?'

'Oh yes.' I saw the same glint of anger as I'd noticed the day before. 'Single, and singular.'

'How was dinner?'

The smile returned. 'Educational, as always.'

'On whose part?'

'Mutually, I would say. He told me that he had humoured me for long enough and that it was time for me to prepare myself for my future in the family businesses, and for the responsibilities that I'll inherit one day in Nigeria, when I succeed him as emir. I told him that he looked pretty healthy to me. I added that I couldn't possibly leave Jonny in the lurch, especially now that his career is secure for the next two and a half years, at least, and that he could go and . . . the rest I leave to your imagination.'

It didn't take me long to work it out. 'That sounds like a full and frank discussion. How did he react?'

'My father and I have been having such conversations for the last year and more, since I turned twenty-five.'

'You're twenty-five?' I exclaimed. 'I thought you were Jonny's age.'

'No, I entered college as a mature student. I did work with my father for a couple of years after I left Charterhouse. I persuaded him to let me study in the US, but now my course is over, he wants

240

me back. Each time we argue about it he gives me a little more rope, as he puts it, but it's getting short. We've agreed, more or less, that I'll stay with Jonny for the rest of the Tour season, then we'll re-examine the situation.'

'Are you going to tell Jonny that?'

His eyes widened; they were green, like his dad's, I noticed for the first time, but less vivid. 'Of course; it wouldn't be honourable to do otherwise. Where is he, by the way? Still sleeping it off?'

'Swimming it off, more like; not that we drank a lot last night. He's on the beach. You'll find him easily enough; there won't be many people there today.'

'Good. However, first I should move into my new home, yes? Can you show me where it is?'

'Of course.'

I led him back across the square and introduced him to his landlord, then went down to the car park, to help him with the rest of his luggage. It included Jonny's golf clubs, and a holdall that Uche said was his also. I offered to take it all to my place.

'The grip, yes,' he agreed. 'It's mostly clothing from the sponsor. But the clubs, they're the caddie's responsibility, always. I'll fit them into the penthouse, don't worry.'

I took the bag from him and went home, to get on with my day. I tried to clear my mind of all the craziness that had filled it over the previous twenty-four hours and to switch it back to working woman mode. I made the call to the manager of Miles's winery. He'd been advised of my appointment as a director of the company, and of my future involvement, so it didn't come as a surprise to him. I hadn't been sure how he'd react, but he was fine. We had a brief chat, during which he told me that he was looking forward to having someone on the ground that he could run things past, rather than having to make all his reports and proposals in conference calls to California. We agreed that I'd visit the bodega the following morning, and then I turned my attention to more mundane things, like the mountain of laundry that had built up during the week of the tournament. Jonny, God bless him, had said he'd do his own, but there was no point in separating everything out, so I ran it all together.

Besides, I recalled one of my father's few profundities, that he'd shared with me on my eighteenth birthday. 'They say, Primavera,' he'd pronounced, 'that the way to a man's heart is through his stomach. That is, of course, nonsense. A man's heart is reached most assuredly through his underpants . . . by that I mean by washing, and above all ironing them for him, together with all his other garments. Ironing is the domestic task that man abhors the most, and if you relieve him of it he will be your servant in everything else.'

My old man is right about most things, but that one hadn't worked with Oz. Tom was too young to be trusted with an iron, so I resolved to see how my nephew would react. I was putting the second load into the condenser dryer, down in the cavernous garage, when I heard the phone ring up in the kitchen, a couple of floors above. I ran upstairs and snatched it from the cradle, out of breath as I answered.

It was Shirley, or as she called herself, graphically, 'The Prisoner of fucking Zenda'.

'Alex Guinart's just left,' she said. 'I guess you know what he came to tell me.'

'Yes. Hence the jailbird crack, I imagine.'

'He says I have to be accompanied everywhere I go, Primavera,' she complained. 'He's been all through the house, inspecting the windows, checking the alarm system, and more than that, he's had me look for anything that Patterson might have left behind.'

'Did you find anything?'

'Not a bloody thing. He's even taken his clothes out of the laundry basket.'

'Did you do his ironing for him?' I asked.

'Hell no!' she barked. 'Mine is mine and his is his; that's what I told him from the off.'

'My dad would tell you that's why he's left.'

'Eh?'

'Never mind.'

'Right enough,' she reflected, and I imagined her smile, 'your dad is an odd bloke. But whatever the reason is, he's gone and that's an end of it. I'm over it. I'm not living like this, though, taking coppers with me to buy a baguette in the morning. Come and eat with me tonight, love, eh?'

'Shirl, I would, but I've got the boys.'

'Bring them. They can swim.'

I weighed that up. 'No, sod it. I'll feed them, then Jonny will Tom-sit for me, I'm sure. I'll come up on my own.'

I hung up and returned to my role as domestic deity. I had just dumped a load of ironed clothes in Jonny's room when he returned from the beach, using the back stairs as I'd told him so that he could get rid of the sand in the shower that I'd had installed for that purpose, one level above the garage, but below the house itself.

'Where's Uche?' I asked him.

'I left him on the beach,' he replied. 'There are a couple of Swedish girls down there, and he thinks he's pulled.'

I frowned. 'Does he need them both? Does sharing with friends mean nothing to the man?'

He laughed. 'Uche does many things for me, Auntie P, but he doesn't procure women.'

'Are you going back down there?'

'No. There's stuff I need to do. First and foremost, I have to get myself a practice base. Having won there, I'll have the courtesy of Girona for the next year at least, but I had a call this morning from the club where you and I played last week, offering me a slot as its official touring pro. I'll need to talk to Brush about that, but it's still only six thirty where he is. Before I speak to him, I have to get ready to go on telly. I had an email on my iPhone from the Tour press officer. The BBC want to interview me for the Scottish news tonight, and for the breakfast programme tomorrow; plus, the Tour wants something for its own website. They're going to roll the three into one. There'll be a crew and a reporter here in an hour . . .' something must have shown itself in my eyes, for he paused, then added quickly, '. . . not here, at the house, just in the square.'

'It's okay,' I told him. 'You can use this place if you want; just don't identify it, or us, that's all.'

'Nah, we'll do it in front of the church. Location doesn't matter to me; the important thing is that I'm in uniform, in the right clothing, wearing the right sunglasses, with every sponsor's logo on display for the camera.'

'What if they only shoot close-ups?'

'They won't. The press officer says that even the BBC understands commercial reality.'

I smiled. 'Go on then. Turn yourself into a walking advertising hoarding. I'll knock us up a salad while you're doing that.'

Lunch, on the terrace, was interrupted by two phone calls from newspaper reporters. Jonny dealt quickly, but willingly, with each of them; there had been three others in the course of the morning, he told me.

'I thought you guys just used Twitter and Facebook these days, and let the newspapers pick that up.'

'Not me. I have a Facebook page, yes, but I'd like to hang on to something of a private life, so Twattering is out.'

I kept out of sight while he became a TV star. I stayed on my private terrace, reading the autobiography of a former prime minister of Great Britain; as I'd hoped, it helped me to doze off, and when I awoke, the whole circus was over and the clowns had gone.

Jonny was on the phone as I tottered back into the living room. 'Yes,' I heard him say, 'I'll do that,' as he ended the call.

'Do what?' I asked.

'Accept the offer from Pals,' he replied. 'Brush said he could probably have got me a touring pro engagement from Girona, or from half a dozen bigger clubs in the UK, but that it's more important to go where it feels right. So I'll call them, and from tomorrow I'll practise there every day. Brush says he can fix me up with some pro days there, when I can fit them in.'

'What are they?'

'Simply put, wealthy amateurs who fly in to play a round with me then fly away again. It's similar to what we do under the sponsor deals. He's renegotiating them, incidentally.'

'Good for him.' I smiled. I was taking to the mystery man, by the minute. 'Where do you play next?' I asked.

'Portugal, next week. I could go to Wales tomorrow, but we would barely have time for a practice round before the tournament. Brush says there's no better way to get demoralised than to win one week and miss the cut the next.'

'Speaking from experience, is he?'

'Hardly,' he chuckled. 'Clive says that Brush never won a tournament, or even came close.' Just as he'd told me. 'But he's right, for all that. To be honest, Auntie P, mentally, I'm wasted. I'll pull out of Portugal too, if my head isn't right by next Sunday.'

I reached up and ruffled his hair. 'Then you make sure it is. You can start by beating your cousin at a couple of video games tonight. He always wipes me out; I reckon that defeat will be good for his soul. If you don't mind staying in with him, that is: otherwise he's bound for a girlie night at Shirley's.'

'Hah! Where his soul would be seriously at risk. Sure, that's fine by me. Uche can join us; Sweden didn't quite work out as he'd hoped.'

'Fine. I'll make dinner for three in that case.'

'No, you won't,' he shot back. 'I need to cook, or I'll forget how.'

I took him at his word. I showed him where the pots and pans were and what was in the larder and in the fridge. I'm American in my attitude to those. I saw a TV series last year in which the anti-hero kept a body in his SMEG for the best part of two episodes, without having to cram it in at all; that's the size I like.

I went back to my book. I'd finished it by the time Tom got home from school, so I was well rested by the time I got to Shirley's place. She wasn't. For all that she'd said that she was over Patterson already, the process of mentally washing that man right out of her hair had taken a lot out of her. She was clad in the sort of garment that used to be called a catsuit, but wouldn't have suited any feline I ever saw, and wearing the sort of slippers that your granny used to give you for Christmas, with imitation fur trimming and inch-thick rubber soles. She hadn't bothered to attend to the black circles under her eyes; indeed she was wearing hardly any make-up.

Shirley has an open kitchen and when you're invited there for dinner, you can usually scent what's on the menu as soon as you walk through the front door. That night there wasn't even the faintest whiff of salad dressing.

I didn't have to point that out. 'I've got nothing done, Primavera,' she moaned. 'I've been so bleeding busy that I've lost track of time. Don't worry, you won't starve: I'll knock something up.'

'Let me help,' I said. 'What have you got?'

'Steaks, burgers, sausage, the makings of a salad; that's what I was planning.'

'Okay, babe,' I declared. 'Tomorrow is war but tonight we barbie! I'll go and fire up that gas contraption outside, you do something about your slovenly appearance. You look like a fat old lioness in that thing. You have a million dollars, woman, so make yourself look like it.'

She grunted something obscene, but shuffled off in the direction of the stairs nonetheless. I did a fridge audit, peeled a few potatoes, cut them into chips and switched on the deep fryer. By the time she re-emerged, looking once again like the Grande Dame I know so well, we were in 'ready to go' mode, the garden table was set for two and there was a bottle of pink cava in a bucket right in the middle.

'That's better,' she declared, as she took the glass I handed her and made its contents disappear faster than an unsuspecting celebrity snorts a line of coke for the hidden tabloid camera. 'I couldn't believe what I saw in the mirror. "Fat old lioness" was putting it mildly; more like a grizzly bear that had fallen through a tree.'

'What made you so busy?' I asked.

'I've been on the internet all afternoon.'

I frowned. 'Trying to trace Patterson?'

'Hell no. Bugger him. No, I've been sorting out an escape plan from this place, and from Alex's insistence on having cops follow me to the toilet, more or less. If Mr Cowling can do a runner, so can I. I've booked myself a cruise. Late booking; I leave tomorrow.'

'Where are you going?'

'As far away as I can get. I fly to Singapore first off, get on a ship there and spend three weeks on the ocean wave. Don't ask me where we'll visit, 'cos I don't remember. I'll be out of here, and that's the main thing. Let our Alex try and park a police car outside that and see how he gets on.'

'Do you need a lift to the airport?'

'Thanks, love, but no thanks. I'm going first class; that means they send a car for me. Bloody decadent, I know, but like they say, I'm worth it.'

I refilled our glasses. 'You sure are, gal. Now, since you're going to be waited on hand and foot for the next three weeks, you can burn the burgers and the sausage. I'll finish the chips and the salad.'

I enjoy my girlie evenings with Shirl, whether they're at her place or mine, or occasionally on neutral ground; hair is let down, drink is drunk and truths are told. The selfish part of me was glad that Patterson was gone, since his arrival, and Shirley's absorption in him, had put them under threat, but most of me was sorry for her, and angry with him, whether he'd been at fault or not. We ate and talked and laughed as usual that night, but through it all, his recent presence still hung around, like settling dust in the air after a big storm. I tried not to talk about him, but I couldn't keep it up.

'How did you meet him?' I asked, when the ice-cream dishes had been scraped clean of anything scrapeable, and as Shirley poured Drambuie into two great glass globes, then desecrated it with ice cubes made from tap water.

'I told you,' she replied. 'On the internet, after my best boy Tom showed me how to get on to the site.' She paused. 'Here,' she added, 'if you ever decide to have him christened, can I be his godmother?'

'That's a decision he'd take for himself, but if I were you I wouldn't buy a new frock for the occasion. You're his fairy godmother as it is; settle for that. But back to my question: I know he put you on-site, but once you were there, how did you and Patterson get together? Who made the first move?'

She raised her goblet to her lips. 'He did, I suppose,' she murmured. 'It wasn't one of those sites that works at random. It was much more personal than that. You write a bio, then upload it, with all your details and a photo. You enter criteria: the sort of person who attracts you, and the things that would turn you off. Well groomed, big dong, yes, scruffy, small dong, no; loves classical music, no, tone deaf, yes; that sort of info. You can either be reactive, that's go a-hunting, or you can be demure, and sit and wait, as I did.'

Demure? I thought, but I let her continue.

'I wasn't there long before the site moderator sent me an email saying there was someone who'd like to make contact and asking if I'd like his details.'

'Like the size of his dong?'

'No, you daft bat; that comes later. His personal profile, a little bit of background, and his likes and dislikes.'

'How did they describe him?'

'Public servant, retired.'

'I wonder how they vet their clients,' I mused.

Shirley snorted. 'That's self-evident. Not too fucking well. There was I, starting to think that I'd found someone who was capable of looking after me, only for him to be some chickenshit bastard who hasn't got the guts to tell me to my face that he doesn't really fancy me, or who fucks off at the slightest whiff of a possibility that somebody might have got on to his past.'

'Is that what Alex told you?' I asked.

'Yes. He said that there was a good chance that pickpocket bloke had been trying to find out who he was. They were working on that theory, and that Patterson had twigged to this. Now I've got Starsky and fucking Hutch parked at my back door, suggesting to anyone who might be wondering that I know where he's gone when I really don't have a clue, and if I did wouldn't give a shit. I pointed that out to him, but he said he'd rather err on the side of caution if it was all right by me.'

From that, it seemed Alex hadn't told her about Christine McGuigan's murder. *Why should he?* I supposed. It was all over that morning's press, and the presumed link to the other had been made public, but for all her years in Spain, Shirl can't read either Castellano or Catalan worth a damn, and he knew that. Why alarm her more than necessary?

'Did you have any hint he was going to leave?'

'Course not. I dunno what the hell he thought. That I'd tie him to the bedpost if I twigged he was thinking about it? He really didn't know me, Primavera, did he? The only thing I wanted from him was commitment. At the first sign it wasn't there I'd have driven him to the airport myself.'

I nodded agreement, for I knew that to be true.

'And yet . . .' She stopped. 'No, I'm chasing things that aren't there.'

'Go on,' I prompted. 'What were you going to say?'

'Nothing.' She hesitated. 'It's just . . . When we arrived at your place for dinner on Friday, there was a moment then, when I thought he was acting as if he'd been rattled by something. But

251

that was all; just a moment, then he was his usual smiling self. You didn't notice anything, did you?'

'No, I didn't,' I told her. But I couldn't have, could I? Because they'd barely arrived before I was outside punching lumps out of the soon to be late Christine McGuigan, for a reason that had turned out to be significantly off the mark.

Fourteen

Shirley's chauffeur-driven lift was coming for her early next morning, so we called it quits around ten thirty, after a stiff coffee for the road. In case you're wondering, Shirley drank most of the cava and I didn't finish the Drambuie, so I was okay to drive.

The house was quiet when I climbed the stair from the garage. I looked in on Tom; he was still awake, and reading. He's a traditionalist in that respect: Susie gave him a Kindle reader for his tenth birthday, but he prefers real books. He had the self-satisfied smile of a winner on his face. 'Jonny might be a champion golfer,' he told me, 'but he's rubbish at the PGA Tour on X-Box.'

'What about Uche?'

He shook his head. 'His thumbs don't work at all.'

I left him to dream of his triumphs, and went downstairs to the front terrace, to look out on to the square. La Terrassa was still open, and the guys were sitting outside. I went across to join them. Jonny offered me a drink, but I stuck to mineral water, like him, since I didn't fancy alcohol, and I knew that another coffee would keep me awake.

'How's Shirley?' he asked.

'Disappointed. Let down. Steaming mad. Mystified. Any one of those, maybe all of them. But she's not going to brood over it.' I told him about her cruise plan, then I had to explain to Uche about the crisis, and Patterson's vanishing act, since Jonny hadn't mentioned it to him.

'Perhaps it's all a charade,' he suggested. 'When she gets on board he'll be waiting for her.'

'If he is, he'll walk the plank. You can be sure of that. Shirley doesn't play silly games, and she doesn't take prisoners either.'

'Ouch!' he chuckled. 'Remind me to be very polite to the lady when she gets back.'

'Hey,' Jonny called out, suddenly, 'you had a call earlier. Man, English.'

'Name?'

'Didn't leave one. He said he'd tried your mobile, but it was off.' (True: I didn't want to be disturbed at Shirley's, and if Tom had needed me he had the landline.) 'I asked him if he wanted to leave a message, but he said it wasn't important.'

'Journalist, possibly?' I suggested

'Don't think so, he wasn't pushy.'

'So not a salesman either. Ah, bugger him. If he's keen he'll try again tomorrow.'

The three of us discussed our plans for the next day. I told them about my trip to the winery. The guys were going to Pals in the morning, to practise and for Jonny to confirm his touring pro relationship. His manager had been at work during the evening, negotiating terms on his client's behalf. He told me what they were: not much money, in the first year at least, but he had pre-emption rights on the practice ground over even the club teaching pro, and he could play the course whenever he liked, with his guests at half price.

I left them to enjoy the prospect of a quiet day, and hit the sack. I slept like a brick, and woke early the next morning, clear-headed and full of enthusiasm, feeling as if I had a hangover in reverse. I wondered about it for a little, then remembered Jonny's home truth over dinner at Can Roura, about me having withdrawn into my place of safety. The trip to the winery, even though it wasn't very far, only to the slopes on the far side of the bay, was a step outside, and it was exciting me, without giving me the hang-up that the consulate job had, through the requirement that it involved handing over Tom's care to someone else.

I chose a business suit for the visit, a lightweight dark number but with a skirt rather than trousers. There's power dressing and then there's overpower dressing: I was the absent owner's sister-in-law, and however enthusiastic the manager had sounded on the phone, I didn't want him to get the idea that I was there to intimidate him.

As it turned out, I couldn't have even if I'd been so inclined. The boss man, whose name was Manolo Blazquez, would not have been intimidated by Attila the Hun. He was the manager by title, but he had owned the company before selling it in the hope of extra investment, and of access to new markets. He was also its principal oenologist, its production director, one of the most respected in all of Spain.

Miles had tied him into a five-year earn-out, with the final price related to performance. They had spent the first eighteen months or so getting to know each other. One thing my brother-in-law had learned about Manolo was that he was a better wine-maker than he was a manager, but he didn't want to take the risk of antagonising the heart and soul of his investment by parachuting in some guy with an MBA and an attitude. That's why he had asked me to take on the role. 'You'll be a director,' he'd told me, 'but I don't want you to direct. Support, suggest, cajole where necessary, but don't give him the impression that he's no longer the man in charge on the ground. This is a three-generation family business, and he's proud of it.'

He was indeed. The former owner of Bodega Blazquez was a stocky man in his fifties with hair that was more pepper than salt, and with wine in his blood. He had an eye for the ladies as well, I could tell, but he had the good sense to keep it hooded as he welcomed me to his oak-furnished office, in a stone building that had once been a farmhouse. In fact, his father had been born there, as he told me during a quick lecture on the foundation and evolution of the business. The tour he gave me showed that it had grown indeed, into something pretty substantial, with factory sheds that were less than twenty years old, and modern equipment, some of which had been bought with new money injected into the business by Miles.

'At this moment,' he told me, when it was over and we were lunching in the boardroom, 'I sell pretty much one hundred per cent of my annual production as soon as it is confirmed. Most goes to our major wholesaler in Emporda, but I hold some back for direct sales to the public and to supply local specialists like your friend Ben Simmers. Often, though, I sell whole vintages years ahead of their maturity date, to hotel groups across Spain. However, I believe that our quality is such that we can double our sales and our profits by tapping into new foreign markets, through Mr Grayson's connection with the business.'

'That'll mean doubling your production, won't it? Is there spare capacity in this site?'

'No,' he admitted, 'but I have plans. They will involve more investment, and the purchase or leasing of more land so that we can increase our capability. I have mentioned this to Mr Grayson, and he has told me to put it before you.'

'Fine,' I said. 'Go ahead.'

'Not now,' he replied, 'not today. I would like to put formal proposals to you and to Mr Bravo.' He was another guy I had still to meet; he was at sub-board level in the bank that represented Miles in Spain. 'What I would like to do, Mrs Blackstone, is to have meetings with you every fortnight, either here, or I will come to you in St Martí.'

'Here will be fine,' I declared, 'unless I can't make it across for any reason; if my son were to need me, for example.'

'Very good. In that case I will make my presentation to you and to Mr Bravo in two weeks' time.'

I thought over what he had told me on the drive back to St Martí. Blazquez had, it seemed to me, something of the entrepreneur in him, but he didn't strike me as being a gambler. His insistence on having the finance guy sit in on our meeting struck me as prudent. He had plenty to gain by increasing profit, but as much to lose by under-performing. Bravo's role would be that of a risk assessor, as well as a banker.

I was still pumped up by the meeting when I put the car away and climbed up and into the house. It was three thirty and the place was empty; that didn't surprise me, since Jonny had warned me that he and Uche were likely to spend all day at Pals, on the range and in the small gym that the club's owners had just installed.

I fed and watered Charlie, priority number one, then took a bottle of water from the fridge and strolled out on to the front terrace, my mind still full of product ranges, output volumes, margins and so on. I wasn't thinking of anything else as I glanced down into the square, and so it took me a while to realise that someone, a lean, grey-haired man, was waving at me from a table in front of Esculapi.

I did a triple take. On first glance I thought, *vaguely familiar*, on second, *no, it can't be*, and on the third time of asking myself, *Jesus Christ, it is!*

'Mark,' I shouted. 'Wait there!' I left the water bottle on the table, ran downstairs and out through the front gate. Charlie decided that he was coming too and I didn't have time to argue, so the pair of us crossed the square to where he was sitting.

He smiled and glanced at the bouncing Labrador as I took a seat. 'Faithful hound, huh?'

I looked for the elbow crutches that he'd used the last time we'd been together, but I saw only a stick. Knowing him, I reckoned it probably had a sword in it 'That's him, but what the . . . Mark, what are you doing here? How did you get here?'

'Eurostar to Paris, then TGV to Perpignan, and finally by hire car down here. My consultant in London isn't keen on me flying.

The remission is stable for now, but we don't know enough about the new drug regime to be certain of its reaction to air travel.'

'There are worse ways to travel than French trains,' I said. 'But what about my first question? Why are you here?'

His MS has affected his facial expressions; the muscles seem to work more slowly than those of a well person. He became sombre, in stages, as if he was taking off one mask and putting on another.

'It's necessary,' he replied. 'I was asked to come. Those people you asked me to find, the soldier surgeon and her sister, the daughters of your mate's missing boyfriend. I traced them, no problem, but when I did I rang alarm bells like you would not believe. You are into something, Primavera, that nobody wanted stirred up. Now it has been, I've been engaged, retained, to get all the bees back into the hive.'

'What do you mean, retained? And why you?'

'By whom? Her Majesty's Government, and others, including Interpol. Why me? Because it's what I do. I call myself a security consultant, as you know. That has a multitude of meanings and connotations, but among them . . . I'm a freelance. My background is military intelligence and the security service. I haven't been in the field for years, since way before the MS thing developed, but in this case, I've been asked to come out here, first to put you right about a few things, then to go on from there, as far as I need to. All of them revolve around your friend's absconded partner.'

'Patterson Cowling?'

He looked around, checking that there was nobody else in earshot: early summer Tuesdays are quiet in St Martí, so there wasn't. 'That's the guy,' he murmured.

'The retired spook.'

'That's your assumption,' he said, 'but you're wrong; about this man at any rate. Patterson Cowling was a specialist in pro-Palestinian groups in the Middle East. He was MI6, but he was an analyst, never had a foreign posting, and worked anonymously at Vauxhall Cross, the HQ building in London. He did indeed have two daughters, Major Fleur Cowling and Ivy Cowling, now Mrs Victor Benson. I called my Ministry of Defence contact yesterday and asked where Fleur was based. Reasonably enough she wanted to know why I wanted to find her so I told her that something had come up involving her father. An hour later, no more, I had a home visit from two guys, a detective chief superintendent and a DI. We had a bit of ritual dancing, but they'd been briefed on my status, and on your earlier approach to your mate Dale, so all they wanted to do was tie the two of us together. Once they understood the background, they were able to open up to me.'

My mouth felt dry, possibly because it was hanging open slightly. I mouthed the words, 'Agua con gas' . . . fizzy water, in English . . . to the tall waiter standing in the doorway. He understood and nodded.

'Open up about what?' I demanded. 'If Patterson isn't, or wasn't, a spook, then what the hell is he and why is everyone so excited about him?'

'For a start,' he began, pausing as Antonio placed a bottle and a glass on our table, then beneath it a bowl of water for Charlie, 'he isn't even Patterson. The real Mr Cowling died from viral meningitis over a year ago. The man you met went, until recently, by the name of Robert Palmer.'

'Then I have to let Alex know that,' I declared.

'Who's Alex?'

'He's a friend of mine. He's a cop and he's looking for Patterson, Robert, or whoever the hell he is today.'

'You can't tell him,' Mark said firmly. 'You can't tell anyone.'

'But I must; he's involved in a double murder investigation, and he is the guy in the firing line if it isn't cleared up.'

'Then maybe I can help him, but not directly. This has to stay with us, Primavera, for the moment.'

I took a drink. 'Tell me why,' I said quietly.

'The two guys who came to see me; they're attached to the Central Witness Bureau. It's a unit that supports and co-ordinates the work of witness protection units up and down the country. Robert Palmer is one of their clients.'

It took me some time to absorb that new twist in the tale. When I'd analysed the information in my head, I asked, 'What's his story? Can you even tell me, since you want to keep it from the Spanish police?'

'I can tell you, but, at this stage, you alone. I've been hired by the Bureau to come out here, investigate and do what's necessary to maintain Palmer's cover, but I've been given very limited discretion to recruit local help as I need it. That's you, Primavera. You did sign the Official Secrets Act when you took that consulate job, didn't you?'

'Yes.'

'That's fine; it binds you for life.' The advice was unnecessary. I'd already been reminded of that fact, fairly recently. 'In the beginning,' he continued, 'Robert Palmer was a business executive.

261

He was sales and distribution manager for a large pharmaceutical firm, until he was well into his forties. Then he had an idea; he turned entrepreneur. He started his own drug company, UK registered, but with its factory in Bulgaria, thanks to very generous start-up grants in the wake of the collapse of the Soviet bloc, and he developed markets all around the world. At first his products weren't very sexy: aspirin, ibuprofen, antacid tablets and liquids, free market stuff, all nice earners enough to get him established and known. However, after a couple of years he moved on to what had been his real intention; he stepped across certain lines. He began to copy other products, the kind that were covered by international patents, and sold them out of Bulgaria, through a second company he'd set up there, into areas of the world where regulation and copyright enforcement is lax or non-existent.' He paused. 'With me so far?'

I nodded. 'Yes, he's a crook.'

'Mmm. Not really, not at that stage. But . . . this new activity brought him to the attention of someone he hadn't anticipated; someone who very definitely was a crook. He was made an offer which he decided he couldn't refuse. He expanded his facility in Bulgaria and began producing recreational drugs, some legal in certain markets, but others outlawed everywhere, of which ecstasy was the most common. Once he was set on that road, he couldn't get off.'

'But he was a willing partner?'

'He had a few million reasons to be willing,' Mark said. 'The new activity was also successful. The products were high quality. Palmer was never involved in distribution; his associate handled that side of it and his network must have been good, because nothing illegal or even dubious was ever traced back to Bulgaria.'

He smiled. 'Now we get to the really interesting part. About three years ago, his new partner encouraged, or coerced, if you believe him, to move on from there. He told him that he'd found a remarkable young chemist who had developed a new way of synthesising human growth hormone that made its use absolutely undetectable by anti-doping agencies, and therefore, you can imagine, of enormous commercial value. Palmer started production immediately. The stuff was a huge success; he couldn't make enough of it.'

'Where did it go?'

'Interpol guessed that it was sold globally, but even now, they don't know for sure.'

'But is the stuff illegal?' A reasonable question, I reckoned. 'It might be outlawed in sports, but is it against the law?'

'Its manufacture isn't; there are recognised HGH brand names. However Palmer's product isn't licensed anywhere in the world, and if it was its sale would be controlled, for sure. Off-prescription sale of HGH gets you five years in federal prison and a quarter-million dollar fine in the US. Carry it undeclared internationally in your luggage, and you'll wind up in the slammer in many countries. Whatever, the stuff that Palmer's factory produced was a black market drug, and because of its unique property, it would never have been licensed.'

'But he got away with it for a while?'

'Yes,' Mark conceded, 'because he was based in Bulgaria, and because it was all under the radar. He was only detected, and the product was only discovered, because one of his Bulgarian managers swiped some of the HGH, took it across the border and sold it to the coach of a Greek football team, who, as luck had it, was under police surveillance as a suspected doper. Honest to God, the stuff was so good and so effective, that nobody even knew it existed until then.' He paused. 'The smuggler thief talked his head off, and the thing became an Interpol investigation, Greece and Bulgaria both being members. The trail led straight to Robert Palmer. He was arrested in Hove, where he lived . . . alone, by the way: he didn't have a wife, let alone two daughters.'

'What about the genius chemist?'

Mark smiled. 'Ah, he got out from under. The Bulgarian factory was raided, and the production of the stuff was shut down, but he was long gone. There had been a tip, a leak from the Interpol office in Sofia. The only people they found were production staff who thought they were making multivitamin pills and phials, not ecstasy and HGH. In fact the chemist was never there. The production process was set up on the basis of written instructions to the local staff. Nobody ever saw him; they still don't know who he is.'

'And Palmer?'

'When he saw that he was in deep trouble, he started to bargain. He claimed not to know anything about the distribution network, but he was able to tell Interpol that the business had gone transatlantic by that time and that the growth product was being sold in volume into the USA, across several sports, from college level up. You can imagine how excited that made the American Drug Enforcement Agency.'

I nodded; having lived there for a while, I surely could.

'They weighed into the investigation, heavily. However, Palmer was able to persuade them that he was just the producer . . . he wasn't doing anything against Bulgarian law, but small details like that don't deter the DEA . . . and that the big prize was his partner, whose interests, he said, stretched into Central and South America, and included major money laundering for drug cartels, plus other stuff. Palmer said that this man had a network of distributors and informants across the western world. He said that he himself hadn't been worried about being nailed in Bulgaria because several government officials, police officers, and a key Interpol agent had been on the guy's payroll. This was borne out, of course, by the leak before the raid.'

He took a sip of water, before continuing. 'Palmer was lawyered up by this time. His brief proposed a deal; he said that Palmer would name the partner and testify against him, in return for immunity from prosecution . . . the ecstasy and sodium oxybate, the date rape drug also known as GHB, were his Achilles heel, as it turned out . . . protection and a new identity when it was all over. There was a conference in Lyon, at Interpol headquarters, and not least because of American insistence, that deal was done, and signed off, all legal and unbreakable.'

I sensed that Mark was tiring; he'd had a hell of a journey. 'Do you want to take a break?' I asked him.

'Not yet,' he said. 'I must finish this. After that, Palmer was installed in a safe house in East Anglia, and given two handlers, one American, a DEA agent called Beau Lucas, and one Brit, a senior secondee to Interpol from the Met, called Graham Metcalfe.

The whole thing was kept desperately secret, for there was one thing still to do. For any prosecution to succeed, the investigators needed a second witness, and Palmer would not reveal his partner's name until that person was secured.'

'Did he have somebody in mind?'

'Oh yes. He told his interrogators, after his arrest, while he negotiated his deal, that there was one person and one person alone who could help bring his partner down, but that the only way to reach him was for Palmer to make contact and set up a meeting. That he would do after the deal was signed; nothing before, not a word.'

'And they bought that?'

'Of course they did,' he laughed. 'The Americans were bricking it. The HGH chemist was still out there. There was nothing to stop Palmer's buddy setting him up in business somewhere else, and putting the integrity of global sport at risk.'

'The Stars and Stripes rule, okay,' I murmured. Ever the cynic. 'What happened next?'

'From the safe house, Palmer made the contact; in confidence. His handlers weren't involved in it.'

'How did he manage that?'

'Through Facebook, would you believe. They used fake identities to communicate. When it was sorted he told Lucas and Metcalfe that a meeting had been arranged. The three of them would fly to Malaga and go to a hotel called the Silken Puerta; the witness would be waiting in room 106, which they would have booked in Palmer's name.'

'And was he?'

'We'll probably never know, not for sure. The handlers wouldn't go along with all of Palmer's arrangement. They explained to him there's a reason for calling a place a safe house. They insisted that only one person would go to bring the witness in, because that's all it would need, and it wouldn't be Palmer. In fact, Graham Metcalfe assumed it would be him, but Lucas pulled agency rank and went.' He drew a deep breath and I sensed tension in him. 'It was kept so tight that they didn't tell anyone outside the loop, not the Spanish bureau of Interpol, not the Guardia Civil, not the local cops, nobody. If they had . . .'

'What?'

'Beau Lucas might still be alive. They might have cracked the whole operation. But they didn't. They kept it undercover. Lucas was supposed to call Metcalfe at a certain time, to confirm that contact had been made and they were heading home. He didn't, but that didn't set the alarm bells ringing, not right away. In fact nothing did, until a chambermaid let herself into the room, and found what was left of the guy. He'd been shot, close range, with a sawn-off. The room was covered in feathers; turn up the sound on a telly,' he said, 'and a pillow makes a pretty effective silencer.'

'Let me guess,' I ventured. 'His face was blown off.'

Mark stared at me. 'How the hell did you know that?'

'Lucky guess. You finish yours, then I'll tell you mine.'

'It was as you said. There was nothing left to identify the body, nothing at all; his wallet, watch, clothes, face, were all gone. So they assumed that he was Mr Palmer, the man who'd booked the room. They'd have gone on thinking that if Graham Metcalfe hadn't called the Guardia after the third missed check-in call, to ask if anything had occurred at the Silken Puerta.'

'What about the witness? Was he killed too?'

'Almost certainly, but Lucas was the only body found in that room. Dead American, though, so you can imagine the fall-out from that. The DEA shoved Interpol and everyone else aside. They closed the hotel and put their own CSI team in there, everyone but Gil fucking Grissom, but maybe him too. They analysed everything; practically tested the feathers for fingerprints. After three days, they established that there were two different blood types in the room.'

'The previous guest cut himself shaving?' I suggested, wryly.

'If he did, it was deep enough for it to spray on the wall. They searched the entire hotel after that, inch by inch, item by item, until they found a laundry trolley with blood smears inside, matching the others in the room. So the witness was killed there, it seems, but the body was taken away. Next question. Why take the risk?'

That was a no-brainer even for me. 'Whoever did or ordered the killing couldn't afford to leave it behind; that would have been a bigger risk. Defacing . . . literally . . . Lucas was a delaying tactic, or maybe no more than the killer's trademark. Eventually, he'd have been identified, even if Metcalfe hadn't blown the whistle straight away. But no way could the other body have been left, because it would have led investigators straight to the target: identification couldn't have been ruled out.' I paused as I saw the flaw in my thesis. 'But no, Palmer knew, knows, who the witness was.'

'That's right. And Palmer wasn't, isn't, saying anything. He refused to accept the certainty of his contact's death. He saw Lucas's killing as a warning to him to stay silent. He may well be right too.'

'And Interpol? How do they see it? They can't be happy about Palmer's silence.'

'It doesn't matter, Primavera. Without that second witness, Palmer's testimony would be worthless. Sure, they're desperate to know who his partner is, but the deal he was given was legally drawn up and witnessed, and it wasn't contingent on him naming him, something he's consistently refused to do without the guarantee of him being taken out of play, permanently.'

'Couldn't that be arranged?'

'Hah! Are you suggesting that the Americans might take direct action? No; another US administration might have, but this one doesn't seem to have the balls for that sort of thing. Anyway, too many other nations are in the know. Instead, Uncle Sam's gone home to watch his own back yard and Robert Palmer's been dropped into the witness protection programme. Patterson Cowling died at exactly the right time. Because of the career he'd followed, he was a non-person. With the co-operation of MI6, the Home Office and the Justice Ministry, the Met witness unit took over his identity, and gave it to Palmer.'

'Why?' I asked; something in me was offended that the original Mr Cowling hadn't been allowed to stay dead.

'Simple,' Mark replied, bluntly. 'Because it was a hell of a lot easier than creating a new one. He stayed in the safe house for a while, getting used to his new self, then they turned him loose to get on with his life. Graham Metcalfe transferred from Interpol to the Central Witness Bureau as his handler, to keep an eye on him, just in case at some time in the future a new witness turns up, and Palmer can be pulled in to earn his freedom properly. Metcalfe was one of the two guys who visited me yesterday morning, by the way.'

'Do the Cowling daughters know about this?'

'Yes. They had to be told. But they have no idea who Palmer was or where he is.'

'Did they give him a new face as well?'

'No, they just fattened him up and gave him a different hair colour, and contact lenses that make his eyes blue instead of the distinctive brown they were.'

'I see.' I frowned. 'So someone who'd known him before, and saw him again, might think they recognised him, but couldn't be sure?

'I suppose. Why?'

'That's part of my story,' I said, then checked my watch and saw that it had just gone five. 'But first things first; any minute now ...'

Right on cue, a brown figure crested the hill on his bike, skidded to a halt at our front gate and jumped off. 'Hey,' I called to him. So did Charlie, in his own way, and ran to greet him.

Tom came across to join us, his face a-glisten with a light sheen of perspiration. There's a speed limit on the cycleway from L'Escala to St Martí, but it means nothing to him, unless it's busy, in which event he keeps it more or less in sight. 'Hello, Mr Kravitz,' he exclaimed, forestalling an unnecessary introduction. I'd forgotten that they'd met, in London, three years before.

They shook hands, like adults, and he dropped into a chair. Our visitor said nothing at first; he just gazed, that was all. When he did speak, it wasn't the usual platitudes about being big for his age, or looking like his father, or like me, both being the case; no, it was a question. 'What do you want to be, Tom?'

'Mum's always asking me that,' he replied. 'I don't know yet.'

'Don't worry about it,' Mark told him. 'Neither did your dad, until the day he died.'

I cut into the exchange. 'Are you taking Charlie for a run as usual?' I asked him.

He nodded, then jumped up. 'Yes. Come on, boy. Where's Jonny, by the way?'

'Still at work, I suppose; him and Uche both.'

'He didn't even ask why I'm here,' Mark observed, as he watched him remount his bike.

'That's like his father too,' I said. 'Oz was curious about everything, but often he kept it to himself.'

'Or hired people like me to satisfy it for him.'

'True, but Tom doesn't have that luxury. When he gets round to it, he'll ask me about you, and he knows that I'll tell him. No secrets in our house.'

'None?'

Sharp question; Kravitz had helped me out of some difficulty I'd got into a few years earlier, involving my cousin Frank. I'd never told Tom about that; he'd been too young, and for some of the detail, he always will be. 'None that involve him,' I retorted.

'Ready to spill this story to me?'

He caught me off guard; my mind was still somewhere else, in

Shirley Gash's swimming pool, three years before, as it happened. 'Pardon?'

'Your story?'

Back to the present crisis. 'Yes, sorry. How did I guess that Beau Lucas had his face blown off, you ask? Because that's what seems to happen when your Mr Palmer's involved.' I gave him a rundown of everything that had happened in the eight days gone by, from Patterson Cowling's introduction as Shirley's new partner, to the attempted theft a few metres from where we were sitting at that very moment, and the dramatic incidents that had followed, leading to Patterson's disappearance, and to his unveiling as Robert Palmer as was.

'That's why I asked if his appearance had been changed. It seems to me that somebody might have —'

'Yes,' Mark picked up, 'might have thought he recognised him, but not been sure, so he sent in people to try to find out. Has the first victim been identified yet?'

'No. The police aren't even close.'

'But it's only the police who are looking? The Catalan people, these Mossos d'Esquadra?'

'Yes.'

'What have they got to go on?'

'Blood group, DNA and a photograph taken on a mobile phone. That was published in the local papers and shown on television. Not a whisper of a reaction, from what I hear from Alex, other than a couple of women who hoped it might be their missing husbands.'

'Then Graham Metcalfe and his DI, Harry Ferguson, need to

get hold of it. The search should be at a different level. What about the woman, McGuigan? What's known about her?'

I tried to recall as much as I could of what Alex had told me. 'She worked in Ireland until a little over a year ago, as a TV sports reporter, legit, union member and everything. Then she dropped out of sight, and showed up in Spain, calling herself Christy Mann and scratching a living feeding video to shit websites and celeb photos to any tabloids that would buy them.'

Mark smiled. 'Sports reporter,' he repeated. 'And she relocated in a hurry at the very time Palmer's Bulgarian factory was busted. As I said, we know nothing about the distribution network for the HGH, but it was global, Palmer said, and those two facts about Miss McGuigan would fit, if she was part of it.'

'Might he have known her?'

'Not according to him. He's always insisted that he just made the stuff, and that the only two people he knew on his partner's team were the man himself and the witness.'

'What about the genius chemist?' I asked. 'Didn't he know him?'

'He said he wasn't allowed to meet him. This was a very secure operation, Primavera, so that makes sense. Just as it makes sense that McGuigan was involved in distribution in Ireland; a woman with contacts and freedom of movement across the world of sport.'

'Too right it's secure,' I pointed out. 'These two people were sent in to try to identify Palmer. They failed and, not only that, they drew attention to themselves in the process. Now they're both dead; no chances taken.'

'Agreed,' he said. 'It's no wonder the man ran. He put his trust in Metcalfe and in Ferguson, believing that they'd given him the sort of new identity that couldn't draw attention . . . and they had; a dead intelligence officer, for God's sake . . . only to find himself in more danger than ever.'

'And maybe not just him,' I whispered, as I considered the caution of the man who was after Palmer, and his ruthlessness in closing down any potential threat. 'If Patterson's mate even suspects that he might have told Shirley about him . . .' I whistled. 'Going on a cruise is the smartest thing she could have done. Mark, did Metcalfe and his boss know about her, and their relationship?'

'Of course they did. The Central Witness Bureau actively encouraged it. The reasoning was that he'd be even safer as part of a couple of obscure nobodies with a nice quiet backwater lifestyle. After Palmer picked your friend from all the lovelies on the website they vetted her before they let him make the approach. Don't worry about her. She'll be regarded as under protection, just as much as he is, probably even more so, since she's completely innocent. On a cruise, you say? Give me the details: I'll tell the minders where she is and she'll be looked after discreetly wherever she is.'

'For how long?' I exclaimed. 'For ever? This isn't just about your employers bringing Palmer back inside the safety net. They've got to find this partner of his and deal with him, through the courts or otherwise.'

'Agreed, but that dictates we have to find Palmer first, and find him alive. When we do, I'm sure he'll realise that the rules have changed, and that he has no option but to help us nail the guy. But if we don't, if the other side get to him and kill him, the threat to Shirley won't go away.'

'Then shouldn't we go to Alex Guinart? His interests are the same as ours. He has two murders to solve, and we're both heading in the same direction. He's looking for Palmer too, if only as a witness. We're all after the same man.'

'No,' he said firmly. 'I have a pretty broad remit from my clients, but one thing I've been specifically forbidden to do is involve local law enforcement. This thing is out of control because of systemic corruption. Robert Palmer's partner had a paid informer within Interpol, for Christ's sake. If he could penetrate them, he could have sources within any police force. If I contact your friend, he could find out about me. And through me, you'd be brought into the web.'

I raised an eyebrow. 'You're saying that by telling me all this you've put me at risk?'

'No, my dear, you did that yourself when you started asking questions about the man. If I'd let you carry on stumbling around in the dark, you might well have walked into the path of a shotgun and wound up with half your head missing.'

I wasn't so sure about that: I'd only wanted to kick Patterson Cowling's arse on my friend's behalf. I'd had no interest in Robert Palmer, or in undetectable performance-enhancing drugs, or even in dead DEA agents. But there was no point arguing, not then anyway. The game was afoot and I was in it.

'Well,' I persisted, 'if you're not going to link up with the best cop I know in these parts, what are you going to do next?'

'I'm going to report back to Graham Metcalfe, who's controlling me on behalf of all the agencies involved, his own, Interpol and the DEA, and fill him in on what's been going on here. He'll investigate Christine McGuigan's past in Ireland; he'll look into her known contacts, bank statements, phone records, everything that's traceable. He'll also get hold of that photograph of the first victim and try to identify him.'

'How will that help?'

'We'll know that if it does. Alongside that, though, he'll pull in all the resources at his disposal and do a very big computer job. He'll look at flight records and hotel bookings in Malaga on the day of Beau Lucas's murder and then we'll do the same for this area, over the last couple of weeks, and find out how many names pop up twice.'

I nodded. It made sense. And then I thought of something that made even more. 'Perhaps you can narrow it down a little,' I suggested.

'How?'

'Where was Robert Palmer when he took off?' I asked. 'He was at the golf tournament. And consider this: he didn't leave home that morning planning on doing a runner, because he left his passport on Shirley's dressing table. So, instead of looking for one person in a whole region, why not establish who was at the Catalan Masters, all of them if that's what it takes, even spectators who paid their entry money by credit card, then see which of them was in Malaga?'

Mark's facial mask seemed to stretch as he beamed. 'Your old man would have been proud of you,' he said.

Fifteen

I offered Mark a bed for the night . . . even with Jonny in residence I still had a couple of spare rooms . . . but out of politeness only, for I didn't expect him to accept. His presence would have begged too many questions, but also, there was the potential problem of the stairs. While his remission was remarkable, given the lows he had experienced, he carried the stick for a reason.

'Thanks, Primavera,' he said, 'but I've checked into a hotel in L'Escala; the Nieves Mar. It has a lift, so everything's on one level, effectively. Suits me.'

He headed for it, to contact his controller, while I headed home to cook for my boys, and one more, since I'd told Jonny to bring Uche for dinner. I'd picked up some steaks on the way back from my business visit, so there wasn't a lot of preparation to be done, just some baking potatoes to wrap in tinfoil and stick in the oven, and some onions and peppers to be chopped ready for frying in oil. Mind you, my fingers were at risk as I did the chopping, for my mind was still whirling with everything Mark had told me.

Until that afternoon, Robert Palmer had been a rock singer,

dead way too soon, one of my favourites; sometimes, when I threw a moody, as I did with monthly regularity in those days, Oz used to call me Sulky Girl, after one of his songs. But suddenly he was someone else, someone with a shady past and an endangered present.

The man had quite a story; pity it could never be told. Some life, some rebirth. Quite a glib talker, Mr Cowling had been; he'd taken me in, and when it comes to people, experience has made me hard to fool. Patterson the Second was so glib that he'd even talked his way into a new life. Yet why did he need it? That was the one problem I still had with Mark's account. Once the second witness had been taken out of play, why hadn't he simply led Interpol and the Americans straight to his former partner? 'That man's arm must be very long indeed,' I mused.

Such contemplation came to an end when Tom arrived back from his run with Charlie, closely followed by Jonny. Yes, Uche was coming, he said, but he'd gone home to shower first.

'How's your new practice base?' I asked.

'Excellent. Lena gave it her seal of approval, so everyone's happy.'

'Lena's still here?'

'Yes. Lars isn't playing in this week's tournament either, so they've kept the rental house on for another week.'

Dinner was delayed. I'd rubbed tomatoes and garlic into the cut loaf I'd bought, and I was ready to put all the rest together, but one ingredient was missing. Uche. After the third check of my watch, I frowned at Jonny. 'You did tell him seven thirty sharp, not seven thirty for eight?'

'Yes,' he insisted, heading for the door. 'I'll go and chase him up.'

He returned ten minutes later, unaccompanied. 'I'm sorry, Auntie P,' he said sheepishly. 'He's not there. He's probably pulled; he was on the phone to those Swedish girls we met yesterday on the beach. He's a bastard for that. His cock works like a divining rod, only it's not water it sources. He follows wherever it points.'

'An observation I hope you won't share with your cousin,' I told him, with an attempt at severity. Then I shrugged. 'Bugger him. Wherever he is, the menu won't be as good. Come on, let's eat, before the tomato bread dries out.'

For once, our dinner table discussion wasn't all about golf. Very little of Jonny's shop was talked, in fact; instead, Tom started to quiz me about my trip to the winery, and I found myself giving them a rundown on the product range and then on the production process. I even found myself opening a bottle of one of the high-end reds, although Tom wasn't allowed a demo of that, only a sniff.

He didn't ask about Mark until we were almost finished. I'd known that he would, eventually, and when he did, it was straight out. 'Why is Mr Kravitz here?'

I can't lie to my son. If I ever do, something will break, irreparably. 'He's on business,' I replied; the answer that I had prepared.

'What does he do, this chap?' Jonny asked.

His cousin chuckled. 'He's a secret agent.'

'Tom!' I protested. 'Don't exaggerate. Mark's a security consultant. He's here on assignment, that's all, and he looked me up.' See? Not a word of a lie.

'Mmm,' he murmured; that's my son's way of saying, 'And the rest!'

Uche was still absent without leave the next morning. Jonny got no reply when he went to knock him up. He was more than a little angry, for his clubs were in the penthouse, but I persuaded the owner to open it with a back-up key, so that they could be liberated. 'We are going to have serious words, Mr Wigwe and I,' he declared as he lugged the massive bag back up to my place. 'He's on ten per cent of a chunk of money, and he's got to realise that you don't just earn it at the weekend. Wednesday morning on the practice ground is as important as Sunday afternoon on the course.'

I calmed him down with a promise that when Uche showed I would tear a piece off him myself, then sent him on his way to Pals.

I'd arranged to meet the 'security consultant' for coffee at his hotel. As it turned out, the coffee was for one; Mark isn't allowed any strong stimulants, so he had plain water. He was hyper nonetheless. I could tell that he had news and that he was keen to share it with me.

'Your pickpocket's been identified,' he said, quietly, as soon as I'd been served at our terrace table, beside the hotel pool. 'He is, or was, Bulgarian, and he hadn't been seen for over a year, not since the raid on Robert Palmer's factory. His name was Ilian Genchev, he was an agent of Interpol in the Sofia bureau and he was assumed to have been the leak, given the timing of his disappearance.'

'That's quick work,' I commented. I could tell that he was

pleased with his team's progress, and that praise was in order . . . but only so much. 'I assume that he left his name behind along with his country.'

'Yes, of course.'

'Have your people come up with the identity he assumed, or with a last known address?'

'No,' he admitted, 'but give them a chance.'

'Fine, but until they establish those things, does knowing who he was take us one step forward?'

'Not yet, but come on, Primavera, it's confirmation that he wasn't just some fucking petty thief. It rules that out completely.'

'Okay, so we've shuffled an inch or two forward, but essentially we're still stuck on square one.'

'That's a pretty negative way of looking at it.'

'But not incorrect?'

He sighed. 'No.'

'What about McGuigan? Have they made any progress with her?'

'No. It's still early days there. You have to remember that the game's changed in the last twenty-four hours, and my task with it, thanks to you. I was brought in to warn you off searching for Robert Palmer, but the information you gave me stood that on its head. Now we need to find him.'

'If he's still alive.'

'I'd bet that he is,' Mark said. 'He'll be hidden away somewhere.'

'What makes you so confident?' I asked.

'He strikes me as the sort of guy who'd follow advice. People like Palmer aren't simply given a new passport and credit card and told to get on with it. There is a certain amount of training; absorption of every detail of the new persona's background, education, career history, family names and professions, and so on, but it doesn't stop there. Subjects may also be told what to do if their cover is blown and they're out of reach of their handlers.'

'For example?'

'As a rule, they'd be advised to have a bolt-hole identified and ready for emergency use; a safe house by another name. Ideally the witness protection people will know where it is, so they can locate the client once he's gone to ground and get him to safety.'

'From which I guess that Palmer doesn't have one, or you'd be heading there right now.'

His face shifted into something that might have been a smile. 'He doesn't have one that Metcalfe knows about, but . . . everything you've told me he's done, the way he made his escape and what he did once he was clear of the course, it says to me that he did have a plan.' He looked at me. 'Primavera, what can you tell me about his movements when he was here?'

I stared back at him. 'Not a lot,' I replied. 'I only met the man the weekend before last, then our Jonny turned up out of the blue and I was swept up in looking after him and in the golf tournament. The only movements I know about were between L'Escala and the course and back again, and to St Martí for dinner a couple of times.'

'Can you remember anything he might have said on those dinner dates, about places he'd been to or seen around here?'

I thought about his question for as long as it took me to draw a complete blank. 'Nah, nuffink. Sorry, Mark, can't help. We need Shirley for that and she ain't here.'

'No, but . . .'

Whatever it was that he was about to say was cut off short. His eyes moved from me to a point over my right shoulder, and registered annoyance.

I stared to turn, but a voice told me who had distracted him before I got there. 'Primavera,' Alex Guinart began. 'Excuse me, but can I have a word?' He spoke Catalan.

'And a coffee if you play your cards right,' I retorted as he reached us.

'I don't have time,' he said, brusquely. 'I was on my way to St Martí when by sheer chance I saw your jeep in the car park. Is your mobile battery flat?'

He was using his cop voice with me; I didn't like that. 'No, it's switched off. I know that most people have forgotten you can do that, but I haven't.' He looked at Mark, as if he was about to ask him for his passport. 'This is my friend, Mark Kravitz,' I told him, in English. 'I've mentioned him to you before. Mark, this is local law enforcement, Alex Guinart. From his expression, either his piles are killing him or there's something he desperately wants to tell me.'

I had indeed told Alex about Mark, and I'd described his profession in general terms. He softened a little and they shook hands. I nodded towards a vacant chair. He yielded and pulled it across, but even as he sat, I could see that he was still agitated.

'What's up?' I asked.

'Do you know a man called Kalu Wigwe?' he countered, sticking to English.

'Yes, I do. I met him on Sunday at the golf tournament. He's a wealthy Nigerian, an emir of part of that country. He's also Uche's dad. He offered to take me for a ride in his great big plane, but I reckoned there would be a fare involved and I didn't fancy paying it. What's he done? Propositioned the mayor's wife?'

'He hasn't done anything.' He looked at Mark. 'This is in confidence, okay?' he asked.

'You may rely on my discretion, sir.' The reply was impassive; it was also in perfect Castellano.

'A couple of hours ago,' Alex continued, relieved to be free to speak his own language, 'he was kidnapped at gunpoint from his aircraft, in the private section of Girona Airport. His absence wasn't discovered until forty-five minutes ago, when ground staff went on board to find out why the plane was making no move to meet its booked departure time, and why the crew weren't responding to radio messages. They found them tied up and gagged. When they were freed, they told us what had happened. They were expecting Mr Wigwe, at eight thirty. Fifteen minutes before that his son arrived, pointed a gun at them, made them lie down and secured them. He bound them hand and foot then dumped them in the galley, which is lockable. The rest they didn't see but heard well enough. Kalu Wigwe arrived, voices were raised, and then there was silence. Nobody saw them leave but one of the airport workers told our people that there was a car parked on the concourse by the steps; an old battered Seat Ibiza that had once been white. It didn't occur to him to ask the driver what the hell it was doing there, but he did give us a description of the man who was waiting behind the wheel. A white man, oldish, but still with dark hair, wearing a blazer with gold buttons.' He frowned at me. 'Who the hell does that sound like, Primavera?'

I stared at him, absorbing what he had just told me and coming to terms with the implications. 'Who does it sound like?' I mimicked. 'You know bloody well,' I replied, 'but forgive me if I deal with the "what" of the situation. My nephew's pal, his bagman, has turned out to be a gun-toting kidnapper, and I've let him mix with my son. I've made him welcome in my house, treated him like family. I've been betrayed; let me deal with that for a little, Alex.'

Then I looked at Mark and I could tell that his mind was exactly in synch with mine and that we had reached the same conclusion. It looked as if one very big question had just been answered, but for sure, it had been replaced by a whole new set of riddles. 'Well?'

My friend nodded. 'I reckon my remit has just been overridden,' he murmured. He looked at Alex. 'Same basis?'

'What do you mean?'

'What I'm about to tell you is between us,' he said, 'okay?'

The acting intendant frowned. 'I'm a police officer, Mr Kravitz. I can't make that promise.'

'With respect, Mr Guinart, you're an investigator, so you're bound to have confidential discussions all the time, with informants and the like. Just listen to what I have to tell you and we'll see where we go from there.'

'Yes,' he murmured, cautiously. 'We'll see.'

Alex took off his uniform hat and sat back in his chair, as Mark launched into the story of the colourful background of the man he had known as Patterson Cowling. He told it from the beginning, meticulously, ensuring that every chapter was understood before moving on to the next. He omitted only one piece of information, the background of the man whose identity Robert Palmer had been given, but that really wasn't something that 'local law enforcement' needed to know.

When the tale was told, Alex took a single huge breath, then exhaled, loudly. 'And you want me to keep this thing among the three of us,' he said. 'Not tell my bosses. Are you crazy?'

Mark nodded, affably. 'Probably. But how would their being in the loop help us at this stage?'

His eyes widened, then he laughed. 'Help "us"?' he repeated. 'Mr Kravitz, Mark, I hate to remind you, but this is Spain, my territory, so there is no "us", just me, and my investigation; my double murder investigation which has just been complicated still further by a kidnapping.'

'Sure, Alex, this is your patch. But you're wrong; I do have a locus here. I'm working for two agencies, one of them being Interpol, of which Spain is a member; I think you'll find that gives me a fair bit of clout. I don't want to be rude, threatening even less, but I could make a phone call and within half an hour you would be taken out of the game. Trust me, I could, but I don't want to; because other people would get involved and we don't have time to wait for them, because you're Primavera's friend, and because from what she's told me, you're a damn good cop.'

'Thanks,' Alex said. 'But I'm a cop with a career and a family. I don't want to join the private sector, as a security guard in a bank, or driving an armoured car. I have a problem with this.'

'Or an opportunity, depending on how you view it. You're the man in charge here, yes? The senior investigator?'

'Yes.'

'So you call the shots?'

'To an extent,' he conceded, warily.

'Then work with me on this. What I've just told you, about Robert Palmer; the great mystery, the secret he's keeping, has been the identity of his partner, the man from whom he's hiding, in fear of his life. Now, put these facts together: last Sunday, he disappeared from the viewing stand at PGA Catalunya, at the very moment that Kalu Wigwe walked into the driving range. This man, this rich and powerful man, has just flown into Spain, ostensibly to support his son's player in the championship, but also in the wake of the murders of Ilian Genchev and Christine McGuigan, two people believed to have been hired to confirm Palmer's identity.'

Alex raised a hand, palm out, like a traffic cop. 'Hold on, hold on, hold on,' he exclaimed. 'Who the hell is Ilian Genchev?'

'That's not really important,' Mark said, dismissively. 'This is. Now, three days after Palmer fled, a man who fits his description as closely as you'd need for a provisional identification, at worst, is involved in kidnapping Wigwe from his plane. So,' he continued, 'Mr Senior Investigating Officer, what are we entitled to suspect from that?'

He sighed, a concession of sorts. 'I get it,' he murmured. 'Mr

Wigwe may well be the man Palmer's partner, or so close to him that he will recognise him for sure, even as he is today.'

'May be?' I protested. 'Alex, it's a bloody certainty.'

'No,' Mark intervened. 'It's not; Palmer may have had other enemies. But it's highly likely. If we ever want to know for sure, we'll have to find Kalu fast, for I don't believe he'll survive this. But there are other questions, Primavera, you know that.'

'Too right. What the hell is Uche doing snatching his father from his plane? Could we be wrong? Could Uche be Palmer's partner?'

'No chance, he's too young.'

'Then why is he hand in hand with Palmer?'

'Yes, that one's valid, and one more. Why did they take him off the plane at all? They had a gun on the crew; they could have flown out and taken him anywhere, but they chose to stay in Spain. Something else is going on here. Alex, if we track them down, you get all the answers and you close off all your investigations. Will you work with us, for now?'

He frowned. 'For a very little while,' he decided. 'If only because I see nothing else to do. What do you need from me?'

'Contact your office; tell them that the matter of the kidnapping is in hand, that you have new information and that you're following it up.'

'That's all?'

'Yes. While you're doing that, I'll make a call, and Primavera, so will you. I want to know as much as I can about Uche. Clearly there's more to him than first impressions tell you.'

'Do you want me to speak to Jonny?'

'Let's keep him out of it. I reckon that Graham Metcalfe can find out more than Jonny knows. No. Remember what I was saying about bolt-holes? Well, I want you to track down Shirley Gash, wherever she is, to see if she can help with that. Can you do that?'

I nodded. 'With luck. She should be in Singapore just now; her cruise liner isn't due to sail until tomorrow. If I contact the company she's sailing with, they should be able to tell me what hotel she's in.'

And then my common sense switched itself on. I checked my watch and realised that where Shirley was it was late afternoon. As Alex went outside to call in from his car, and Mark went inside to phone from his room, I took out my mobile and hit her entry.

There were a few more clicks that usual, but I got a dialling tone, rather than straight to voicemail, usually a good sign. She picked up a few seconds later. 'Girl,' she squealed, 'you'll never guess where I am. I'm in the bath.'

'I didn't think that was your "on the toilet" voice. You got company?'

'Don't be daft; I've had enough of that for a while. I'm happy because I've got this wonderful room with a bath that lets you see right out over the marina.'

'Go on then; stand up and wave to the sailors.'

'I just did, but I'm way too high for anyone to wave back. Now,' she went on, 'have I got news for you. You'll never guess who I'm having dinner with tonight.'

'Patterson.'

'Huh. Cow. Try again.'

'Mac Blackstone.'

There followed a couple of seconds of atypical silence. 'How the . . . How did you know that? Ah, I can guess. He's been in touch with Jonny.'

'Maybe he has, but not since I saw him last. That was a shot in the dark by me. I remembered that he and Mary have just been cruising, and that he was heading back there.'

'Yes, and they've just got off the ship I'm on. I sail tomorrow, they go home. He's had a great time. She looks as if she'd only enjoy an execution.'

'Her step-grandson would agree with you. But I didn't call you for your social diary. I need to ask you something.'

'If it's about him,' she said, firmly, 'I'll make a point of not remembering.'

'Shirl,' I said, 'hear me out. This is serious. If I tell you it could be a matter of life or death you'll think I'm being melodramatic, but I'm not.'

'Whose life or death?'

'Uche's father. Maybe Uche's too. Maybe your bloke's. We don't know for sure.'

I had her attention. 'What do you need to know?'

'I want you to think about anywhere you were with Palmer, probably not in L'Escala, but maybe not too far away, somewhere different, somewhere he was interested in.'

'Excuse me, but who in the name of Agatha Christie is Palmer?'

'Slip of the tongue, sorry. I have a CD of his in the car just now.'

'Just as well. I don't think I could have taken another secret. Let me think.' I heard water ripple in the background. 'We went to Mas Torrent. How about that?'

Mas Torrent is a very posh, very public and very expensive hotel. 'I don't think so.'

'Mmm. In that case, there's only really La Central.'

'What's that?'

'It's a spa hotel, up near Darnius, close to the reservoir. We went up there for a couple of days, week before last, while I was getting ready to show Patterson off in L'Escala high society.'

'I don't know it.'

'I'm not surprised; it's quite hard to get to, five kilometres along a very dodgy road. Mind you, it gets worse beyond the hotel. I'd think twice about taking a car up there, all ruts and bumps and rocks.'

'But you went up it?'

'Yes, on our first morning there. We walked up it following a sign that said there was a restaurant up there. We were on the road for an hour and more, uphill all the bleedin' way, but somewhere we must have taken the wrong turn, for we never found the bloody restaurant, only this old abandoned house. The track was windy all the way, until we came to a fork; we reckoned that we went right when we should have gone left. We should have known, 'cos it got even worse after the split.'

'House?' I repeated.

'It had been, at one time; it was an old stone building.'

'How did you know it was abandoned?' I asked.

'Holes in the slate roof, half the windows broken, no electricity, no proper sanitation, no running water, just a well outside; I have an instinct for these things, my dear. The odd hunter might have stopped there, in fact that's probably what it was, a hunter's lodge, but it hadn't been occupied since Franco's time.'

'Did Palm . . . Patterson say anything about it?'

'Yes,' she chuckled, 'he made me laugh. He said it was a pity Robin Hood wasn't Spanish, 'cos the sheriff would never have found him there.'

Sixteen

Mark was gone for so long that I asked for another coffee, and Alex joined me. 'You're not going to let me blow my job with this, are you, Primavera?' he asked, quietly, as he ripped his way into the wrapping of the obligatory biscuit that came with his double espresso.

'No,' I told him, making a promise to myself that I wouldn't. 'Mark knows what he's doing, and he is as well connected as he says, but at the first sign he's reached a dead end, you and I will drive to Girona and I'll put everything that I know and that he's told you on the record, and after that, if you like, we'll go to your headquarters and tell the whole story there.'

'That might not get me out of trouble.'

I smiled. 'We'll be economical with the timeframe if we have to.'

'This Genchev. Who's he?'

I told him. 'So you see, it is international. Also, we'll be able to link the two murders here with the killing of the American DEA man in Malaga last year. That will give the Mossos big bragging rights over the Guardia Civil. You won't be in trouble, you'll be teacher's pet.'

As I spoke, I saw Mark making his way around the poolside, steadying himself on his stick, but looking thoughtful as well. 'Pleased with yourself?' I murmured.

'Pleased with Graham Metcalfe,' he told me. 'He must be plugged into every database in the world on this thing. It took him ten minutes to produce Uche Wigwe's life story. He's aged twenty-five, the eldest son and heir of Kalu Wigwe, Emir of Kanaan in Nigeria, and of Sonya, family name Odalonu. Uche was educated in England, at a prep school in York from the age of six, and then at Charterhouse School. From there he went to Massachusetts Institute of Technology where he majored in and graduated *summa cum laude* in . . .' he winked at me. 'Guess what, Primavera?'

'Chemistry.'

'Go it in one. His tutors at MIT said he was near-genius level. They had him marked down as a potential Nobel Prize winner, and universities the world over just love to produce those. They offered him the chance to do a PhD, and yes, you guessed it, on the synthesis of hormones, only for him to turn them down. He dropped out of sight for a while after that, surfacing again two years ago as an MBA student at Arizona State University, with the stated ambition of getting on the golf team, which surprised the coach there, because he wasn't exceptionally gifted at the game, despite having a personal tutor. Instead of playing, he hung about the team, caddying for a few of them, before settling for the bag of the brightest and best, Jonathan Sinclair. The rest we know.'

He smiled at me, expecting praise no doubt, but all he got was a frown. Something he'd said had thrown a switch. 'His personal tutor?' I repeated. 'Did Metcalfe put a name to him?'

'Hey, come on,' he protested. 'The database isn't that good.'

I got to my feet and walked around the pool. My back was to them as I dug out my mobile, and selected Jonny's number. I wasn't sure he'd reply; I thought he might have been switched off on the range, but he must have had it on vibrate, for he picked up. 'Auntie P,' he greeted me. 'Has the bastard shown up? If not, when he does, you might like to tell him he's fired. I suspect you'll be better at it than me.'

'Sorry, Jonny; that's a job you can't delegate. Are you sure you don't want to sleep on it?'

'No. You know I've been thinking about the longer term? Well, I've been speaking to Clive Tate. He's found me a guy who's looking for a bag. He's free now, but won't be for long, and he's giving him a big build-up.'

'You have to make the decision that's right for you,' I said. 'But no, Uche hasn't turned up. It seems he had family business to take care of. But I don't want to talk about him. There's something I need to ask you. It'll seem odd, but nonetheless. Remember you told me that Brush Donnelly found your coach for you?'

'No,' he contradicted me, at once. 'If I said that, it's not quite what I meant. Brush approved Lena, but that was never an issue, for she's one of the best. Strangely enough, it was Uche who introduced us. He said that his dad had hired her to work with him.' He paused. 'Does that help?'

'Does it ever. You go hit another few hundred balls.'

I went back to the guys, feeling more than a little smug. I was going to tell them what I'd just learned, but Mark didn't give me the chance. 'Did you find Shirley?' he asked, urgently.

'With the greatest of ease,' I replied. 'The call was worth every euro too.' I recounted her story, complete with Robert Palmer's comment, then added one of my own. 'Sounds like a bolt-hole to me.'

'It's all we've got,' Mark agreed. 'Do you know that area?' he asked Alex.

'Yes. I went hunting up there when I was a kid.'

'Fancy doing it again?'

The cop face returned. 'Hold on. If there's a chance that's where they are, I can get a whole squad up there.'

'Just what we don't need: a Catalan SWAT team.'

'Come on, man. We've got a kidnap victim there and a probable double murderer, triple counting the American in Malaga.'

'Who?' I exclaimed, intervening.

'Uche Wigwe, who else?'

'Uche never killed anybody,' I protested. 'Why the hell would he?'

'Good question,' Mark agreed. 'Uche never met Robert Palmer, so how could he have recognised him? He didn't send Genchev and McGuigan to try to identify him, so how could he have killed them?'

'Then who did?'

'That's the big question. Maybe Kalu gave them their orders, from Nigeria, but he didn't get here until after the second murder, so he didn't shoot anyone either, not personally.'

Alex shrugged. 'So I send in a team, we arrest everyone who's there, and we get the answers.'

'You get bodies; that's the only certainty. We have a man with a gun, we have a man with a secret, and we have a man with whom they both seem to have a grievance. If you send people in there with big boots, Kevlar helmets and assault rifles, someone, maybe all of them, will die. I was sent here to secure Robert Palmer, and to make him safe. That's still my objective. I don't care about the Wigwes, father or son. I propose that you and I go up there, Alex; first to establish if they're in the building at all, and then to find out why.'

'How do we do that?'

'In my experience, the best way is to ask.'

'Are you forgetting Uche's gun?'

'You're a cop. Your uniform's bullet-proof, because only a lunatic would shoot at it.'

Alex frowned. 'Yours isn't. Or is that stick all the protection you need?'

'I'm still here,' Mark pointed out, cheerfully. 'And I'll bet I have a lot more experience than you of situations like this. If I wasn't here you'd probably fly in someone like me, as a negotiator.'

'Shit! Okay, we go up there and we do what you say. But the decision on calling in back-up will be mine. You may be here to protect Palmer, but you're a civilian, a foreign national, and my first task will be to protect you.'

'Boys,' I said, quietly, 'if I may interrupt your pissing contest. If either of you think you're going up there without me, then take a reality pill.' They stared at me. Alex started to speak but I cut him off. 'I'm coming, end of story. You don't seem to realise that I'm the only one of us who's actually met all of these people. Two out of the three aren't remotely dangerous, and the third? Last seen, he's been rendered harmless and anyway, if he's what we think he is, he gets someone else to do his close-up work.'

'And what if that person gets there before us?' Mark asked.

'I've got a feeling that's what this whole kidnap thing is about, don't you? In which case . . . let's get a fucking move on.'

Alex let out a great sigh. 'What's the point of arguing with this woman?' he moaned, then stood. 'But before we go, I have to ask this, and I'd appreciate an honest answer. Mr Kravitz, are you carrying a gun? That I couldn't allow.'

The reply was instant and firm. 'No, I'm not; search me if you want to be sure. I can still hit a target with a rifle, from a prone position, but my MS makes me useless with a handgun. I'd be dangerous to everyone except the person I was trying to shoot.'

We took my jeep. The car that Alex had arrived in was an ordinary saloon, and from Shirley's description of the road we'd be tackling, a four-by-four would be needed. I didn't need directions to get to Darnius, since it was only forty minutes from L'Escala, but I'd have driven right past the turn for La Central if Alex hadn't been there.

The road to the hotel should have been labelled 'Proceed at your own risk'. Most of it was single track and every one of the many bends seemed to be blind, but at least it had a hard top. That ended as soon as we reached La Central and crossed the tiny, narrow bridge that sat just beyond, with a yellow sign advertising a restaurant in what had once been Robert's Mill, and with an arrow pointing the way.

We began the ascent, and it didn't long for me to wonder what the hell a couple of sixty-somethings had been doing walking up a small mountain like that. Winter rains had left deep ruts in the dirt surface and once or twice I had to steer around the remnants of fallen trees. There was woodland on either side of the camino and some of it was pretty thick. Once or twice I thought we might be in among it, so narrow were some of the twists and bends. It could have been worse, though; in muddy conditions I wouldn't have gone much further than the hotel, but spring had sprung early in Catalunya and we'd enjoyed almost four weeks of sunny weather.

It took around fifteen minutes to reach the fork that Shirley had described. When I saw it I could see how they had got it wrong. There was another restaurant sign, but without an arrow. Guesswork, if you weren't smart enough to work out that there were no windmills in woodland country, only watermills, and that no rivers run in ground as high as that which we'd reached, far less along a track that continued to climb for as far as I could see.

I hadn't thought that driving conditions could get any worse, but they did. The way grew narrower and rougher; the jeep even bottomed out a couple of times, despite its underside being normally well clear of the ground. I had to concentrate even harder, so I was more than a little annoyed when Mark, in the front passenger seat, patted my arm.

'What?' I snapped.

'Ease off, Primavera,' he said. 'There's a dustcloud up ahead. I think there's another vehicle ahead of us.'

I stopped, and looked. He was right; the surface was bone-dry and I could see billowing dust in the distance, the same sandy-grey colour as the fine film that had formed on my hood. As far as I could judge, it was a few hundred metres away, and heading in the same direction as us.

'Ten minutes earlier and we might have been waiting for them,' I murmured.

'No,' Mark contradicted. 'They'll have come straight here from the airport, and I don't imagine they've just nipped out for an early lunch. Someone else . . . unless of course this is a through road; that we don't know for sure.'

'It isn't,' Alex volunteered from the back.

'Then wait. Roll down the windows and listen.'

I did as I was told. Funny thing, but even although we were in the middle of a wood, there was no birdsong, only the sound of a high-revving engine in the middle distance. And then there was nothing. 'He's stopped,' I whispered. Why did I whisper? No idea.

I reached out to turn the engine on once more, but Mark stopped me. 'We can't,' he said. 'We could hear him, so . . . We're on foot from here.'

'Are you okay with that?' I asked.

'As long as it's not too far. If I start to struggle you two go on.'

We climbed out of the jeep and set out up the track. In truth we travelled almost as fast as we had on wheels, sticking to the side of the road and avoiding the deepest ruts; some of them looked like small ravines. We'd gone a couple of hundred metres when we reached the other vehicle, the one we'd been following. It was a mid-range Volkswagen saloon, new, metallic blue beneath the dust, totally unsuited to the terrain, as out of place as Rudolf Nureyev in a Wild West saloon. Incongruous also because there were two kid seats in the back.

I looked ahead and I could see why the driver had stopped. The nose of another vehicle was sticking out from a gap between two

300

trees that might have been intended as a passing place. It hadn't been new for some years. It was a crappy old off-white Seat, the kind that a car hire company will only keep in the hope that a renter might write it off, or steal it.

Mark had fallen a few metres behind. 'Careful,' he murmured as he caught us up. 'Let's go steadily. This changes things.'

We walked on, but slowly, taking care not to kick any loose rocks and send them clattering. We'd only gone for another fifty metres when the forest on our right track opened out into a clearing, in the middle of which was an old stone building, but not so derelict that it didn't have a front door, through which a man was stepping. We had the briefest glimpse of him, but it was enough to tell us that he was very large, and that he was carrying something in his right hand, an object with a polished wooden stock.

Before any of us could react, he was inside the old house. 'That's a sawn-off shotgun,' Alex exclaimed. 'This is where I send for back-up.'

Neither Mark nor I tried to stop him as he reached for his phone. Then, from inside the house, there came a crash and a yell, then another . . . We waited for the blast of a firearm, but after that there was only silence.

'Hold off on that, Alex,' Mark murmured. 'We may not need the heavy squad.'

'If not, then what do we do?' he asked.

'I'm going in.'

'You can't,' I protested. 'You don't know what's happening in there.'

'I can guess, though, and so can you. Somebody's about to be killed. What's the worst that can happen to me? I might die ahead of schedule, but not by that much.'

He set off for the house, walking briskly, using his stick. 'Bugger,' I muttered, and went after him. 'Shit,' Alex hissed and fell into step alongside me, drawing his service pistol from its holder.

There was no shotgun fire as Mark threw the door wide and stepped into a big open area. In fact the weapon was on the floor, not far from its wielder, who lay face down, with an egg-sized lump on his right temple, and with his hands secured behind his back with a plastic tie. The egg had been laid, I realised, by the bloodstained object that dangled from the fingers of Uche Wigwe's left hand as he stood over his captive. It was one of Jonny's lob wedges, a match for the club that had won him the championship three days before.

In his right hand my nephew's caddie held a revolver. It was pointed at the head of the fallen assassin; at the head of Lars Martinsson.

Alex raised his own gun, but Mark waved to him to lower it, as he stepped up behind Uche, and patted him gently on the shoulder. 'You're not going to use that, mate,' he whispered, and took the pistol from him. 'You're not the type.'

'That man killed my mother,' the Nigerian told him, in a voice as hard as the stone of the walls, 'and that man there, my father, ordered it.'

He stared across the room in the direction of an old wooden chair, under a window. Kalu Wigwe was tied to it. He was alive but he'd been beaten about the head, and beaten bloody, for there were streaks of gore all over his flight suit.

Robert Palmer, the man I'd known as Patterson, was standing beside him; he met my gaze as I looked at him.

'She was your witness?' I asked him. 'Kalu's wife?'

'She was more than my witness,' he replied, 'much, much more.' His voice seemed to have changed with his name; it was hard, strained, and not all that far from hysteria. 'Kalu took me to Nigeria, four years ago,' he continued, 'to show off, no doubt, to impress me, to let me see that he really is a prince out there. Sure,' he snorted, 'and he's also a fucking criminal, who isn't just into designer drugs. He's involved in money laundering, international fraud, slavery, and he even finances Somali pirates for a cut of their ransom money. He thought he was sure of me, and financially he was. I'd left my scruples behind a long time before. Oh yes, Kalu and I got on great. Then on that trip, he introduced me to his wife, to Sonya.'

He shrugged. 'As I explained to Uche when I went to see him on Monday night, things happen that you can't control. That's how it was with Sonya and me. It might sound corny to you, but we fell in love. We saw each other whenever we could; we used to meet in a different city every time, Rome, Miami, London, always when Kalu was off screwing around, and that's something he did a lot. Didn't you, you fucking monster. Flashy, cheap women everywhere, but you treated Sonya, who was pure gold, like . . .' He punched the bound man, harder than I'd thought he ever could, hard enough to produce a small scream even in his semi-conscious state.

'Enough,' Kalu moaned.

'Enough!' Alex ordered, sharply.

'No. Not nearly enough,' Palmer shouted back.

'Hey,' I intervened. 'Robert. Didn't you tell me a few days ago, when you were someone else, that humanity is essential, and that needless cruelty is inexcusable?'

'This was necessary. It was justice,' he protested, but I knew I'd got to him, and in the same moment I knew too that the naturally kind person with whom I'd had that discussion was the real whoever-he-was.

'How the hell did you find us?' he asked, more quietly.

'With help,' I replied, then took him back to the story. 'How long did it take Kalu to catch on?'

'He got suspicious of Sonya about two years ago, but he didn't know it was me she was seeing, until we set up her escape through Malaga.' He sighed, and I could hear the despair in it. 'It turned out that setting it up through Facebook wasn't as clever as we thought. Sonya made a mistake. She used her home computer, and by that time Kalu was checking everything. So when Sonya went into room 106 in the Silken Puerta, he and Lars were waiting for her. They thought they'd be killing me as well; they were disappointed when only Beau Lucas, my American minder, showed up. Poor Beau; nice guy.' He winced. 'They got her body out of there in a cart, then put it in a big suitcase and took it back on board the plane. Those fucking Kiwi pilots!' he hissed. 'He made them fly low over the Atlantic, so he could chuck her out. They'll deny it, but they knew what he was up to. They're lucky, those guys, that all they got was tied up for a few hours. I'd have wasted them, but Uche said no.'

'And Lars?' I asked. 'I take it he spotted you at the golf course. Had you met before?'

'Yes, a couple of times at the factory.' He looked at Mark. 'Who are you, by the way? CWB? Interpol?'

'Both,' my friend replied.

'Who're you working for here?'

'Everybody. You were a little short of the truth with Interpol, Palmer, weren't you?'

He nodded, with a smile that was slightly embarrassed. 'Just a bit,' he admitted. 'I told them that I only made the stuff, but I knew a little more than that. Kalu made sure I did, enough to tie me in, but not enough to be a threat to him.'

He pointed at the giant on the floor. 'Lars was part of the route for the HGH into the US sports market. Before he became a crap golfer, he had an early career in the Swedish military, and Kalu found him useful for other work. I'd no idea he was in Girona, and I never saw him there. But he saw me, that first day we went there. He wasn't certain, but he got in touch with Kalu, and Kalu told him to find out for sure. The Bulgarian and the Irish woman were both in Spain; they had to relocate after my place was busted and the HGH network was shut down. He sent Genchev, then the girl, first to nick something from me, then to take a closer look than he could risk. When they failed . . . you know what he did to them.'

'When did you realise you'd been rumbled?' I asked.

'For sure? Not until Kalu walked on to the practice ground. I saw him and he saw me, and I got out of there.' He looked at me, with an expression that was almost a plea. 'Primavera, I'd run away from my old self. I never stopped grieving for Sonya . . . oh, I knew she was dead; I knew she had to be . . . but I became a different man, literally. I met Shirley, I found a new life, one I'd thought was beyond me, and I'd truly given up being Robert Palmer. I wanted to be clear of Wigwe; that's why I refused to give anyone his name. If I had shopped him, I'd have been tied to him forever, and probably he'd have slithered out from under and I'd have wound up in a suitcase myself. But it wasn't just fear: I was happy, honest, I really was. Then the bastard turned up and I realised that I couldn't be, not really, until he was dead. So I went to see Uche, and I told him what had really happened to his mum.'

I turned to him. 'You didn't know?' I murmured.

'No, Primavera,' the younger man replied. 'I knew that my father was capable of most things, but not that, no, I didn't believe that. His story to my brothers and me was that she had died in a boating accident, while we were all away studying, and that her body had never been found. I didn't believe it, of course. I suspected that either she had run off, or he had sent her away. Now, I see I should have known, but I wouldn't allow myself to, or maybe I couldn't. I suspect I was hiding from the truth . . . until Robert came to see me and I knew I couldn't hide any longer.'

'And so we set this up,' Palmer continued. 'Kalu had told Uche when he planned to leave, early when there was very little traffic at the airport. So we snatched him; it was easy. We were able to drive straight in, and up to the plane.'

'Where did the gun come from?' Mark asked.

'It was mine; I brought it with me, just in case. I kept it in Shirley's safe, in a lockable box; I told her there were bonds in it.' His eyebrows twitched, and the corners of his mouth flicked upwards in a brief smile. 'I never imagined I'd need it, but it came in handy this morning. It impressed Kalu, that's for sure. Didn't it, mate?' He paused. The bound man's traffic signal eyes turned towards him. There was no arrogance left in them, only pain and fear.

'We brought him here,' his captor went on. 'We made him admit to everything . . . he isn't really very brave, by the way, not nearly as brave as his son; a few whacks with that golf club and he was screaming at us to stop. When he was finished, we knew everything. That was when we made him call Lars and tell him to meet him here, to get rid of me once and for all. We had the opposite in mind, and everything was going our way until you three showed up. Why the hell didn't you just wait outside for a minute longer?' he growled. 'I'd have killed them, even if Uche had bottled it. Now they're both going to walk out of here.'

'Looks that way,' Mark agreed. He looked down at Martinsson, who was fully conscious once more, still face down, but aware. 'But when you do, big fellow, you're going to sing for your supper, aren't you? You're going to tell the whole story to Interpol, you're going to admit to killing Genchev and McGuigan, and in return you will not be extradited to the US, and you won't be executed for Beau Lucas's murder.' He drove his stick, hard, into the back of the Swede's neck. 'Aren't you?' he growled.

'Yes, yes!!!' the fallen killer yelled.

'That's the deal, then.' He turned to Alex. 'I think you should take this one outside now,' he suggested. 'Uche will help you, I'm sure.' He watched as the cop and the chemist hauled the former Scandinavian golf champ to his feet and dragged him from the room, from the old, dark house, into the bright day outside.

'There you are, Mr Cowling,' Mark said, easily. 'You can relax.'

'How do you work that out?' Palmer retorted. 'How long will it be before this thing here hires someone from his jail cell to finish me off?'

'You wouldn't do that, Mr Wigwe, would you?' Mark asked.

The traffic signal eyes locked on to his. 'Oh yes,' he hissed. 'That is exactly how it will be. This man will go into a meat grinder, feet first. My oldest son will watch him, and then he will follow. Lars's children too, if necessary. That's why he'll change his mind about giving evidence.' He smiled, through the blood and the broken teeth. 'You people have made certain of that, of all of it.'

Mark took a few steps forward, to stand above Kalu in his chair. As I watched him, I felt my heart heading for my mouth, as I had a premonition of the immediate future. 'That's not quite how it'll be,' he murmured, then put the pistol he had taken from Uche against his father's forehead and blew his brains all over the wall behind him. As easy as that. I didn't scream, but Palmer did.

'You see? It's cheap to talk about killing people,' Mark told him. 'Even about killing yourself. Doing it, though . . .'

He had tossed the weapon on to the floor by the time Alex came charging back through the front door, his own gun raised and held in both hands. He pointed it at Mark's chest. 'What the hell have you done?' he yelled.

'Followed orders,' my other friend said, as I took in what I had just seen, and as Robert Palmer wiped furiously at the blood that had splattered over him. 'My remit was extended this morning, as soon as the Americans heard what we'd turned up. You're not here, Intendant Guinart. You didn't see this; you've never met Kalu

Wigwe, only his son, and the man you've just arrested after he confessed to two murders. Now either shoot me, or put your gun away. Either way, I don't give a toss, but it'll be better for you if you do as I say. It would be more grateful of you too, considering that I've just made you a hero.'

I pulled myself together, got hold of Alex and drew him away, back outside, where I hugged him until he'd stopped shaking.

Uche didn't say a word. He looked at Palmer, as he emerged with Mark, and Palmer nodded. That was all.

'What about . . . ?' I nodded towards the house, as I looked at Mark.

'I have to make a phone call,' he told me, 'that's all. Nothing will be left behind.'

He did, and then we headed back down the track. I gave Alex the keys to my jeep, since it was the only vehicle there that was capable of taking a six-foot five-inch handcuffed man, and two escorts: him, and Mark at the wheel.

'What about me?' Palmer asked his saviour, as he reached the first vehicle, the one he'd blagged from the care hire company.

'Nothing. You weren't here either. I didn't call you Mr Cowling by mistake, a couple of minutes ago. You still are him, and if you choose, you always will be.' He took in the man's doleful expression and smiled. 'Don't feel so sorry for yourself,' he said. 'You've still got Palmer's money, rather than some spook pen-pusher's pension.'

'Let me give you some free advice,' I added. 'Get yourself on the first plane to Singapore, look for a hotel overlooking the marina, and check the guest list. Get there before Friday and you'll find a large lady waving at sailors from her bathtub. Tell her I sent you and that she should let you in.'

He blinked. 'Anything you say, Primavera,' he murmured, as if he wasn't quite sure what he was hearing or doing, but reckoned that the smart thing would be not to argue.

'And me?' Uche followed up, solemnly.

'How do they address an emir in Nigeria?' Mark asked him.

'Sir, would be the usual form,' he replied.

'In that case, sir, you've just inherited. If I were you I'd get to Girona Airport, hire new air crew . . . you two desperados were right not to kill the Kiwis; that would have ruined everything . . . and fly back to Lagos as soon as you can get a take-off slot. You have two brothers to look after, from what I gather, and a lot of cleaning up to do within your family business.'

'But what about . . . the human growth hormone that I made for my father? My sadly late father?' he added, without a trace of grief in his voice

'What about it? All you did was invent a synthesising process for a naturally occurring substance. That might be hugely profitable for certain people, but I think you'll find that it isn't illegal in itself. As I see it, the only law you've broken is a small one involving kidnapping, but the Mossos d'Esquadra won't be following that up. Get out of town, mate.'

Uche looked at me. 'But Jonny . . .' he began.

I tried not to smile, but didn't get close. 'I have some bad news,' I advised him. 'Jonny said to tell you: you're fired.'

Seventeen

I never saw Mark Kravitz again. When I called the Nieves Mar later that day, I was told that he'd checked out. I didn't call him, because I decided that for a while, silence between us would be best. Things you regret; too many people to whom I never said, 'Safe journey onward. Your touch upon my life was fair and good.'

Three months ago I had a phone call from a stranger who introduced himself as Detective Chief Superintendent Graham Metcalfe. He told me that my friend had finally run out of treatment options and that his MS had moved on to a new, aggressive and irreversible phase, and he explained that Mark, being Mark, had decided not to hang around for the inevitable but instead had taken an overdose of carefully stockpiled sleeping pills, washed down with a nice claret, from a very good year. At once, I remembered what he'd said to Patterson Cowling, in the abandoned house, about it being easy to talk about killing, even killing yourself, but . . .

Patterson Cowling? Yes, that's who he is again, as far as the entire population is concerned, indeed as far as the whole world is concerned, apart from a few spooks and two women who will never meet him, although the General Register Office says that he's their father. He took my advice, he made it to Singapore on time, and joined Shirley in her first-class suite. I'm sure she gave him hell for putting her through same, but the man she got back was the one she'd known, and they are now in the process of living happily for as long as 'ever after' lasts.

Uche Wigwe? The new young Emir of Kanaan? He did the right thing, for him and for his family. He sold all his father's legitimate assets and shared them with his brothers. He realised that there are more things in life than the endless pursuit of cheerleaders, and now he's back at MIT, doing that PhD. I've no idea of the subject, but as my nephew says, it won't be bloody golf, that's for sure.

Lars Martinsson? He pleaded guilty to two murders, motive for both simple robbery, and was sentenced to twenty years, half of what it could have been, for cooperating with the Spanish police and prosecutor. No charges were ever brought against Lena Mankell. I know, Mark's friends at Interpol will know, and I'm sure Uche must know as well, that she was an important link in Kalu's distribution network for his son's super-HGH, maybe the key link throughout the US. But since the existence of the stuff has never been public knowledge, it would have been counterproductive for her to be accused of anything. However, she did quit as a swing coach, and she has since returned to Sweden with her kids. I'm told that she now has a job as a club pro. That'll be handy for her when Lars is transferred to his home country in a couple of years, to serve out his sentence.

Alex Guinart? He brought my jeep back that evening, and swapped it for Lars Martinsson's car, which I'd used to get myself back home from the hills above Darnius. He was still shaken up by Mark's execution of Kalu Wigwe, but he had become wise enough in the ways of the darker world not to mention it. It's a secret he and I share, and it's made our friendship even stronger. He's become a star, as Mark promised he would. His promotion to intendant was confirmed (Hector Gomez didn't return to work; he took early retirement instead) and he's seen as a blue-eyed boy in Barcelona.

Jonathan Sinclair? He hasn't won on the European Tour since his debut, but he hasn't missed a cut either, so he's made money every time he's played, the first objective of any professional. He and his new caddie, Logan Miller, have a good relationship, and his game hasn't suffered from the loss of Lena Mankell, thanks to her replacement as his swing coach, Clive Tate, who took over a couple of her old clients, and who has a wise silver head on his shoulders.

Jonny still lives with me, but that will change very soon. He's found himself a very nice girlfriend, the daughter of a hotel owner in Figueras, and next month he will move into a house that he's bought on the edge of the golf course at Pals. She isn't moving in with him, not yet, but his domestic independence will make their life, shall we say, easier. His Grandpa Mac is very pleased too. I don't know what gives with him and Mary, but we've seen a lot of him this summer and nothing of her.

Tom Blackstone? The rock on which my life is built? That analogy doesn't work any more, because rocks don't grow. He and

I stand at the door of great change. I chanced to see him naked one morning last month . . . neither of us is an exhibitionist, but we're not prudishly shy either . . . and couldn't help but notice that things were slightly different. Since then, I've been reading up on puberty in boys.

And James Brush Donnelly? The mysterious, enigmatic Brush, acknowledged by Jonny's contemporaries as one of the best managers on tour; what of him? He remains a stranger, although that may change when Jonny returns to Arizona this month to play in his first PGA Tour event. Even now, I know nothing about him, beyond what Clive Tate told me, although we did speak once. Jonny had left his mobile upstairs while he went down to the garage to fetch something from his car. It rang, I picked it up. The voice on the other end had been through so many cells and satellites that it sounded almost artificial, but certainly American. I told him that Jonny was elsewhere, and couldn't help adding that it was rather late where we were. 'Hey, I'm sorry,' he drawled. 'I keep forgetting that you guys have daylight saving.'

And that has started me wondering . . .